CONSPIRACY OF MAGIC BOOK THREE

# FEARLESS MAGIC

## MEGAN CREWE

*To my daughter, may you be fearless with your own magic*

# CHAPTER ONE

*Finn*

There's nothing like a global catastrophe to put one's personal problems into perspective. If someone had asked me even half an hour ago what the worst part of losing my magic was, I'd have pointed to the sense of isolation from the community I grew up in or the sting of remembering dreams I no longer had any chance of realizing.

I'd have been wrong. Now, standing in the midst of the mess of broken stone that had once been the center of operations for the North American Confederation of Mages, I was experiencing the worst part with wrenching intensity.

The world was falling apart. Sobs and pained gasps carried from all around me. People were *dying* within my reach—and all I could offer to help them were my bare, magicless hands.

Scree rattled under my feet as I clambered across the hill of rubble that covered the entire city block. A burnt chalky smell filled my mouth and nose. The warble of the magic, which minutes ago had whipped up so frantically that even my burned-out senses had been able to hear it, had faded in the chilly

December air, but now and then another windowpane cracked or a wall dented with a thud.

Rocío had warned everyone she could that the magic that flowed around us all through the world was faltering—that spells aimed at destruction were agitating it and weakening it at the same time. The mage insurgent attack on this building must have pushed it over some final line. That mysterious living energy was lashing out like a wounded animal, and possibly wounding itself more in the process.

A short distance away across the rubble, Rocío knelt by a large chunk of limestone. As my girlfriend focused her concentration on the stone, her dark hair rippled along her shoulders with the continued niggling of the magic. She murmured under her breath. Sweat gleamed on her forehead with the effort of her casting, but the chunk eased slightly upward and to the side with the rhythmic rise of her voice and motion of her hands. The second she released the stone, she dove into the gap she'd uncovered and reached for the person trapped there.

My legs itched to join her, to see what assistance I could offer, but a sharper pang held me back. I had no magimedical 'chantments at my disposal anymore, and I was hardly familiar with Dull first aid. All I'd contribute was a distraction.

A muffled groan rose up through the wreckage ahead of me. I picked my way over as quickly as I could.

A woman lay in a dip, partly hidden under a couple of pieces of limestone that pinned her legs in place. Though her eyes were closed, her chest rose and fell with hitches of breath. So many scrapes marked her pale face that it took me a moment to realize I knew her. She was one of Dad's colleagues—she'd been at our house for my parents' dinner parties at least once or twice. I groped for her name but didn't find it in my scattered mind.

It wasn't as if she'd care about formal greetings at this particular moment. I hunched over and grasped one of the rocks holding her down. My fingers fumbled for a second before finding purchase. I hauled the stone backward, my shoulders straining. With one more massive heave, it lurched free, and I tripped and fell onto my backside.

I scrambled up, ignoring the jab of pain, and went for the second stone. As I yanked it to the side, the woman stirred, her eyelids fluttering, her expression dazed.

Should I try to move her, or leave her there? A siren wailed in the distance, the professional emergency workers on their way, but the thought of simply abandoning her until they arrived made my gut twist.

"Finn!" My mother's voice rang out from behind me. She and Dad were hustling my way, their long shadows rippling over the rubble in the late afternoon light. They must have followed me from the hospital, where we'd been reeling from my granduncle Raymond's death when the insurgents had attacked. Other people emerged from the buildings around us and farther down the street, wary but moving toward anyone injured they could see.

The sight of my parents hit me with an uncomfortable punch of relief strung through with horror. *I* had nothing to do with the insurgent attack… but I had to shoulder some responsibility for Granduncle Raymond's death. He'd only come out of the Confed building during the protest I'd helped organize because I'd forced his hand. If he hadn't stepped outside, a rogue member of that protest wouldn't have had the chance to catch him off-guard.

Perhaps I should take some blame for the catastrophe around me as well. Would the insurgents have attacked if they hadn't seen the Confederation weakened as one of its leaders lay dying?

Dad and Mom had no idea how deeply I'd gotten involved with the Freedom of Magic League's protests and other activities. I'd lied to them and gone behind their backs so many times in the last few months, but other than their own horror at the situation, all that showed in their expressions as they reached me was concern for my wellbeing.

This was hardly the time to dwell on my transgressions. *Inter arma silent leges*, as Cicero so aptly put it. Many more lives hung in the balance with every passing moment.

I motioned to the half-conscious woman. "I got her free, but I don't know what to do for her now."

A lot of the color had already drained from Dad's face, but he turned even more sallow when he saw his coworker sprawled there.

"You did well for a start," he said with a quick squeeze of my shoulder. "Let me scan her and see if there's anything else we can do before the magimedics and the emergency workers get here. They should be close by now."

He and Mom knelt on either side of the woman. Both of them sang out lyrics under their breaths with puffs of condensation, Mom beginning at the woman's feet and Dad at her head. Their features tensed; their voices grew louder. They were struggling to conduct the frantic magic just as Rocío had.

Mom paused. "Her leg is broken. Finn, can you find something straight and sturdy that we can use as a splint? It'd probably be best to move her to a spot that's more stable if we can manage it without exacerbating her injuries."

"I'll look." I swiveled around as Mom took up her chant again. A broken chair back protruded from the wreckage several feet away. I dashed over and tugged it free to find one of the wooden legs already dangling by a few splinters. I broke it off completely with a jerk of my hand.

I rushed back to the prone woman, tugging my scarf from around my neck. "Here," I said. "Use this to bind it on."

"Perfect." Mom flashed me a tight but genuine smile as she took the scarf and chair leg. She set the splint against the woman's shin and whispered a lyric that I suspected would become a numbing spell.

Dad had balled his own scarf against the back of the woman's head, which he'd eased up from the broken stone beneath her. A streak of blood was spreading across the fabric.

"Hold this here?" he said to me.

I dropped down beside him to press the makeshift bandage against the wound. Dad murmured a 'chantment to slow the bleeding as much as he could. For an instant, despite the worried voices all around us and the cold air burning down my throat and into my lungs, I felt oddly calm.

I might not have magic, but the three of us were working together as a family toward a goal we had no trouble agreeing on. That sensation was very different from the way I'd interacted with my parents in recent weeks, and I couldn't help welcoming it. Perhaps I hadn't made a total ruin of those bonds.

Then my mind flashed back to the splintered stone from the Confed building archway plummeting to pierce Granduncle Raymond's chest, before—to the terrible glowing mask of the group Rocío had called the Bonded Worthy rising in the dust over the destroyed building mere hours later. So many other people had been working in the Confed building when it had collapsed. So many of them would be buried too far or be too injured by the impact for us to save them. Nausea squeezed my stomach, chasing the momentary peace away.

Dad swiped his hand across his forehead. He intoned another melodic line, but his casting sounded strained.

"The attack shook up the magic too," he said. "It keeps shuddering away from me when I try to conduct it. Whatever technique those mages used, it was awfully powerful." He glanced around as if confirming the insurgents weren't lurking nearby, ready to launch another assault.

"I don't think they damaged the magic on purpose," I said.

"It was a side effect they probably didn't even expect. From what Rocío says…"

When Dad's gaze jerked to me, startled and puzzled, I let my voice trail off. I glanced toward Rocío where she and a couple of other rescuers were easing a man away from the rubble.

My parents had only just met my girlfriend. They knew only a fraction of what we'd been through together in the Mage's Exam or what she'd had to endure after making Champion and being conscripted into the Confed's special ops division.

Thanks to the 'chantment the examiners had cast on me, I couldn't tell them the most of the rest, if it was even my place to try. How could I explain the exact nature of magic or how our own military actions were affecting it when I couldn't offer much of the reasoning or proof? The parts I *could* share tended to make Rocío seem delusional.

"Never mind," I said. "It's not as if it matters to the people who've been hurt." It was just one more span in the divide that had been growing between me and the rest of my family.

Dad watched me for a moment longer, but the arrival of the first wave of emergency vehicles saved me from answering any questions. Ambulances pulled up on either side of where the rubble spilled across the street. Paramedics and magimedics alike streamed out. Within seconds, they were shouting to us civilians who'd thrown ourselves into the fray, giving orders about how we could best contribute.

One of the magimedics called for all the mages to assemble around him while he laid out a strategy to tackle the catastrophe. I took a few steps toward him before it registered that he couldn't possibly mean a Burnout mage like me. As my parents went to join him, I drifted toward one of the regular paramedics. She pointed me to the open back of one of the ambulances.

"There's a bunch of blankets in there. Cover up any of the

people you see who've already been removed from the wreckage. We don't want them going into shock."

I grabbed as many of the thin but dense blankets as I could carry. Quite a few figures sat slumped along the fringes of the strike zone. The falling rubble must have struck many random passers-by who'd been traveling through this part of the city. I offered a blanket to an older man hunched by the open driver's side door of his car, the hood of which had been bashed in by a limestone boulder, and then I moved on to a girl a little younger than me who had one hand braced against her bruised forehead and the other clutching her swollen ankle.

"Thank you," the girl said before she'd even looked up. When she did, I could tell the moment her gaze snagged on the crisscrossing black Burnout mark that must have been partly visible on my left temple, below my hat. Her expression tensed with more than just pain, and she shrank back an inch.

I hurried on before I made her any more anxious. Thanks to the Confed, mages who failed the Exam were marked as failures for anyone to see—failures who'd challenged the fate the authorities had decreed for us. In some people's eyes, that made us seem dangerous. Of course, for all I knew, the girl was simply one of the many Dulls who were still nervous of mages in general, whether or not we actually had any magical ability at our disposal.

The mages who'd gathered together were spreading out across the rubble again. Rocío caught my eye and gave me a nod as if to reassure me that she was all right. Her tan face was drawn, her shoulders stiff with tension as her lips moved to form a casting. Whatever she sensed in the magic, it propelled her toward a heap of broken stone that contained a smashed desk and scattered books. Their pages ruffled in the wind.

More ambulances roared up, flanked by several police cars. A few of the uniformed officers scanned the wreckage with a different sort of grimness in their gazes.

"Hey!" one officer shouted with a sweep of his arm. "We can't have anything worse stirred up here by all your spells and things. I don't want to see any magic cast by regular civilians. Uniformed responders in official capacity only."

I stared at him. Didn't he know that most of the people we were trying to save were civilian mages themselves? I doubted they shared the same fears.

A couple of the other officers were nodding. "Hell, anyone who isn't trained move right out until the professionals have had a chance to survey the area," one added. "The last thing we need is more injuries—or another building coming down on our heads."

It wasn't as if a stray, unfocused spell could accomplish that by accident. The Confed building could only have been destroyed by an immense, concentrated magical assault. I supposed I couldn't blame the Dull forces for being ignorant when the Confed spent an awful lot of time making sure they stayed that way by restricting access to any sort of magical teachings.

When I glanced at Rocío, she was frowning, but she eased away from the body she'd been uncovering in the rubble. She hugged herself, rubbing her arms through the sleeves of her coat as she headed toward me.

"Why shouldn't we be helping?" she muttered when she reached me, with a glance toward the Dull authorities. "I can do more, faster, than they can on their own."

"They must be even more shaken by that display of magic than we are," I said. "They probably think it's the best way to keep the situation under control."

An officer motioned for us to move farther away, and we wove through the scattered wreckage to a clearer section of the street. Mom and Dad caught up with us there.

Dad touched my arm. "I'm not sure there's much else we can do here right now. We should get back to the hospital and see if they need any help. Your grandaunt is waiting for us."

The knot in my stomach tightened. My grandaunt Phyllis had just gotten the news that her husband had died. With everything else they'd had to worry about, I wasn't sure she or my parents even realized I'd been *at* the protest where Granduncle Raymond had been attacked yet. It would come out sooner rather than later, though, once news footage of me confronting him on the steps began circulating—if it hadn't already.

My gaze slid along the street and caught on a familiar blue mohawk. Mark, one of my collaborators from the Freedom of Magic League, was standing by the corner. He saw me, and his eyebrows shot up. He waved for me to join him.

"Finn?" Mom said. There was that concern again, as if I couldn't be more than an innocent victim in this scenario.

I swallowed hard. I'd picked my side this morning. Possibly I'd picked it weeks ago when I'd first stolen information from Dad's work files to help an earlier League protest. I didn't belong with the Confed or my family anymore.

"I'm sorry," I said with a quick glance at my parents that only provoked another jab of guilt. "There's something else I have to do." I turned to Rocío. "Come with me?"

"Of course," she said immediately. I grabbed her hand and tugged her along to meet Mark.

"Finn!" Dad called after me. A sudden, irrational panic shot through me that he might try to stop me by force, and I picked up my pace to a run. Rocío fell into step beside me. The guilt prickled sharply through my chest, and then we were dashing around the corner with Mark, out of my parents' view, and into the new life I'd chosen for myself.

# CHAPTER TWO

*Rocío*

The magic wouldn't leave me alone. The strands of it that had been nagging at me while I was trying to help people out of the rubble chased after me down the street. I kept up with Finn and Mark, doing my best not to let the constant twitching and tugging at my hair and skin distract me. The energy had calmed down a little since its epic flailing right after the mage insurgents had launched their attack, but distress still radiated off it.

*I'm* trying *to fix this. Give me more than five seconds, will you?* I thought at it, as if the magic could understand me. It might be alive in some way, maybe even conscious enough to respond to my feelings when I opened myself up to it, but it wasn't exactly capable of having a conversation.

"I'm glad I bumped into you," Mark said to Finn, a little breathless. "Luis is getting as many of us together as he can for an emergency meeting."

"Understandable," Finn said with a shudder. He turned as if to introduce me to the other guy.

The magic rippled across my shoulders, some of the winter air seeping under my coat collar with it. Then it lurched as if startled. The glass covering a streetlamp across from us shattered.

Mark flinched and swore, stepping closer to the buildings as if they offered any real protection. As I glanced around for other signs of damage, I caught a movement from the corner of my eye.

The soldier who'd been assigned to follow me—both for my protection and to make sure I didn't skip out on the promises I'd made—was coming around the corner after us. In the chaos, I'd almost forgotten about her and Secretary of Defense Zacher, the man who'd assigned her to shadow me.

She'd picking up her pace to catch up with us. If she did, she'd probably haul me back to Zacher and the rest of the Dull military leaders.

My first, overwhelming instinct was to run for it. I'd made my deal with Zacher before the magic had gone wild. I'd already told him how his people could help: by keeping the magical special ops forces out of any combat. There was a lot more chance I could do something good here than stuck at the Pentagon.

He'd barely believed what I'd told him about the magic—he wouldn't see how much it needed me now. I was the only one who really understood what was happening to it. I needed a chance to regroup, take stock, and figure out what I could do on my own. If Zacher complained about it later, I could reasonably say I'd gotten caught up in the moment and hadn't been thinking about anything except the attack.

"This way," I whispered to Finn and Mark, careful not to let the soldier realize I'd noticed her. I yanked Finn with me into an alley between two of the buildings, and Mark hurried after us.

The second we were all hidden in the shadows, I reached out to the quivering thrum of energy in the air. I intoned a line from an old song under my breath. "Jugando al escondite en el bosque anocheció." The magic jittered away when I tried to bend it around that harmony. I concentrated harder, putting all my focus into conducting the erratic shivers that flowed like a faint electric current around me.

My skin tingled. The walls on either side of us and the sky overhead grayed slightly. Mark sucked in a breath to ask a question, and I jammed my finger to my lips to warn him to stay silent.

The soldier jogged into the alley. We flattened ourselves against the rough brick wall beside us. A few flakes of snow drifted down and landed on my face with tiny nips of cold. The woman frowned and strode forward—right past us. The conjured illusion I'd cast hid us from her searching eyes.

She would assume we'd run farther down the alley. While she was trying to track me down in that direction, we could continue on our way.

As soon as she'd loped out of view, I motioned to the others. "Show us where to go," I murmured to Mark. "But let's be quiet about it. I'll dispel the casting once we're inside."

He nodded, but he was watching me warily now. Because of the memory suppression the examiners inflicted on everyone who failed the Exam—even Finn, to some extent, despite an insider's attempt to help him—Mark didn't recognize me from the trials where we'd been in the same group. Finn had talked about how strange it was hanging out with our fellow survivor when he had no clue who we were, and now I could see what he'd meant firsthand.

I hadn't gotten to know Mark all that well in those few days anyway. I guessed starting over from scratch shouldn't be that hard.

"This is Rocío," Finn said. "She knows more about what's going on than anyone in the League will. And she's, ah, my girlfriend."

He took my hand, a faint warmth traveling through our

gloves. Mark raised his eyebrows, but he didn't comment, only nodded.

"If anyone can help us with… whatever we need to do next, it'll be the League," Finn said to me as we hurried on through the streets. "There are a few people in the group who are mostly looking to stir up trouble, but Luis, the guy in charge, I trust completely."

Reading people was one of Finn's strengths, so if he gave the guy a vote of confidence that emphatic, I'd trust him too. I hadn't had a chance to meet this League since Finn had started working with them, having been overseas on special ops duty most of that time, but he'd told me plenty. The Burnouts and Dampered mages who'd be at this meeting had shown they were willing to put their necks on the line to challenge the Confed and demand a better future for themselves. I couldn't ask for better proof of their bravery and strength than that.

And between the Bonded Worthy making good on their threats of violence and the magic reacting in kind, we might need a heck of a lot of both qualities.

Mark led us to a bus stop where we caught one heading north, toward Harlem. Once the bus had rumbled forward, with no sign of my soldier shadow behind us, I released the magic I'd used to disguise us. Mark slumped in his seat with a sigh.

"This whole thing is crazy," he said. "Luis asked me to scout out the Confed building because I was the closest person he managed to reach. I had no idea it was totally *demolished.* Who the hell did that?"

"Terrorists." Finn looked to me. "Right? They conjured a face like the mask the one insurgent was wearing on the news."

I grimaced. "It has to be. There are a—"

My throat clamped tight around the words. The silencing 'chantment the examiners had placed on me still prevented me from talking about my special ops experiences. "We were expecting something like this," I finished, much more vaguely. "Sorry. I can't talk about it."

I gestured to my neck, and Mark's eyes widened. "You were in the Exam too, huh?"

The corner of my mouth curled up in a pained half smile. "Yeah, but I can't talk much about that either."

"She made Champion," Finn said with a weird mix of pride and dread in his tone. He knew how hard I'd worked to win the Exam my way—and how horrible the real role of Champion was.

Mark's gaze slid from me to Finn and back again with obvious curiosity. But now that we were relatively safe for the moment, I had something else to take care of.

"I've got to check in with my parents," I said, digging out the prepaid phone I'd gotten during my stealthy journey back into the country. "Make sure they're okay." What if the magic's backlash had spread all the way down to Brooklyn?

Mom picked up on the second ring. "Hello?"

The sound of her voice sent relief rushing through me. "Mom, it's me. Are you okay—is Dad? I don't know if you've heard—"

"Oh, Dios mio, mija. They're saying there was an attack downtown near the college. I'm so glad to know you're okay. The magic has been acting strangely—it knocked over an electrical pole on our street, and it feels… strange. But we're fine. You *are* all right, aren't you?"

"Yes." Guilt mingled with my relief. The Confed had given Mom the same official story about my role as Champion as they gave everyone: that we won a spot in the Confed's college so we could study for magical careers. No one except the examiners—and maybe not even all of them—and a few select higher-ups in the Confed knew the truth: that we were launched straight into military operations on the front lines of international conflicts. My parents had no idea that I'd spent most of the last few months investigating terrorist activity in eastern Europe.

And I was kind of happy about that, as much as I hated lying to them.

"I'm with friends," I added. "We're safe, trying to find out as much as we can about what's going on. I can't talk for very long right now. I just wanted to make sure you were okay."

"You look after yourself. Surely they'll let you come home for a day or two with all this going on? It's almost Christmas anyway."

"I don't know. I'll see. If anything happens, you can call me at this number, okay? The—the college is at least being looser about communication while they're sorting things out."

As I tucked the phone away with a squeeze of my heart, Mark got up. The three of us stepped off the bus onto a residential street with a row of brick walk-ups not much different from my street in Brooklyn. Mark led us past a squeaking gate up a flight of steps to a heavy-looking door. He rang the buzzer.

"Who's there?" a voice barked over the intercom.

"Mark. I've got Finn and a friend of his with me."

The lock clicked over. We went down a dim, musty-smelling stairwell into the basement apartment. At least it was warmer than outside.

Maybe thirty people were already gathered under the apartment's low ceiling, clustered in smaller groups around the spartan living and dining rooms. Finn headed straight to a twenty-something Latino guy with dark curls that reached the bottoms of his ears and a middle-aged Black woman whose braided hair clinked with wooden beads as she turned to greet him.

"Luis, Tamara, this is Rocío, my girlfriend," Finn said quickly. "She's been working toward the same sorts of goals as the League on her side of things, as one of this year's Champions.

Rocío: Luis and Tamara. Luis put the League together, and Tamara spearheads a lot of the initiatives—anything we get involved in, they're leading the way."

"With plenty of help from Finn." Luis gave me a warm smile, but his forehead furrowed as he met Finn's eyes. "We haven't been able to track down Ary. Are you sure— The news was saying—"

"She was the one who pulled down that archway on my granduncle," Finn said firmly. "Or at least she got one of her friends to do it. It's the same trick she was planning before—and I *saw* her. That terrorist group, the Bonded Worthy or whatever, just took advantage of the situation."

My gaze skimmed the figures around the room and stopped with a lurch on one that was all too familiar—a guy with a square-ish face topped with messy red hair. Callum. *He'd* been in the Exam this year too, and he'd tried to kill both me and Finn more than once. I snatched Finn's arm.

He glanced at me and saw where I was looking. "It's okay," he said. "He's… well, he's not a different person, but he's been playing fair since he joined the League. He even helped me a little. He doesn't remember how far he let the examiners push him."

Of course the guy didn't, but *I* did. And even if he'd gone to extremes because of the torture the examiners had put us through, some part of him had been willing to go to those extremes. I'd keep my distance, thank you very much.

Several of the League members were squished onto a sofa in front of a TV, watching news footage of the Bonded Worthy's attack. "Is this for real, Mark?" one of them called over.

"Hell, yeah. The entire Confed building is in pieces." Mark ran his hand over the shaved portion of his head beside his spiky mohawk. "I don't know how many people are going to make it out alive."

A young woman leaned over the back of the sofa. "So, it *was* terrorists, right? One of those groups the Dulls are always ranting about? Why would they go after the Confed building?"

Finn held up his hand to get people's attention. "I brought someone who should be able to answer questions and help us figure out how we want to proceed from here. Rocío was trying to stop a disaster like this from happening." He checked with me. "If you're okay with explaining whatever you can?"

My heart started to thump harder, but I nodded. They had a right to understand—and they'd be able to do more to fix the situation if they did.

Everyone in the room turned to watch me. I worked out what I could actually say around the silencing 'chantment. Generalities were usually the way to go.

"There are insurgent groups made up of mages who don't like the way the Confed's military division has messed with their countries or them," I said. "I don't know exactly what they were hoping to get out of this attack, but I'd guess they saw it as retaliation."

"Are they going to hit us again?" someone asked nervously.

"I don't know," I had to admit. "I think they'd probably at least wait and see how we respond... And now that they've revealed that they're here, everyone in the Confed who can be spared will be tracking them down. They might be fleeing the country as quickly as they can." We could hope.

"Or they could smash a bunch more buildings." The guy who'd first called to Mark squinted at me. "How do you know more about this than what they're saying on the news? It sounds like you're just guessing."

"I—" My throat closed against saying anything definite. Me lleva.

"Hey," Finn said. "Believe me, she knows what she's talking about."

I inhaled slowly, and my balance wavered. It was still

afternoon, but I hadn't exactly slept well last night, and I'd done a lot of casting, under a lot of strain, trying to help as many people as I could today.

Finn noticed my reaction in an instant, because that was just him. He set his hand on my back, reassuring and steadying at the same time, and pitched his voice lower. "I'm sorry. I didn't mean to put you on the spot. If it's too much—"

"Hey!" shouted someone near the TV. "They've got someone from the Circle on the news now."

We both looked over. On the screen, a woman was giving an interview outside the stone face of a building I didn't recognize, her gray hair pulled back tightly from her papery face, her expression weary but resolute.

"I want to assure all of you that the Confederation is doing everything we can to apprehend the culprits responsible for this horrific attack and see them brought to justice," she was saying. "And also, rest assured that the attack has nothing to do with any mages within the Confederation. *We* keep careful control over who can and cannot practice magic precisely to avoid catastrophes like today's, and we'll continue to do that to the fullest extent of our ability."

Finn went rigid beside me even as I gritted my own teeth. They'd tried to take my magical ability from me even though I'd never been anything like a danger to society. What would this woman have said to explain the cruelties they put us through in the Exam?

And Finn had just gotten a promise from the Circle that they'd meet with the League leaders and discuss relaxing their policies around Dampering and the Exam. Were they going to use the attack as an excuse to back out of those negotiations? I couldn't imagine how he'd feel if all the protests and the risks he'd taken with his family got the League nowhere.

"The mage community of North America revealed itself to

those of you without magic specifically so that we could help you in times of need," the woman went on. "It only makes sense that we take the lead in tackling magical enemies like these. We'll be meeting with government officials shortly to discuss all the ways we can strike back against the organizations of terror these criminals represent."

Oh, no. No, no, no. A chill washed over me from head to toe.

I knew what she was doing. She was courting the public's favor because anyone who'd already distrusted magic would be even more wary of mages now. But didn't they realize that fighting back with more magic would only make things worse?

The League members were still focused on the first part of her speech. "There go all the promises they made this morning," one girl muttered. "Why would we expect anything different?"

"We can't let them use this attack as an excuse to crack down even harder on mages like us," someone else piped up. "We'll be even worse off than when we started."

"Hold on," Luis said, moving to the front of the room. "They're panicking and saying what they think the Dull viewers want to hear. We can't know for sure how much of this they mean. And if they do try to go back on their promises, we'll just remind them of those. It's public record now."

"As if the public cares," someone muttered.

Finn raised his head. "Some of them do," he said, even though I could tell he was shaken by the newscast too. "We had a hell of a lot of support this morning. If we—"

All at once, the magic spasmed around us. A tremor shot through the ground beneath our feet, making the TV stand and the light fixture overhead rattle. A glass toppled off the table to smash on the floor.

The energy wrenched a cry from my mouth, shoving me with so much force that I stumbled and fell to my knees. Magic ripped through the room, searing and then freezing, racing along my nerves. Images burst into my head, ones I could sense were real although carried from a long ways away: the blaze of an explosion tinged with magical light, a toppling wall, a shriek, the stuttering of a machine gun.

I huddled on the floor, clutching my arms over my head to shield myself from the magic's battering. It wailed on and on, its natural harmony warped like the world's worst musician sawing off-key on a violin's strings. Something crashed just outside the building we were in.

They'd done it. The fragmented scenes that flashed through my mind told me that with glimpses of flame and a smoky, bloody flavor that coated my mouth. Someone had launched the special ops assault I'd come home to stop. The people I'd trained with, worked with, and dozens more from the bases across the world were at that moment battering insurgent hideouts and magic itself at the same time.

Finn's best friend Prisha would be out there, and Leonie, the other girl from our tentative alliance in the Exam who'd made Champion. I'd promised them I'd do whatever I could to make sure they didn't have to go on that suicide run.

They might already be dead.

My vision turned watery. I closed my eyes. The magic tore at me again, not so much a desperate child begging for help as a being at the end of its rope, striking out in every direction in the hope of hitting something that would bring relief.

A hand came to rest on my side. Finn's voice warbled through the frenzied energy streaming around me.

"Rocío. I'm here. What can I do?"

Nothing. None of us could do anything. Hopelessness closed around me for a few suffocating seconds. Then I clenched my jaw against it.

No. We were still here. The magic was still here, crazed or not. There had to be something that would make a difference.

The initial raging outburst was simmering down. I eased up my head to look around. The crowd had scattered to one end of the basement apartment, away from the windows, one of which held only broken shards now. A rush of winter air coursed into the room.

"Is it over?" someone asked.

"Not yet," I said hoarsely. The magic was quaking more than lashing out now, but it still ran over my skin in an erratic tempo that turned my stomach. Outside, snowflakes whipped around in a wind I suspected was more than simple air currents.

I wasn't sure I'd be able to cast through this discord. I was a little afraid to try. My hand came up instinctively to grasp the sunburst necklace Mom had given me right before I'd gone into the Exam. The tines, some of them slightly melted from the trials we'd faced there, bit into my palm, helping me narrow down my thoughts.

Finn knelt beside me, his face even paler than usual. "There was another attack?"

"The one... not here." I coughed to clear my throat. My lungs constricted as I gripped my necklace harder. "They launched it after all. Maybe I should have gone back to Zacher. Maybe I could have talked him down."

"No." He looped his arm around me in a partial embrace. "This isn't on you. The Dull government probably set the operation back in motion the moment they heard about the attack on the Confed building. You said that was the deal, didn't you? As long as no one attacked us, they wouldn't attack anyone."

"That's right." Even Zacher might not have been in a position to stop it. People got hurt, and the first thing they wanted to do was hit back. Just like the magic was hitting us.

A ripple of energy slammed into my cheek. I winced, my

teeth nicking my lip, and suddenly I tasted blood for real, not just as an impression from some distant battle.

The military had launched their attack—and people must have felt the aftershock through the magic all across the world. That was *proof* of everything I'd told Zacher. How could they deny it now?

Just like before, my instincts balked at the thought of reaching out to the Dull officials. *You can't trust those pendejos,* my older brother Javi would have said. *They're only looking out for themselves. They don't understand magic, and they don't want to.*

I couldn't deny he'd been right about most of the Dull authorities. But Zacher had at least tried, and if anyone could do something to stop the magic's blustering from getting any worse, it'd be the people who could call the shots on the Confed's entire military division. I knew from experience it wasn't the Circle who had the final say there.

I needed to have faith in my own judgment. *My* instinct, under that first knee-jerk distrust of every authority figure, was to try. Because Lord knew what would happen to us if I didn't try everything I could.

I pushed myself onto my feet with Finn helping me keep my balance. "I need to talk to Zacher now," I said. "The Dull government must be getting reports—they *have* to see that all the attacks are damaging the magic."

"*Damaging* the magic?" Callum repeated in a skeptical tone. In my daze, I'd almost forgotten our audience.

"Get the TV back on," Luis said with a gesture. "We need to find out where they've hit now."

I shook my head. "It's not here. It's— I don't have time to explain it all, but when we use magic to destroy things, to kill people, it throws the magic out of harmony. We've done it so much since the Unveiling that it's just… breaking down. That's why it's going wild like this." I waved my hand toward the broken window. "I'm pretty sure what we just felt is because of something that happened on the other side of the *ocean*. But maybe I can stop that from happening again."

I felt for my phone in my pocket. The magic crackled around me like static, itching in my ears.

Finn eased me over to the door. "Do you know how to reach him?" he asked as we stepped into the more private space of the basement stairwell.

"I think I can get him on the line. Maybe you should go back and talk to your League. They probably think I'm delusional, but they know you."

Finn nodded with a jerk of his head. "I guess—Zacher won't know anything about the operatives overseas yet, will he?"

He was worried about Prisha, of course. I grasped his arm. "As soon as I hear anything about them, I'll let you know."

"Thank you." He gave me a quick but determined kiss, there and then pulling away before I had more than a second to kiss him back. "You've got this," he said, with that unshakeable faith he'd always seemed to have in me. Then he disappeared back into the apartment.

I'd only talked to Zacher before via my soldier shadow, who was long gone, but there was always the indirect route. If she'd told him by now that she'd lost track of me, he'd be hoping to hear from me.

I dialed the operator and asked for the Pentagon's public line. The guy who answered sounded absurdly bored considering the havoc his bosses had just ordered. "You have reached the Pentagon. How may I direct your call?"

"I'd like to speak to John Zacher."

There was momentary silence. "John *Zacher*," the guy repeated, sounding a lot more alert now.

I found I had zero capacity left for politeness. "Yeah, the Secretary of Defense. I'm assuming you know of him? If you can't put me straight through to him, get me his secretary or something. Say it's Rocío Lopez calling. He'll want to talk to me."

"I—I'll see what I can do."

He left me with the soft drone of the hold signal. I shifted my weight from one foot to the other.

The other line clicked on with an abrupt, "Hello? Miss Lopez?"

I recognized Zacher's brisk voice. "Mr. Zacher. I'm sorry—I got kind of sidetracked. I think you know what made me think I should get back in touch."

"I did tell you—"

"I know," I said. I didn't want to hear his excuses. From outside the building, another ominous thud sounded, and someone cried out in fear or pain. I cringed and made myself go on. "And *I* told you. If I'm seeing the effects of that attack here, I'll bet you've had a few smashed windows and dented walls out in Virginia too."

"Yes," he admitted. "We have."

"So can we at least make sure no one screws things up even more than they already have? Will the president listen to you if you tell him the Confed's soldiers need to stay out of combat starting now?"

"That's why I'm glad you contacted me." Something about the evenness of his tone sent a prickle down my spine. "I've tried talking to people here, and they're having as much trouble wrapping their heads around all this as I did at first. I think for them to fully understand everything you told me, it's going to need to come from you—not me, not your colleagues here. Will you meet me and a few of my associates so we can talk and perhaps demonstrate in person?"

"Meet where?" I wasn't going to travel all the way down to the Pentagon again.

Zacher must have sensed my uncertainty. "Let's say we come

to you. Penn Station in an hour? We'll meet you by the main entrance."

A busy train station sounded like a safe enough place for a meeting. If his "associates" really needed more convincing than he could manage, and I had a chance to persuade them to stand down on any further attacks, I couldn't say no to that.

"All right," I said, but my mind had also stuck on his comment about *my* colleagues. Three of my special ops teammates had gone AWOL alongside me, and they'd stayed in Dull military custody while I returned to New York. "What about—the guys I came with? Are they all right?"

"Oh, absolutely," Zacher said. "They're getting settled in at the apartment where we set them up—worried about you, of course, but perfectly safe themselves."

"Okay," I said with a little relief. They'd definitely been far from the actual attack, in any case. "Penn Station in an hour, then."

# CHAPTER THREE

*Finn*

No matter how practiced I became at explaining how magic was alive and could be hurt by the ways we used it, I suspected I'd continue to receive disbelieving skepticism in response. It was like trying to convince people that gravity had opinions on international politics.

When Rocío had first suggested the idea to me during the Exam, I'd reacted in much the same way that the League members who were staring at me now. I shifted on my feet where I was standing by the door to the basement apartment, grappling with all the things 'chantments prevented me from saying—or in some cases, even remembering.

"I've seen it with my own eyes," I said. "I've watched how the magic responds to Rocío. I swear to you, there's something there, something conscious, and certain castings weaken it and make it more erratic. Even if you can't hearken it anymore, all you've got to do is look at that broken window to know."

Several people followed my gesture to the window the magic had smashed. By the TV, Mark grimaced. "There aren't any reports of a new local attack, just more general craziness with the magic acting up."

Luis, who'd come to stand beside me, rubbed his jaw. "I can hearken enough to feel that the energy is off-kilter," he said. "And not in a way that seems like a specific casting."

I shot him a grateful smile. The other Dampered mages in the room were nodding.

"What can we do about it, then?" someone asked. "Won't it settle down again on its own?"

"I'm not sure, now that it's been pushed this far." The eerie sound of the wind outside kept the hairs on the back of my neck on end. "The most important thing is for our National Defense division to stand down. Any attacks they make with magic are only going to worsen the situation."

"And the Circle's on the news gabbing about how they're going to send their forces to punish the terrorists every which way," Tamara muttered with a frown.

"Exactly," I said.

"We can't let the terrorists get away with it, can we?" Callum said.

"If going after them right now damages the magic in some permanent way, it sounds like a strategy adjustment is in order," Luis said. "Losing the ability to cast, having the magic run wild like this—it hurts all of us. The League's mission is to try to make sure everyone keeps their connection to the magic. We aren't serving that goal very well if we stand back when everyone could lose it, all at once."

Just then, the door behind me opened, and Rocío slipped back into the apartment. Her mouth was set in a small, grim smile, but I didn't think I'd ever seen her look so exhausted, not even in the fragments of memory I'd retained from the Exam. My heart wrenched.

She stepped close to me so only a few people nearby could

overhear. "Zacher wants me to meet up with him and a few of his colleagues here in the city," she said. "He says they won't believe what I told him unless they hear it from me. I don't know how well that's going to go, but… I've got to give it a shot. He was able to at least delay the one attack."

It couldn't hurt to try. "How soon?" I asked. "Some of us could come with you for backup, just in case you need it."

"An hour," she said. "But I think I'd better go alone. If everything goes well, then having more people along will just confuse things, and if anything goes wrong…" Her voice dropped even more. "I'm having enough trouble controlling castings with all my magical ability. I'm not sure even a Dampered mage with a relevant talent could cast well enough to defend themselves."

A Burnout would be a total liability, someone she'd have to protect rather than someone who could protect her. She hadn't said it, and she wouldn't have, but a shamed flush crept up to my cheeks anyway.

I didn't want to let her go off to face a bunch of Dull military officials alone. This girl who'd done so much to save so many people—the girl who'd owned my heart since the Exam—deserved someone who could stand beside her.

My thoughts tripped back to my conversation with Luis and the others. There were ways I could stand in support of her cause even if not in the same place. I glanced at the leader of the League.

"What if we went to speak to the Circle? Bump up that meeting they agreed to. They offered to speak to us as equals—we should use that. Like you said, our primary mission is to make sure everyone keeps their magical ability. If we can show them that the problem is so dire that even Dampered mages are sensing it, maybe we can persuade them to at least be more careful in how they allow National Defense to get involved."

Luis nodded slowly. "We'll make it a small delegation. Show we expect that there's no need for protests now. The worst they can do is turn us away, and then we know nothing's changed after all. You'll come?"

My pulse stuttered. "Of course." I stood with the League, and the Circle might as well see how fully I'd made that commitment.

"If the Circle is willing to push back against the Dull government's demands, that should help any case Zacher is willing to make for us," Rocío said. The smile she gave me then was sweet enough to light me up from the inside. "If anyone can convince them, it's you."

"All right," I said with all the confidence I could summon, for both her sake and mine. "Let's do this."

* * *

The remaining members of the Circle and an assortment of lesser Confed officials had settled temporarily into the administrative wing of the college. As Luis, Tamara, and I climbed the front steps to the main entrance, I couldn't help remembering the times I'd walked through the halls ahead of us, always assuming I'd do so as a student before long. When I'd thrown away my Chosen status to declare for the Exam, I'd thrown away my future here as well.

I couldn't quite summon anything like regret, only a slight queasiness in my gut. I had no desire to go back to the blithely ignorant Finn I'd been in those days, heedless of the many injustices happening under my nose.

The Circle had brought Confed security to the college with them. We'd waited until the guards on patrol outside had passed before we went in, but another pair stood just inside the doors.

"Hold up there," one said, raising her hand. "Classes are

canceled until next week. If you have official business here, we'll need to see IDs."

Luis and Tamara gazed past the guards into the main foyer with its thick, red-and-orange rug, the mahogany staircases leading up to the second-floor halls, and an immense bronze chandelier overhead. A flicker of awe touched both their faces. They'd grown up in new-magic families—they'd never had the opportunity to simply stroll through the Confed's main buildings.

*Time to put my own familiarity to use, then.*

"We're here on behalf of the mages of the Freedom of Magic League," I said, my chin raised and voice steady. "I'm Finnegan Lockwood. My granduncle Raymond Lockwood and two of his colleagues in the Circle agreed to meet with us to discuss the future of the Confederation. Considering what happened to my granduncle and the catastrophes since, we felt that discussion is more urgent than ever."

Luis quirked an eyebrow at my tone. I was channeling Granduncle Raymond to the best of my ability. His authoritarian attitude didn't come naturally to me, but the guards appeared to be affected by it. They exchanged an uncertain glance, their stances turning a bit defensive.

"I'm not sure the Circle is open to speaking with anyone at the moment," the other guard said.

I fixed my stare on him. "They're here, aren't they?" That would be the seven of them still with us—from what the news reports had said, two members had been in the Confed building when it came down, and they hadn't been recovered. "Let them know that we're here. Speak to Ms. Cunningham—she agreed to the meeting too. You can remind her that we have information they may want to take into consideration."

It might be evening now, but after the disaster and the sentiments Cunningham had been expressing on the news, I wouldn't be surprised if the Circle meant to discuss their next action through the night. I might as well use whatever leverage I had to get us to them. Luis and Tamara didn't know yet what Rocío and I had uncovered about the Dulls' small but definite latent magic ability, but Cunningham, who'd been next to Granduncle Raymond when I'd threatened to go public with the information, did.

The first guard stepped off to the side to speak into her radio. Tamara caught my eye and gave me an encouraging nod. She and Luis would do most of the talking for the League, but at least I'd been able to help smooth their arrival. Gods willing, my presence might lend weight to their arguments with the Circle too.

After a few minutes of hushed conversation through the radio, the security guard waved for us to follow her. "I'll escort you to their room."

We headed up the righthand stairs and down a hall that smelled of wood polish. A few more security guards stood posted outside some of the classroom doors we passed before we reached the end. Our guard knocked on a door there and then opened it.

On the other side, the seven remaining Circle members were sitting around a makeshift meeting table formed by three executive desks pulled together. Papers and books lay scattered on the wooden desktops, and a couple of the mages had computer tablets in front of them. They all raised their heads at our entrance, but no one stood to greet us.

They looked a lot less impressive in this relatively ordinary setting compared to the grandeur of their public appearances. Who were they, really, but seven aging mages who'd grown up in a time before magic was anything but a secret? The twist in my gut eased a little.

Cunningham and the man who'd come out with her and Granduncle Raymond during the protest—Leron, I thought his last name was—perched in their chairs, kitty-corner to each other near the doorway. Their wary gazes lingered on me.

"I hardly think this is the time for us to discuss the exact details of the Exam or admission to the college or anything else," said a woman farther down the desks.

"I think it's the perfect time to talk," Luis said smoothly, his eyes bright. I knew him well enough now to recognize the tension in his stance, but the Circle members probably wouldn't see it through his aura of assurance. "Specifically, to talk about whether you plan to order any of the mages who *are* allowed to keep their magic to fight on behalf of Dull government interests. You said on the news that today's events show why magic use should be regulated. They've also proven that striking back against our enemies using magic endangers all of us."

Tamara picked up the thread. "We've heard that certain types of castings disrupt and weaken the magic. Even those of us who have most of our abilities dampered can hearken how it's reacting to the attacks carried out on both sides today. We want to see every mage keep their magic, and that means there'd better be magic around for them to work with."

None of the Circle members appeared startled by her statement. Rocío had suspected they all must know about the fragile state of the magic.

Cunningham continued to study me, her broad brow knit, perhaps wondering how much else I might have shared with my companions. "We have a commitment to the Dull government," she said. "The most immediate problems must be dealt with first."

Luis motioned toward the window behind her. "I'd say magical energy running wild and smashing up all kinds of things in its path is a pretty immediate problem."

"Better that than another magical assault on the level of this afternoon's," Leron said. "Or—" He cut himself off with a flattening of his pale lips. His beady gaze slid back to me.

"Or what?" I demanded. "I know you've been under pressure from the Dulls, but if you have any extra sway while you're investigating the attack, it can't hurt you to at least *try* to convince them—"

"We will not have our strategies dictated by a seventeen-year-old boy," Cunningham said tartly, pulling her posture straighter with her boxy shoulders rigid. "None of you have any idea of the complexity of the situation, nor is it your place to. But you should at least be able to appreciate that as a massive *magical* assault has been launched on the city, our relations with the Dull authorities are already even more fraught than usual."

"It's not as if they're going to call you terrorists for pointing out a real problem with the magic," Tamara protested.

She might be wrong about that—or at least the Circle members thought she was. A shadow of uncertainty crossed at least half the faces in the room, and a sudden certainty struck me.

They were afraid—afraid of the Dull government, afraid of losing what cooperation and support they had there, afraid of admitting any weakness. They were more afraid of that than they were of permanently damaging the magic.

They weren't going to change their minds unless we forced them to.

Cunningham was already waving her hand to the security guard who'd followed us in. "Escort our visitors out of the building, please. This meeting is over."

I hadn't come here just to be turned away. Rocío wouldn't have given up at the first dismissal. She needed me—and I didn't need to care what the seven people in front of me thought of me anymore.

"No," I said as the guard touched my arm to usher us out. "There has to be a way you can find a compromise, or—"

"I *said* this meeting is over." Cunningham stood up, and the security guard's hand clamped around my elbow.

My pulse thumped harder, but if I was going to play this card in front of anyone from the League, Luis and Tamara were the ones I'd have trusted above anyone else. They'd understand how important it was. They'd always supported Dull involvement with the League.

"Do you really want to turn me away when there's so much you wouldn't want me saying to the people out there?" I asked, catching Cunningham's eyes and then Leron's.

Leron paled. One of the other Circle members turned to him. "What's he talking about?"

"It doesn't matter," Cunningham snapped. *Her* face had darkened with an angry flush. "Take Mr. Lockwood into custody, please. He's just revealed himself to be a threat to national security."

As the security guard reached for my other hand to restrain me, I couldn't restrain a sputtering laugh with no humor in it at all. *I* was a threat to national security? The threat I'd just made only affected the seven people in this room. It could help the rest of the country.

"Arresting me isn't going to keep the truth about the Dulls from getting out," I said quickly. "There are other people who know how your testing for magical potential works—that every person could learn to use magic if you'd give them the chance. If I disappear, that information will only get out faster."

"What?" one of the other men said, flushing even darker than Cunningham had. Panic flashed across the face of the woman next to him. Leron looked as if he'd swallowed his tongue.

He and Cunningham hadn't shared my original threat with the rest of the Circle, then. Perhaps they'd hoped they could contain me before the others found out that the Confed's biggest secret had been compromised.

Luis's head had jerked around. As he stared at me, Tamara let out a dry chuckle. "My God," she said. "It figures."

The security guard's grasp on my wrist had loosened in shock. She wouldn't have known about the testing or the Dulls' magical potential either. I suspected I could break free now if I tried, but this wasn't the moment to snap her back into arrest mode—not while we still had a chance of continuing our negotiations.

"Your best option to control how that information gets out is to work with us—with the Freedom of Magic League," I said. "I can keep quiet as long as I know you're listening to us and making changes. We can figure out this catastrophe together."

"We're not making any deals." Cunningham shoved back her chair with a rasp of its legs against the floor. "Hold them here. Sylvie, you're adept with mental 'chantments. We can make sure none of them ever speaks on this subject again."

A chill sliced through me. I knew how effective silencing 'chantments could be. The woman Cunningham had addressed rose with pursed lips, but she took a step toward us. Whatever she thought about the order, she was going to protect her standing above anything else.

The only thing in our favor was that the Circle hadn't dared to call in any of the other guards, probably worried I'd spread the word to them. No doubt they'd silence the one holding me or wipe that part of her memory when they were done muzzling us.

Then the responsibility would fall entirely on Rocío's shoulders again. I *couldn't* let that happen. The time for negotiating was clearly over, though.

I yanked my arm away from the security guard and spun toward the door. Cunningham cried out a warning. Before I could even touch the doorknob, a hand shoved me down on the floor.

It wasn't the guard—it was Luis, clutching Tamara's shoulder too. A strained lyric tumbled over his lips, his expression going taut with concentration. With a jolt, we dropped straight through the floor.

I landed on my hands and knees at the edge of a classroom full of empty desks, the smack of the impact radiating through my limbs. Tamara swore but heaved herself to her feet at the same time I did. "What the hell?" she said to Luis.

A smile crossed the League leader's lips. Then he swayed and had to catch the edge of a table for balance. "The one skill they left me with was teleportation. I don't have the ability to take us any farther than those few feet, though—and with the magic as unstable as it is right now, even that was harder than usual. Come on. We still have to get out of this place before they lock up our minds, if not the rest of us."

Raised voices already carried through the ceiling from the room above. We dashed into the hall just as someone teleported into the room behind us. Tamara slammed the door, and we bolted for the front entrance.

Veering around a corner, we raced into the path of a young woman with a couple of books clasped to her chest and a loose hijab tucked over her hair. Her dark eyes widened at the sight of us. "Finn?"

A memory jolted loose: her face framed by examiner gray, her murmured reassurance. She was the one—

"Let's go!" Tamara said, yanking both me and Luis with her through another doorway. "There's more than one way to get through a wall."

She urged us on through a lecture hall and hoisted a chair from the end of the row to heave it through one of the arched windows. The glass shattered, clinking onto the ground outside.

Tamara set the chair beneath the window, and we hopped onto it one by one to scramble outside. I dodged a shard still protruding from the frame. This might not be the most graceful way to exit the school I'd once dreamed of attending, but the magic had smashed enough glass today that I couldn't bring myself to feel all that guilty either.

We ran across the short lawn between the building and the sidewalk and came face-to-face with a crowd converging on the college.

I'd been part of enough protests in the last few months to recognize one. The problem was that the dozens of people marching up on the building held signs with slogans like *No magic in our city!* and *Mages = terror!* Several of them were already hollering, their faces twisted with a mix of fear and anger. I stumbled mid-step.

Dad had talked about the anti-magic contingent in the country—the organizations that pushed back against public mage activities and stirred up trouble at any events that went forward. My grandfather had been killed by one of those people before I was even born. I'd seen a few of their demonstrations on the news, but I'd never encountered a mob of this size face-to-face.

Cunningham had mentioned that the terrorist attack was making mage-Dull relations more fraught. Obviously it'd stirred up the ordinary civilians as well as the government. They were blaming us for the insurgents making their city a target.

I wheeled backward, sharply aware of the Burnout mark on my forehead that identified me as some sort of mage. I doubted these people would care about how little magic I could still conduct. For a second, with the stutter of my heart, I felt caught on both sides. Enthen mén Skýllē, hetérōthi de dîa Charubdis. We could hardly flee back into the building.

"This way," Luis said, gesturing toward a side street a ways from the entrance. Shouts rang out after us as we sprinted for it.

The protesters didn't follow us. Their voices faded as we hustled down the street. We still had the Circle's security force to worry about, though. I slowed a little but kept to a jog, watching to make sure Luis wasn't too worn out from his teleportation casting to keep pace.

His brown skin looked slightly gray, but that might only have been the effect of the dwindling sunlight as dusk set in. "Subway," he suggested, pointing to an entrance up ahead. The three of us hurried down the steps and underground.

On the platform, he stopped and leaned against the wall, his breath coming roughly. His gaze stayed on me. "Is it true what you were saying to the Circle? I'm guessing it has to be, from the way they reacted."

I wet my lips. "It is. I found out—I lent Noemi a few of my books on magical techniques, she started practicing, and she managed some small castings. Rocío's seen an entire database where the Confed has all our assessment numbers. The Dulls have a rating for magical talent; it's just at a lower level than the people the Confed counts as mages. I have to assume only a small number of people have access to those figures. This just confirmed it."

"Wow," Tamara muttered. "All this time..." She shook her head, her beaded hair clinking, her expression more rueful than surprised. "How much trouble are you going to be in for that stunt, Finn?"

Dear Zeus, I didn't even want to think about that. It shouldn't matter anyway. I hadn't expected to count on the Circle or the rest of the Confed for anything now.

I forced my mouth into a pained smile. "All the trouble, if the Circle or their security people catch me. So I'll just have to keep away from anyplace they'd think to look."

If I'd wanted to second-guess where and with whom I'd thrown in my lot, that chance was gone. Until we'd decided what to do with this information—until it was out, one way or another, and the Circle no longer had reason to keep me contained—I couldn't even think about going home.

# CHAPTER FOUR

*Rocío*

It was nearly an hour after I'd felt the immediate effects of the military strike overseas, and the magic still hadn't settled down to even the mildly frantic state it'd reached after the Confed building attack. As I hurried through the dusk toward Penn Station, the wind gusted in odd directions. I could hearken the erratic energy racing through it, but even the Dulls could tell *something* was wrong with it. The few pedestrians I passed on the street eyed their surroundings anxiously.

I tugged my hat lower against the deepening chill and tried texting first Desmond and then Sam. No response. Zacher had said my special ops teammates were fine, but I suspected his people had taken away their phones. Although that was a normal thing when the government put someone in a safe house, wasn't it? To protect them from saying the wrong thing to the wrong person?

The street outside the station was unusually quiet. Between the attack and the magic's lashing out, the trains might not even be running. I wasn't sure how Zacher had planned on getting here. It took more than an hour to travel by train from the Pentagon. He might have already been heading to the city, hoping to speak with me as soon as possible.

The lights over the entrance split the dusk with a weak glow, a few spots dark where the magic must have shattered the bulbs. I crept down the stairs into the immense underground concourse. The shops along the sides had all closed for the night, their interiors shadowed. Zacher and four other figures in suits—three men, one woman—waited farther into the room. Otherwise, we were alone.

The eeriness of the empty station locked my legs, but the Secretary of Defense had already spotted me. "Miss Lopez," he called with a small smile, motioning me over. "I'm glad you could make it." His voice echoed off the low ceiling, adding to the unsettling atmosphere.

I inhaled slowly. I was a mage—a powerful one—and I had no reason to think this man was a threat. But still, to ease my nerves, I sang under my breath to the energy around me. The magic twisted and shivered, but as I focused, enough of it condensed around me that if anyone came at me with malicious intentions, the barrier I'd just conjured would deflect their first offensive.

The people flanking Zacher stirred impatiently. I walked over, past a side hallway with blocky beige columns down the middle. I stopped there, still about ten feet away from the group, the back of my neck prickling. Zacher hadn't made any move to meet me.

Maybe I was paranoid, letting the skepticism Javi had taught me take over. But I was sure this time *my* instincts were sounding the alarm too. I wanted to trust the man in front of me, but it'd be ridiculous to throw caution to the wind.

"Hi," I said, with a dip of my head to him and then his colleagues. The way they were watching me, as if I were a rare zoo animal and not a regular human being, didn't exactly comfort me. I shifted my gaze back to Zacher. "Here I am. What did you want me to tell these people—or show them?"

The corners of his smile tightened, almost apologetically. My stomach clenched in response.

"We feel it would be best if you came back to Washington, actually," he said. "With tensions as high as they are right now, and the situation so volatile—"

"For how long?" I interrupted, even though I balked at the idea of leaving the city—leaving Finn, my parents, the people in the League who might be willing to help—on the Dull government's command. "To do what? If I can't say anything here that will convince people, even with the way the magic's been behaving for everyone to see, I don't know what I could say *there* that would make any difference."

Zacher's expression turned even grimmer, and a new trickle of suspicion ran through me. Meeting like this hadn't been his idea. He was following orders just like he was asking me to do—orders I wasn't sure he even liked.

"It's not so much about convincing anyone," Zacher said. "Although there are a lot of people who couldn't make it here tonight who'd like to better understand what you told me. We want you to try teaching. What you were able to accomplish with me in less than an hour—you can see that with a threat like these insurgent groups right on our doorstep, we need every advantage we can get to defend ourselves."

His words took a few seconds to sink in. I stared at him. "You want me to teach more people—your soldiers?—how to use magic?"

The woman with him brightened up at that question, looking happy that I'd caught on.

Zacher nodded. "Our enemies will regroup for another attack. We can count on that. If our people can meet them with unexpected skills at their disposal—"

"No." I backed up a step. The magic wanted me to keep going, tugging at my collar as if it was as frightened by his suggestion as I was horrified. The circular lights overhead flickered. "Don't you remember anything *else* we talked about this morning. If we twist the magic to fight our battles, it's only going to break down and lash out more."

Zacher held up his hands. "It wouldn't have to be aggressive magic. Spells for healing or communication or identifying threats—those would all be useful too."

Using the magic for healing would also help heal the past damage they'd dealt to it. A tiny part of me longed to believe him, but the rest of me knew better. If I went back with him, it wouldn't be Zacher calling all the shots. I'd already served more time in the military than I'd ever wanted to, and I knew to what lengths the officers would go to get what they wanted.

I shook my head. "Even if we started that way, you know they'd want me teaching magical attacks in no time. I can't take that risk."

The man next to Zacher piped up. "With one mass effort, we could subdue the insurgent groups completely and then rest easy."

I shot him an incredulous look. "Are you kidding me? That's what everyone was saying about the attack you just launched." *One decisive strike*, my commander back at the base in Estonia had said. "And you're already talking about another one."

"It'd be our people, following our orders," the man replied. "No need to rely on the Confederation with whatever hidden agendas they have."

Didn't he know how far the Confed bent their priorities to make his military leaders happy? "That's not the point."

"Miss Lopez," Zacher started, his tone soothing but his expression weary.

"No," I said again. "If that's the only reason you asked me to meet you, you've got my answer. I'm not doing anything that'll hurt the magic more than people already have."

I started to turn, and several soldiers in fatigues appeared from behind the columns down the side hall, all of them with rifles pointed at me. My pulse skipped a beat.

"I regret that it has to come to this." Zacher sounded genuinely sorry, as if that helped me any. "But with what you know and what you're capable of, I'm afraid I have to insist that you come with us."

I wasn't going to be much use to anyone dead. Maybe the soldiers had been told to shoot me in the leg to simply stop me from running, or maybe the guns had tranquilizers rather than bullets. I wasn't sticking around to find out.

With my heart pounding my throat, I made a dash for the stairs.

Shots crackled, and my shield shuddered around me. "Careful!" Zacher shouted. Footsteps thudded after me.

"Los de adelante corren mucho," I murmured, urging more speed to my own feet. The barrier I'd conjured quivered and flinched. I sang fresh strands of magic around me, struggling to keep my rhythm through the physical exertion and the energy's uneasy thrum.

I scrambled up the steps two at a time, only to see more armed figures charging to cover the exit. ¡Mierda! For once, I was glad for the magical and physical training I'd endured in the special ops program—without it, I wouldn't have stood a chance.

I gasped one last lyric to solidify my shield the best I could and dove between two of the soldiers. One reached to snatch me and slammed his arm into the conjured wall. The force vibrated through the magic and sent me sprawling onto the sidewalk. I hurled myself up and onward, ignoring the sting in my palms.

A car blared its horn as I bolted across the street in front of it, but that near-collision might have saved me from capture. I threw myself behind a parked truck farther down the road and sang to the magic in a low voice, willing it to draw the darkness closer around me the way I had in the alley earlier today. With night falling, hiding myself in shadows was easier even if the magic still pulled away from my call more than it aligned with the melody.

Soldiers barreled past me, calling to each other as they searched the street. A few passed their gazes over me, but none of them hesitated for even a second. I held as still and quiet as I could, willing the magic not to abandon me.

A voice carried from across the street—the man in the suit who'd pitched the idea of one big attack. "And now we've lost her."

"I told you she wouldn't like the proposal," Zacher replied.

"We can't trust any of these goddamned mages," the woman said. "They only care about themselves. For all we know, she tricked you into calling off that attack, to begin with."

"I know what I experienced," Zacher said tersely. "There's still the other three. They may not be as adept as she is, but we can see what they might offer."

*The other three.* My special ops teammates, he meant. My hands clenched at my sides. What would they do to the guys to force them to teach magical combat?

It'd been my idea to go AWOL, my idea to turn to Zacher. Because of me, the three of them were stuck in the Dull government's custody. I couldn't just leave them there.

"Hey!" the first man said, presumably to one of the soldiers. "Take a few of your men and swing by the New Jersey safe house where we have the other mages. We want to be sure *they* don't go anywhere."

Wonderful. But even if he'd put more obstacles in my way, he'd also given me a chance to find my colleagues in the first place.

I edged over to the end of the car so I could watch the activity across the street. Zacher and the suits left in one direction, and four of the soldiers marched the other way to a gray van with a ladder mounted on one of the back doors, reaching for the cargo rack on the roof.

I zeroed in on that detail and braced myself as the soldiers clambered into the van. The second the doors closed, I dashed across the street.

The engine rumbled. I whispered the magic closer around me to blend me into the shadows as I sprinted the last several feet. Just as the van started to pull onto the road, I sprang up and caught hold of the ladder.

It took another hastily spat out casting to stop from thumping against the back of the vehicle. I hooked my arm around one rung and braced my legs against a lower one. A burn was already spreading through my muscles, but I steeled my mind against it.

This was going to be a long trip, but I intended to make it.

* * *

My whole body ached by the time the van jerked to a stop outside a trio of squat brick apartment buildings. I winced as I detached my arm from the ladder's rung and darted away from the vehicle just as the doors started to open.

A car farther down the curb gave me enough shelter to watch the soldiers emerge. They tramped over to the last building on the block and marched inside.

I approached warily, crossing my arms over my chest against the magic's flailing. It yanked my hair and prodded my face, but I was far from its only target. A low windstorm driven by the tumultuous energy warbled through the streets. My protective shadows kept fraying no matter how often I murmured to draw more magic into them.

Outside the building, I dragged in a breath and turned to another casting from my special ops days. With a lilting lyric, I sent my awareness skimming through the walls to search out any living presence inside the apartments beyond.

There were lots of occupants scattered through the building, which had to hold at least six separate residences. But toward the rear, on the top floor that was three stories up, three people pinged my awareness with their familiarity. Sam, Desmond, and Brandt had stayed close to each other in the same room. I sensed a couple of other people nearby, with more throughout the apartment around them. Ten in total—Zacher had nearly doubled their guard.

I scanned the outer walls and then moved to the next building over, which had a fire escape running along one side. With a magical boost that took twice as much effort as it should have, I jumped to grasp the first platform and hauled myself the rest of the way up with muscles alone. My feet hissed over the metal steps as I hurried up to the roof.

The gap between the two buildings wasn't much wider than a car. I might have been able to jump it without help, but considering how tired I was, I added another boost of magic to carry me across. The energy I called to flinched away from my attempt to conjure a cushion for the landing at the last minute. My feet hit the roof with a thump that left me cringing.

Thankfully, I'd made my jump near the front of the building rather than right over the safe house apartment. After a minute's wait, with my ears pricked, it seemed that my colleagues' guards hadn't caught the noise. I slunk across the roof to the back apartment until I stood directly over the spot where I sensed the guys were.

The three of them might not have as strong a talent as I did, but they still had their full abilities. Even with the magic acting up, they should be able to manage some casting. I just needed to give them an opening to get out of there and let them know help was waiting outside.

I sang a little magic onto my tongue and conducted it into a whisper that I directed straight to Sam's ear. He'd been one of the team leaders in our squad—the other two would listen to him.

"When some of the soldiers leave, make a run for it. I'll cover you outside."

There was no way to confirm whether he'd heard me or if he would follow my instructions. I'd have to go ahead as if he had and hope for the best.

I stalked to the edge of the roof and picked out an alleyway across the street. The magic twisted against the melody I sang into it, but by tightening of my concentration and stiffening my stance, I convinced it to conjure a volley of sound. False gunshots rang out as if from the alley, mingled with crackles like magical attacks. They burst through the air loud enough to penetrate the apartment's closed windows.

Sweat trickled down my back despite the winter cold, but my gambit worked. Seconds later, five of the soldiers hustled out the building's front door. I pushed the conjured sounds farther away to lead them on a bit of a chase. Then I raced back to the other building and down its fire escape so I could meet my teammates on the ground.

I'd just dashed around onto the sidewalk when the three figures spilled through the doorway. I couldn't help smiling at the sight of them. "Here!" I hissed with a wave of my arm, and they veered toward me, panting. I suspected they were as winded from casting spells to slip by the other guards as they were from the run.

Of course, it couldn't be quite that easy. They'd just reached me when one of the soldiers charged out of the building and three more came loping back from their investigations. All four of them locked eyes on us in an instant. Their guns jerked up.

Without a thought, I launched into the casting I'd practiced and honed overseas. I whipped out the words and the magic I conducted with them with all the strength I had left.

The blast of energy knocked the figures to the ground and pinned them there. My own legs sagged under me with a wave of exhaustion. Sam caught my arm before I collapsed completely.

"Let's go!" he whispered to the others. Desmond slung my other arm over his shoulder, and I managed to keep up a stumbling run supported between the two of them.

The first few minutes of the escape passed in a blur. I wasn't sure exactly how far we'd run by the time Sam shouldered his way into a darkened laundromat he must have magically unlocked. We sank behind the closest row of dryers, the stale floral scent of old fabric softener tickling my nose.

"The military was going to try to use you to teach their army magic," I said between ragged breaths. "I had to get you out."

"I can't say I was enjoying the stay anyway," Sam said with a hint of wry humor. "It's good to see you."

I gave all three of them a tight smile. "I don't have much in the way of good news, but at least you aren't stuck in their custody anymore. It turns out Finn has a lot of friends. One of them might be able to help us figure out where to stay."

I pulled out my phone to text him, but my heart was still thumping heavy behind my ribs. If Zacher could pull a turnaround like this on us, was there any chance the Circle had seen reason?

And if they hadn't… where did we go from here?

# CHAPTER FIVE

*Finn*

The only thing worse than the feeling of epic failure was seeing the same hopelessness etched on the face of someone you loved. I'd recognized it in Rocío when Luis's friend had dropped her and her special ops squad-mates off at the New Jersey motel where we'd arranged to meet, and it lingered now as we sat across from each other on our respective beds.

Luis shifted next to me with a squeak of the mattress. The motel was a dingy place where the cash I'd managed to quickly take from my bank account could be stretched pretty far. To keep costs down, Luis and Tamara were sharing the room with Rocío and me, at least until we were sure of the Circle's next moves after the attempted arrest. Desmond and the two special ops guys I'd only met briefly were set up in the next room over, since the desk clerk had made the "max occupancy" rule gloweringly clear. Tamara had suggested that "ladies and gentlemen share with their own," and I wasn't going to argue even if I'd rather have been by Rocío's side.

The news channel Luis had turned on at a low volume

murmured through its commercials. He glanced around at each of us. "So," he said, "we can't expect any help from the magical authorities or the Dull ones. And it sounds like neither of them even trusts the other. That doesn't put us in the greatest position." He nodded to Rocío and me. "You two know more about the big picture than anyone else. Is there anything useful the League can do at this point?"

"I'll stand up if we know what we're standing for," Tamara put in. "But there *are* times when laying low for a bit is the best of a lot of bad options."

Rocío glanced toward the curtained window. A storm still blustered outside, too erratic to be purely the weather. The air carried an unexpected trace of ozone that left me unnerved too.

"I think addressing the harm that's been done to the magic has to come first," she said in her soft but steady voice. "We can't count on anyone else to consider what's best for it. But even if National Defense keeps fighting, we can at least try to offset the effects. Using magic to build and heal strengthens it and settles it down. The more of those castings we can conduct, on as broad a scale as possible, the more it should help."

A lump caught in my throat. "Most of us in the League either can't cast or are limited in what we can cast." I didn't think even magic like Luis's teleportation skill would do much to tip the balance.

"True." Her mouth curved with a crooked smile. "But we've got millions of Dulls in this city, all of whom should be able to cast at least a little with enough training. If we focused that training on the right kinds of castings… even if they can't do very much, not-very-much times several million is a heck of a lot."

"You think we should spread awareness of the nature of the magic and the Dulls' abilities," Luis clarified.

Rocío hesitated. "I'm not sure it'd be a good idea to make a big public statement right away. Even after what I showed the Secretary of Defense, his people sounded skeptical. Dulls have spent their whole life assuming we're almost a different type of *being* than they are… I don't know how easily they'd wrap their heads around the idea without proof. And you know the Circle will do everything they can to stifle the information. We might only get one chance."

"Which means we want it to be a chance with proof," I said, catching her reasoning.

"That's what I'm thinking. You have some Dull allies in the League, right? And they should have family or friends they feel comfortable reaching out to. We could start by teaching a smaller group of people we trust, and get some healing happening that way, and then bring it to a larger stage as soon as we think we've got a strong enough base that the Circle can't deny it and the other Dulls will have to believe it."

Luis clapped his hands together. "I like it. We can definitely pull an effort like that together. I'll just have to reach out to a few people—we'd need a place to hold the teaching sessions that won't be too obvious, and our first students…"

"There's that tutorial leader who's come to some of the meetings," Tamara said, similarly energized. "What was his name…? Eduard. He should have some good teaching strategies if he's willing to pitch in."

I grinned. "That's perfect. And even those of us who don't have our magic can do a little advising… I remember all those early lessons far too well."

I turned to Rocío to share the hope of the moment with her, but her eyes had fixed on the TV, her fingers digging into the bedspread. I followed her gaze, and my stomach lurched.

On the screen was a photograph of me along with an emergency alert saying that I was a wanted criminal—for what crimes, they didn't bother to state—and a contact number for the

Confederation security forces if anyone had information about my whereabouts.

The Circle had sent out a public call to action to track me down. Somehow, despite the way they'd treated me at the college just a few hours ago, I hadn't expected that.

My parents would see this... My siblings. My former classmates. What would they think? I'd already known I couldn't go home. Now I wasn't sure I could even safely talk to them if I'd wanted to.

"Well," I said, pleased that my voice didn't shake. "I suppose that complicates matters a little. I'll just have to be awfully careful not to show my face while we're carrying out these plans."

* * *

Luis motioned around the stock room we'd entered, which was about as big as my living room at home, with a tiled floor and concrete walls lined with steel shelves.

"What do you think? Vihaan said they only come back here for supplies a couple times a day. We could have decent teaching sessions without any interruptions. Not the most comfortable space the League has used, but I don't think we should rely on any place where we've held meetings before."

"I agree." I ambled farther into the space. The overhead light gleamed brightly but with a faint buzzing sound. "Could we bring in chairs?"

"It might be better to have people sitting on the floor," Rocío said, taking in the room with a thoughtful frown. "If we could get our hands on some yoga mats, we could roll them up when we're not here. Less imposition on the store."

Tamara snapped her fingers. "I've got a friend who works at a fitness center. They've got stacks and stacks of those. I bet she could lend us some."

As she and Rocío hashed out the equipment details, Luis's phone buzzed. He glanced at the text he'd received and knit his brow. After a couple of back-and-forths, he motioned me closer. "Eduard—the tutorial leader—will be stopping by in a few minutes, but I think Rocío and Tamara can fill him in," he said, pitching his voice to include the other two in the conversation. "You and I have other business to take care of, Finn, if you're up for it."

I gave him a questioning look. "Sure. What are we doing?"

"I'll explain on the way."

Rocío rushed back to us. "Let me just bolster the conjuring I've got shielding you. The magic is so twitchy, I want to be sure it'll hold."

She murmured the same Spanish lyric she'd used yesterday after we'd told her about our disastrous meeting with the Circle: a casting to ensure they couldn't track us by magical means. A pang came into my chest, watching her work with the magic—partly the awe I'd felt since the first time I'd seen her exercise her immense talent, and partly the memory of the meager ability the examiners had burned out of me.

Even on my best days, I'd never been able to conduct that living energy the way Rocío could, but her expression as she tuned her pitch to the rhythms I could no longer hearken brought up bittersweet memories. There was an entire aspect of the world locked away from me. I couldn't sense so much as a hint of the barrier I knew she'd conjured around Luis and me. The air felt as still and dull as it had since my burning out.

I'd adapted, but I didn't know if I'd ever stop missing it.

I tugged my hat lower and my new scarf higher so no one outside could see any of my face except my eyes. Rocío squeezed my hand, and I gripped hers back in silent reassurance. Then I followed Luis out to the street.

He strode along the sidewalk at a brisk pace, more hurried

than usual. The continuing magic-driven wind ruffled the curls that poked from beneath his own hat.

"What's going on?" I asked. Clearly it was something sensitive enough that he hadn't wanted to involve even Tamara or Rocío.

"I thought you and I should handle this alone," he said. "Too many tempers in the mix might just confuse the issue. Ary reached out. She wanted to talk to me."

My back went rigid. "Talk about what?" I asked. Was she going to invent some excuse for the casting that had killed my granduncle—or pretend she hadn't orchestrated it?

"She didn't say, but there are obviously plenty of things we need to work out." Luis glanced at me. "I know what you saw during the protest yesterday, Finn. I believe you. We won't let her off the hook—I don't approve of attacks on anyone, including the Circle, out of vengeance—but we have to give her a chance to talk."

I supposed my being there would help to hold her accountable. I was fairly sure she'd seen me noticing her in the crowd. It'd been the exact same plan I'd challenged her about a couple of weeks before.

"If the Confed found out she was involved, she'd be in jail," I said. "She's responsible for his death. Even if we don't call it outright murder, she set up a situation where she *knew* someone could be killed."

"I understand that. But we don't have proof, and no one wants to listen to us. Right now I'm mainly concerned with figuring out what she's up to and reining her in if she's not satisfied yet. The rest can come later."

Ary had asked Luis to meet her at Saks Fifth Avenue. When we reached the department store, I could guess why. Even with yesterday's attack and the continuing unusual weather, last-minute Christmas shoppers were bustling through the expansive foyer under the glistening lights. Carols carried from distant speakers, and a hint of pine hung in the air. If Ary got nervous, she could blend into the crowd and disappear as easily as she had during the protest.

I'd been *here* just a couple weeks ago, shopping with Prisha during one of her weekend leaves. My stomach knotted as Luis and I peered through the crowd.

O gods, I wished it were Prisha we expected to find now. I wished I at least knew that she wasn't lying broken and burned in the ruin of a building on the other side of the ocean. Even if she was alive, how long would National Defense keep her over there? How many more attacks would they launch now that the insurgents had hit us this hard?

I had to shove those worries aside when Luis nudged me. Ary had staked out a spot by a column on the edge of the foyer, her boyfriend and one of the other guys from her little pack of followers flanking her. Sometime since I'd last seen her, she'd taken the time to re-dye the streaks in her hair—they stood out bright violet against the smooth black strands.

My disguise didn't stop *her* from recognizing me. Her narrow eyebrows rose to the fringe of her bangs when she caught sight of me heading over with Luis.

"That's ballsy, isn't it?" she said when we stopped in front of her. "Bringing a wanted man?"

I tugged my scarf down to my chin, just far enough to make it easier to speak. "You've done a lot worse than I have," I couldn't help saying.

She grimaced at me. "Oh, really? Last I heard, terrorists had claimed responsibility for that little incident with the Circle mages."

"Ary," Luis said in his mellow way, stepping closer so he wouldn't need to raise his voice over the cacophony of passing shoppers, "if we're going to talk, let's be honest with each other.

You had your Dampered friend cast the same 'chantment on the Confed building doorway that you'd planned to use during the award ceremony before."

"What does it matter? If the guy hadn't gotten jabbed by that piece of rock, he'd have been buried under the building a few hours later, and the terrorists *definitely* did that."

"It matters that someone died because of what you did," I said.

She folded her arms over her wiry frame, fixing her gaze on me. "And you're all worked up about *that*, huh, even though he was one of the people squashing us down? One of the people who *stole* our magic?" She tipped her head so her hair slid back from her own burnout mark.

"Killing people doesn't fix—"

"Talking wasn't getting us anywhere either," she interrupted. "Look at them now! The first chance they got, they doubled down on all the 'restrictions' they need to enforce. Acting like every person they ever Dampered or burned out was a terrorist in the making. Meanwhile, the magic is going crazy out there, and who knows if the actual terrorists are going to blow up the whole city. The Circle only cares about keeping their power."

My thoughts had run along similar lines yesterday during the meeting. I noticed how tense her arms were where she'd crossed them. Her gaze darted over the crowded foyer with more than regular wariness. She was nervous… maybe even a little scared. She worked so hard at maintaining a tough front that I'd missed the obvious signs at first.

She didn't even know as much as we did about why the magic had gone haywire. None of us had any idea what the insurgents might do next. She'd have to be a robot not to be affected.

"I know," I said, letting go of some of my own anger. She'd done something awful, but that didn't mean I had to sink to her level. "If I hadn't challenged the Circle on their decisions, there wouldn't be wanted ads all over the news for me."

"We *were* getting somewhere," Luis put in. "If the terrorists hadn't attacked, we might have gained a lot of ground, and the stunt you pulled could have ruined everything. That's why we work together in the League—to make sure we're all on the same page. If we can't stand with each other, we can't stand up to anyone else."

The twist of Ary's mouth told me his disapproval had hit home. Then her expression tightened with renewed defiance. "It was a gamble, to show them what we're capable of. No one was supposed to *die*. But those are the risks when you're fighting for your own lives." She glowered at me. "Not that the Academy boy here would know anything about that. We've got to keep fighting, keep pushing, while they're off balance, or they'll crush us completely. Don't you see that, Luis?"

Luis's jaw worked, but his voice stayed even. "We're coming up with new strategies, Ary. The main reason I came here today is to find out whether you're still with the League or not. Because if you are, then you can't take matters into your own hands like that again. You either agree with what I stand for and support the rest of us, or you're on your own. I think you know you'd accomplish a lot more if we can find a compromise in our approach."

Was he seriously considering bringing her back into the fold —bringing her in on Rocío's plan? My hackles rose even as guilt churned in my gut. Of course I hadn't liked Granduncle Raymond's policies. I could be upset that she'd essentially killed him without compromising that fact. If I spoke up against her, how many in the League would share her view?

Ary tossed back her hair, but the gesture looked a little too stiff. "I'm not stupid. I just want to know that *you'll* give me a chance to speak without the rich boy getting on my case. Lots of people in the League were happy to see those rocks rain down on the Circle. You know that."

"It might be a while before we can organize a larger assembly," Luis said. "With everything going on and the anti-magic sentiments stirred up even more than usual, we have to operate quietly. Can you accept that?"

"Are you going to loop me in on the work you're doing right now?" She glanced between us. "I heard you've been calling up the Dulls in the League. Especially with the way those assholes are treating us now, we should be kicking them out, not giving them more to do."

"The Dulls in the League aren't marching in the anti-magic protests," I said, restraining a disbelieving laugh. "People like Noemi have contributed plenty."

"Yeah, well, you can't trust a Dull. Those anti-magic pricks beat up a bunch of novices from the Manhattan-Bronx tutorials this morning, you know. Kids. The Dulls are happy to use us when it suits them, but they're always going to be afraid of us underneath. Why should *they* get access to the libraries and all that when people like us, who were actually born with magic, aren't admitted into the college?" She brushed her fingers over her burnout mark with a jerk.

How much resentment would she feel if she found out we were planning to teach Dulls to conduct the magic neither she nor I could even hearken anymore? How would she act on that resentment? A chill ran through me.

Luis inclined his head. "I agree," he said smoothly, as if he hadn't been happily discussing Rocío's plan less than an hour ago. "I was reaching out to our Dull membership to see what they knew about anti-magic activity so we can be ready. When we're prepared to make a decisive move, I'll get in touch with you. It shouldn't be long. I hope you can be patient until then—for the benefit of us all."

Ary shrugged, but a little of the tension had ebbed out of her stance. Luis had managed to diffuse it with his calm composure. It was true, after all, that she'd accomplish a lot more with the League on her side than without them. She bobbed her head in acknowledgment, motioned to the guys, and sauntered out of the department store without another word.

Luis sidled closer. "Sorry. I needed to gauge how much she already knew—and how she felt about it."

"Well, we obviously can't loop her into our current plans. We're going to have to be careful that she doesn't find out from whatever friends she has in the League."

"This *is* going to require more caution than I thought." He let out a huff of breath. "And that means we're going to have to proceed more slowly than anyone will like. I hope your girlfriend is overestimating just how bad the situation is."

# CHAPTER SIX

*Rocío*

The Dull novices sat in three rows on the mats we'd spread over the storage room's concrete floor. Their voices rose and fell in a rhythmic chant that took me back to my earliest magical training at the Brooklyn-Queens tutorial.

"Good," I said softly. I didn't want to distract them from the exercise. I was half afraid my racing pulse would be loud enough to throw them off. The fact that I was helping them at all, encouraging magical talents in people who weren't supposed to have magic, made me at least twice as much a criminal as when I'd only been a special ops soldier gone AWOL. "Now… let's try taking that sound quieter while we bring in the finger movements from before."

At least, I thought that was the natural next step. I glanced at Eduard, the Dampered tutorial leader Luis had brought in to direct our lessons, for confirmation. So far he'd been stepping in only when I prompted him, as if he expected *me* to do most of the directing. I might have a lot more of my magical ability than he did, but I had no experience training other people how to tap into theirs.

Eduard nodded and added in a similarly low tone, "Don't push yourself to search for the sensation of the magic. At this stage, you simply want to open yourself up and be ready for it to come to you."

The energy in the air tremored as it hummed through the room. The windstorm outside was still gusting away, and I wasn't sure the magic had calmed at all over the past day. Some of our students were struggling, foreheads furrowed or lips pulled into a frown, but a few of them smiled. They were getting their first taste of a power they'd never imagined they could reach.

Despite my worries, the sight sent a giddy quiver through me. Before the Exam, before getting shoved into National Defense, I'd dreamed of showing the Dull population how beautiful magic really was. Of somehow convincing them to love it as much as I did rather than fearing it like so many seemed to do. Eventually —hopefully soon—everyone would be able to experience the awe of conducting it firsthand, even if only on a small scale.

Assuming the magic didn't collapse in on itself and destroy a hell of a lot more in the process before we reached that point.

It was hard to help all ten of the students get over the initial hurdle of hearkening the magic while talking to them as a group. Finding a rhythm alone was difficult enough. The exercise went on for several minutes with their low murmuring.

Eduard seemed content to leave it at that, but I prickled with impatience. Hadn't Luis explained that we hoped to have these people casting a few minor spells as soon as possible?

I drew in a breath, centering myself the way I'd learned in my own tutorials. Eduard knew what he was doing. And *what* we were doing was monumental; it wouldn't be good to rush the process.

I wasn't the least patient person in the room, though. My fellow AWOL teammates stood together in the corner near Eduard. We'd asked them to help with the training since they already knew about the Dulls' potential, and they were the only people the League could turn to who had their full magical talent.

Now, Brandt rocked on his feet and took a step toward Eduard.

"Should we move on to something else?" he asked. "Some of them must have gotten it by now."

Sam eyed him warily. I suspected we'd all been uncertain of Brandt's response when I'd explained the plan. In the whole time I'd known him, his loyalty had been to the special ops mages and no one else. To him, both the Confed authorities who'd forced us into military service and the Dull government who pushed for those operations were the enemy. He'd even talked about attacking officials at the White House, as if that would make anything better.

But the guy had taken to this idea with unexpected enthusiasm, smirking at the thought of going behind the Circle's back. "We can teach these people what they really need to know," he'd said. So, I was definitely going to keep a close eye on him, but if he was on board, we couldn't afford to pass up his help. He *had* managed to follow my lead and keep his cool, relatively speaking, when we'd been at the Pentagon.

Since he'd suggested changing up the lesson, I might as well run with that. "We could move on to one-on-one teaching," I suggested. "That should get the people still struggling to hearken up to speed." At the Pentagon, I'd gotten the farthest with Zacher by working with him directly.

"That sounds like a good next step," Eduard said to my relief, and clapped his hands lightly. "All right. Those of you who are uncertain, come up and we'll pair you off with one of the mages here for some individual training. If you have a sense of the magic already, I suppose…" He looked at me as if expecting me to know the best course of action.

"What do you think?" I said. Jumping straight into the castings I most wanted them to learn might be too much to ask.

"I, well…" He hesitated, and I remembered that he'd never had to teach students who were this distant from the magic before, either. Guiding those of us with high enough scores for the Confed to label us as "mages" must have been simpler. And he was putting his livelihood at risk by helping us, with more to lose. After all, I'd crossed into traitor territory days ago.

"I can talk with everyone who's farther along," Finn's friend Noemi volunteered with a grin and a swipe of her hand through her dark brown pixie cut. "Every time I work on this stuff, it gets easier."

I smiled back, warmed by her enthusiasm, which was a lot less suspect than Brandt's. "Okay, great." She'd have a better idea what the nonmagical students needed to pay attention to, having gone through the process herself. I couldn't remember a time when I *hadn't* been able to hearken the magic all around me. I couldn't truly understand what this must be like for them any more than I could imagine what it'd be like to suddenly have sight after years of blindness.

Four of our students, the ones who needed extra help, had come to me and Eduard. I considered the situation and turned to Finn and Tamara, who'd been hanging back on the sidelines.

"Why don't you two help Noemi lead the others through some really basic castings, just to get them used to conducting the magic. We can help this bunch catch up, and then if we have time, we'll move on to the healing castings together." I didn't expect the Dulls to make much of an impact right away, but we could start with things like sealing tiny cracks around the room and move up to bigger goals.

And if that didn't feel like enough, I'd remind myself how

miraculous it was that we could teach them how to cast at all. Ten people sealing little cracks might not soothe the magic much, but if we could pass those lessons on to hundreds or thousands or more, the effect could be amazing.

My former colleagues and I each paired off with one of the students who'd been struggling, while Eduard moved between us observing our work and offering tips. I focused on the young woman I'd waved to join me—a friend of Noemi's who was only a few years older than I was, her eyes ringed with dark eyeliner but bright with excitement.

"I can't believe this is really happening," she said. "I want it to work so bad."

"I'll get you there," I said with all the confidence I could find.

It took three more exercises, with me adjusting her tone and the rhythm of her movements. Then all at once, she sucked in a startled breath. Her eyes popped open to stare at me.

"I think I feel it. Like this weird whispering right up next to me."

I couldn't help smiling at her amazement. "Okay, now let's see if we can get you conducting that energy. It's a little trickier than usual right now... The magic has been shakier since the attacks. But we should be able to manage something."

A half an hour later, I had her making one of the papers in the supply boxes flutter with a lilting verse she repeated over and over. She bobbed on her feet with unrestrained eagerness. "This is so amazing. Oh my God. Thank you!"

It wasn't anywhere near what we needed to calm the magic, but it was a start. Looking around the room, I got the impression all of our Dull students had managed at least a basic casting by now. Finn's group had already gathered around one wall, eyeing the spidery splits here and there in the paint. Did the magic shift and settle just a fraction with their soft castings, or was that wishful thinking?

Unfortunately, it'd taken all our time tonight to get this far. "You can come back tomorrow at eight, and we'll really get you casting," Tamara said as the students grabbed their things. "Just remember to keep quiet about what you've been doing. Don't talk about these lessons outside this room, even with each other. Anyone asks, you were hanging out with friends, that's all. We don't want you getting in trouble for learning this stuff."

The Dulls—well, they weren't exactly Dull anymore, were they?—looked solemn at her reminder. The Confed might come down on them just as hard as on us if our project here was discovered, and we'd made sure they understood the risk before accepting them as students.

If we could get the momentum going, we could take the news public, and they wouldn't have to worry about possible consequences any longer.

As the other students filed out the back door of the shop and into the parking lot, Noemi hung back. "This is incredible," she said to Finn with a glow that turned her somewhat gawky face pretty. "I can't believe we're really doing it."

"Everyone has a right to their talents," Finn replied, with a crooked smile that made my stomach twist with sympathy.

How hard must it be for him to watch these people receive what he'd lost and didn't know if he could ever get back? During my time overseas, I'd seen evidence that at least a few magimedics had the training and skill to reverse the effects of burning out— and presumably Dampering too—but the Circle would keep that information tightly under wraps. I'd have healed every member of the League if I'd had any idea where to start. But attempting magical brain surgery without training seemed like a very bad idea.

We'd campaign for that, too, after we'd dealt with the most immediate problems. Once the Confed accepted that every Dull had the capacity for magic and deserved to use it, it'd be a lot harder for them to argue that anyone who'd been a full mage should *lose* their talent.

"Well, I'll keep helping however I can," Noemi said, still beaming. "Thanks for calling me in on this."

Finn laughed. "Hey, you're the one who made *me* realize it was possible."

Something about their easy rapport made the tension in my gut coil a little tighter with a prick of jealousy. The second I noticed it, I shook off the feeling as well as I could.

Finn was the warmest, friendliest person I knew. He could hit it off with just about anyone, and of course some of those people would be girls. I just... hadn't been in a position to see him chatting casually with any girls he knew well other than Prisha, who'd made her lack of romantic interest in him incredibly clear.

I guessed the way we'd met and the circumstances since then had kept our relationship pretty isolated. *This* was more like the real world. A real world I didn't have much practice with, considering I'd never dated anyone before, let alone had a boyfriend I cared about this much. But Finn couldn't have made his romantic interest in *me* any clearer, so it was a silly thing to worry about.

I felt even more ridiculous for that brief jolt of jealousy when Luis walked into the storage room a moment later. Noemi's gaze shot to him, and somehow she lit up even brighter than before.

Oh. If she had a thing for anyone in the League, it definitely wasn't Finn. Even I could spot that massive crush from a mile away.

Luis didn't look as if he'd noticed, though. "The first demonstration went well," he said. He'd organized a gathering in Times Square, where a bunch of Dampered League members had held signs offering their particular magical skills to anyone who asked. The idea was to diffuse anti-magic sentiments by showing we were helpful members of society, not potential terrorists, and maybe to conduct some constructive magic at the same time… while also drawing the attention of any authorities monitoring the League away from our more clandestine activities here.

"Not too many people took us up on the offers," he went on, "but we didn't have to deal with any militant anti-magic opinions either. How was the first tutorial?"

"Good, I think." I glanced at Eduard, hoping he'd weigh in. When he didn't, I wavered for a second before filling Luis in myself. "It looks like everyone's ready to move on to learning the specific skills I want to teach them. Some of them already started on those. We can bring in some more newbies for an earlier session tomorrow to build our numbers."

"Perfect! I already know who I'll call. I can get started on that tonight." He paused, and the low-key but positive demeanor I was getting used to diminished a little.

"What?" I asked, tensing.

He gave us an apologetic grimace, as if any of this was his fault. "The Confed has expanded their news alerts. They've got photos and warnings about me and Tamara up there now, too. I think it's best if the two of us and Finn don't go anywhere together, even bundled up to hide our faces. So we're going to need to work out someplace new to spend the night."

# CHAPTER SEVEN

*Finn*

When I'd promised myself a couple of weeks ago that I was done hiding who I was, I hadn't anticipated that would lead to me becoming one of the city's most wanted fugitives.

As Rocío used some of my cash to pay for our new room in another cheap hotel, I kept my hat and scarf in place, despite the warm lobby making me sweat inside my wool coat. The clerk looked so bored I wasn't sure he'd have paid any attention to me, but I didn't take the chance. Luis and Tamara had gotten a room at a different place, and Sam and the others had stayed where they were, since there weren't any public alerts identifying them yet. The Circle wouldn't want to reveal too much about what their "Champions" really got up to, after all.

The clerk gave us the keys to a room that looked a lot like the one before: two double beds, a desk with a little TV, a patchy carpet. It even had a similar musty smell under the artificial lavender scent from the most recent cleaning. This wasn't the sort of place I'd stayed in when traveling with my family, but then, I was hardly on vacation.

Rocío dropped onto the edge of one of the beds, testing it with a bit of a bounce. The mattress gave a faint creak, but nothing horrifying. I hesitated between the two beds, the awareness of the sudden, rare moment of total privacy we'd found for ourselves rising over me. We hadn't really been *alone* together since she'd gone AWOL from her post overseas.

We hadn't really had that kind of privacy ever, honestly. In the Exam, there'd been the constant threat of danger hanging over us, not to mention the examiners tracking our every move. We'd talked in an abandoned shop during Rocío's first leave of absence, but considering she'd had to break in for us to use it, it had hardly felt secure.

Here, unless her castings failed, which they never had before, we should be able to relax and just… spend the night together.

Suddenly I didn't know what to do with myself. Should I go sit next to her, or avoid presumption and sit on the other bed instead? Would she want—

Rocío held her hand out to me, making the situation infinitely simple with one small gesture, as she had so often in the past. I sank down beside her, and she tipped her head to rest against my shoulder. My arm went around her without my giving it a thought at all.

Just like that, everything fraught about the catastrophe where we'd found ourselves fell away. Nothing existed except me and the girl I loved, warm against my side, the smell in her hair sweet from the motel's shampoo.

"I feel like I could sleep for about ten years," she said with a sigh. Her body relaxed more fully against mine.

The corner of my mouth curled upward. "We might be able to manage ten hours."

"Assuming the city stays standing that long." She took my

free hand in hers, watching our fingers as she twined them together, mine starkly pale against her light brown skin. "Do you think we're doing the right thing, trying to teach the Dulls?"

"I think it's the best option we've got, considering no one in authority is interested in changing their ways unless we force the issue. And hopefully we'll calm down the magic at the same time. Why? Did something feel off today during the lessons?"

She shook her head lightly against my shoulder. "No. Not exactly. I was just thinking… How is it right that all those mages in the League have lost most or all of their talent, and we're focusing on giving that ability to people who never expected it at all? I wish I could give *you* back your connection to the magic first."

The thought of being able to cast again, to even hearken the whispers of energy in the air, squeezed my heart.

"There's no point in worrying about that, though, is there?" I said. "We *can't* get that connection back. We can teach the Dulls. So, that's what we do."

Rocío was silent for a moment. "I think there is a way to get it back," she said quietly. "When we were— One time, Desmond —" She made a sound of frustration at her inability to get the words out.

"Something to do with your missions overseas," I filled in for her, a giddy lightness rising through me at her first statement.

"Yes. Anyway, from what I saw, the magimedics—a few of them, anyway—have techniques for restoring the part of your mind that hearkens magic. I don't know exactly what they are, and I definitely wouldn't attempt anything myself without proper training, but the Circle knows it's possible and who can do it. If we put pressure on them for that…"

I hugged her a little tighter, my exhilaration fading. "And we'll put pressure on them the way you're already planning. It'll be easier to expose everything else they've kept secret once we start with the biggest revelation."

"It just isn't right that you have to wait when you never should have lost your talent in the first place."

I couldn't help thinking of all the effort I'd put into developing that ability—all the hours poring over instructional texts and performing exercises and practicing, practicing, practicing—and how little I'd been able to do with it in the end. My abilities had been much weaker than anyone else in my family, and weaker still compared to what Rocío could do. A pang of that past shame echoed through me. I let my voice come out wry to cover it.

"I don't know. It wasn't as if I ever made very good use of the talent while I had it. Maybe it makes sense for people who've never had it to take their shot before I get a second chance."

Rocío's head jerked up. She stared at me, frowning. "Do you really believe that? That it's somehow fair that the examiners *took* the magic away from you?"

"Well, I…" It was a lot harder to gather my thoughts when she was looking at me like that, so pained on my behalf. "I'm just saying, if we're going to talk about who's the most deserving, clearly it's the people who haven't already proven how mediocre a mage they are."

"Hearkening the magic isn't something you're supposed to *earn*," Rocío protested. "Would you say it's okay for the government to go around cutting people's hands off for not being master builders? You could cast. It doesn't matter how epic your skills were."

"Or weren't."

"Do you think the Dulls we're teaching are going to have epic talents? They don't even have a strong enough connection to sense the magic at all without a bunch of guidance."

"What do you think I had?" I burst out. The knowledge that

had been gnawing at me since Rocío had first told me about the Confed's database clawed up to the surface. "My parents could encourage my abilities from the day I was born. We can't possibly know whether I'd have shown any knack if not for that. The Confed never measured *my* magical capacity. What score do you think I'd have gotten? It might have been a nine, just below the threshold for calling me a mage at all. It might have been a three. I could be weaker than most of the Dulls, with the same training."

Maybe the only reason I'd been allowed my talent in the first place was because my old-magic name had protected me from judgment—like it had so many other times.

"I've seen you cast," Rocío said. "Your talent wasn't *that* weak."

"How do you know? We have no idea what someone like Noemi might be capable of if she had every advantage across her entire life."

"Finn…"

I let go of her hand to rub my face. "We don't have to talk about it. We can't know anyway. If there's a procedure for reversing the Dampering and the burning out, then we'll fight for that for everyone when it's the right time."

Rocío's expression was still tense. "I just don't like the way you're talking. It's one thing to joke around, but—to really think you don't even deserve the connection you had— You should believe in yourself more than that. Look at how much you've accomplished. You've done a heck of a lot that has nothing to do with your family."

"It's not that big a deal. And look at how much *you've* accomplished." My observations from this evening's training came back to me. "You're the most powerful mage I've ever met, you talked down the entire Dull government—temporarily, but still—and you keep backing up to let people from the League take the lead, even with your own plan."

"That's different. I don't think I'm incapable; I just know there are people with more experience or specific skills. This is too important for me to try to do everything when someone else may be more qualified. I don't want to screw everything up."

Her mouth snapped shut with those last words, and she winced as if she hadn't known they were going to come out. "Okay, maybe I'm also a little nervous that I don't know what I'm doing. But this is so huge."

I pulled her to me again, tucking her head under my chin. "I know. And *you* know that no one is expecting you to take on *everything*, right? I'm just saying… You understand what the magic needs better than any of the rest of us. You've seen firsthand what the military is doing. You took a stand during the Exam and got most of us through it alive. What if stepping up and taking charge—with all of us right behind you—is what's most likely to fix this disaster?"

"I don't know," Rocío mumbled into my shirt. "It's just so *much*. This is the future of the whole world we're talking about."

My throat constricted. "I realize that. I'm not saying you have to take on more, only that I think you could and I'd be there supporting you. My point was mainly that… maybe having doubts about what we're capable of is normal?"

"Okay. Fair enough. I just…" She looked up at me. "I love you. I think you're amazing. I'd fight anyone who tries to say otherwise—including you, apparently." Her mouth curled into a sheepish smile. "I don't want to argue with you, though. Not right now. There's enough awfulness out there as it is."

"I don't want to argue either." All at once, my heart felt so full that I could believe I might be the amazing person she saw in me. "We'll have plenty of time to hash out the accuracy of our self-confidence when this is all over. I hope. Right now, I just want to—"

She tipped her head at the perfect angle for me to trace my fingers along her jaw, and nothing in the world made more sense than pressing a kiss to her lips. Rocío kissed me back, her hand coming up to slip behind my neck. Just like that, all the angst of the conversation gave way to the stirring of other feelings—many of them heated in a very different way.

I kissed her again, trailing my hand down her side. The possibilities of the night ahead, with just us in this room, dizzied me. I had to stop, breathless, to clarify a few things.

"I—I'm not saying we're necessarily going to do this, or that we necessarily should—I mean, not that I wouldn't want to— Ah, the point is…"

Rocío waited with an amused arch of one eyebrow. I finally spit out what I'd been trying to get to. "I haven't gone all the way before, not with anyone. Or even particularly close to all the way."

"Neither have I," Rocío said. "So, I guess neither of us really knows what we're doing?"

"No," I said, with a little laugh of relief at her response. "That would appear to be the case."

"Then let's not worry about it. We'll take it as it comes. If it feels like we're moving too fast, then we'll stop. There's no rush, right?" She smiled. "And if we both feel ready, then we'll figure it out as we go."

"Right." My heart thumped faster at the thought that all those possibilities might become real tonight, that she might be looking forward to them just as much as I was. I lowered my face so my forehead grazed hers. "I love you too."

Her smile widened, and then she was kissing me again, and thinking no longer seemed all that important.

* * *

I'd been expecting to hear from Luis around ten in the morning. I hadn't expected him to start the call with, "Someone's looking for you."

I sat back in the wobbly wooden chair at the hotel room desk where Rocío and I had just finished a late breakfast. My gaze caught hers, and I couldn't help grinning, pretty much the same way I'd grinned when I'd woken up cuddled next to her this morning. She beamed back at me like she had several times since, with a hint of a flush in her cheeks. It'd have taken pretty dire news to shake my good spirits.

"Well, yes," I said to Luis. "I believe most of the state is currently on the lookout, thanks to the Circle's efforts."

He chuckled. "That's not what I mean. A woman came around when we were getting started with our demonstration this morning, asking if anyone could pass on a message to you. She said you'd know her from the Exam."

From the Exam. My pulse skipped a beat. "Did she give her name? What did she look like?"

"No name, but the guy who tipped me off said she looked around mid-twenties, Middle Eastern or maybe Southeast Asian, brown coat, one of those head scarfs on. I'm not sure if that rings any bells?"

It did. In the fragments of memory I'd retained when the examiners had tried to bury them all, I found the image of a young woman in a hijab who'd said she would try to help me— the same woman I'd briefly crossed paths with at the college the other day. Was that why she was reaching out to me now?

"I know her," I said slowly.

"Well, she said that she'd like to talk with you, and you should meet her at your dad's favorite pastry shop at noon if you're up for it. Hopefully you know what to make of that. Do you need any backup?"

"No." I had more backup than the League could offer in the girl sitting across from me.

Rocío watched me curiously as I hung up. "What was that about?"

The silencing spell still held me in its grip—but I could talk around it to some extent. Rocío already had the gist.

"You know how I didn't lose everything like I'd guess most of the other examinees did?" I said with a motion to my head. "It's because—I couldn't have done it on my own."

"Someone at the Exam helped you," Rocío supplied, catching on quickly.

"She reached out to the League. She wants to meet with me."

"About what?"

"I'm not sure," I admitted. "But she did put her job on the line before… And I saw her at the college after the Circle had moved in there. She might have heard something there that she wants to pass on."

Rocío swept the wrappers from the takeout she'd picked up for us into the garbage can. "Are you sure we can trust her now? If they found out what she did, they might have forced her to lure you in."

I mentally weighed what I knew about this woman and the circumstances. "It didn't seem the Circle was even suspicious about that, but of course it's hard to tell. I don't think we should turn down the chance to get whatever information she has. We've just got to be careful about it. Will you come with me? Be ready to arrange a quick exit for us if things go sideways?"

Her smile came back with enough warmth to send another tingle of happiness through me. "Of course. We always make a good team."

Dad's favorite pastry shop was a little place in Lenox Hill.

When he'd brought me and my siblings there for Sunday brunch or mid-afternoon snacks, he'd told us how, back in the day, he had come there with his own parents. Granduncle Raymond had sometimes joined us, as I gathered he'd joined Dad's family in the past. That ghost of a memory lingered as I eased into the shop at a quarter to noon.

I sat at a table with a stone-tiled top. Loosening my scarf just enough that I didn't swelter, I took in the buttery smell and the bouncy pop song playing faintly over the speakers—crackling slightly now and then as if reacting to the wind blustering outside.

Rocío slipped in a few minutes later and positioned herself in a corner where she could watch without obviously being with me. When I blinked, the light around her blurred. I could only see her when I concentrated on looking right at her, knowing where she was. No one else would have noticed her at all.

The two of us could hardly fend off a full contingent of Confed soldiers if this woman brought one, but we could hope Rocío would pick up on any threat before we were cornered. I folded my hands on my lap to keep them from fidgeting and ordered a slice of peach pie.

The woman walked in, alone, at noon on the dot, sweeping her gaze over the café as if she was just as nervous about anyone I might have brought along as vice versa. She wore a trim, lilac-purple pantsuit with a darker purple hijab, a little of her dark hair peeking from beneath its loose folds. After a moment's hesitation, she sank into the chair across the table from me.

"I'm glad you came, Finn," she said in a smooth but cautious voice.

Every sign suggested she'd come with benevolent intentions at risk to herself. When I glanced at Rocío, her nod reassured me even more.

I shifted forward in my chair so I could speak quietly. "Before we talk about anything else, I should thank you. I know you've already helped me once. I—I don't know your name, though."

The woman blinked at me, and then understanding lit her face. "It's always the small details that go first," she murmured, seemingly to herself. "Out here in the real world, I'm Salma Khalil."

Then she would have been Examiner Khalil when I'd known her before. The Exam wasn't why we were here now, though. At least, I didn't think it was.

"Why did you ask to see me?" I said.

The waitress brought over my pie, and Salma fiddled with her fork until the other woman left. She gave me a faint smile. "I've seen that I was right to believe that you'd take a stand if you knew there was one to take… even if there was a loss along the way. I'm sorry about your granduncle."

She was the first person outside of my family and Rocío who'd bothered to say that since his death. My nerves settled a little more, even as the condolences sent a pang through my chest. "I didn't want that to happen."

"I didn't think you would have. I'm hoping…" She inhaled sharply. "I don't like the way the conversations among the Confed leadership have been going since the Bonded Worthy's attack. I know this League you're involved with has pushed for an alternate approach… You might have already seen on the news that the president is coming to visit the Circle at the college this afternoon. If you can sway even one member of the Circle beforehand, it might make a difference."

Of course it would. But— "How are we going to sway a member of the Circle in the next four hours?" I asked. "They're trying to *arrest* me."

"I happen to know... When you work closely with the upper echelon, you pick up on certain things. They present a united front, but I'm aware of at least a few occasions when Mr. Leron protested some of the more restrictive policies. He's definitely more liberal-minded than most of the others."

"He didn't seem that way when I talked with the Circle before."

She spread her hands. "It's hard for all of us to speak our minds surrounded by people who might see us as traitors. But if you or your associates could speak to him alone, without the pressure of the others looking on, you might get somewhere with him. And I think I know where you can find him this afternoon to do just that."

# CHAPTER EIGHT

*Rocío*

The little Dull-run tea shop wasn't the kind of place where I'd have expected to find a member of the Circle. That seemed like at least a little proof that the information the examiner had brought to Finn was true.

She'd said she'd observed that Mr. Leron often popped out of the building to indulge in a quick cup of tea at this place before important meetings—and you couldn't get much more important than a conference with the president of the Dull government. Sure enough, an hour before the scheduled meeting, he ducked inside with a jingle of the bell over the door.

I stayed in my corner for the first few minutes, the magic I'd gathered to disguise my presence jittering in time with the warble of the wind outside. The currents flicked the scents of the various tea leaves my way, the varieties alternately bitter and sweet. Leron asked for a fancy-sounding blend and sat with his cup and saucer at a table near the side wall, less than ten feet from where I stood. His thin features relaxed as he took his first few sips.

This was the moment to go over to him and make my case. It'd had to be me because Finn and the other League leaders would have risked too much just showing their faces, and I was best able to speak to what the magic needed, anyway. Not that Finn had been happy about that. He'd gone back to the hotel to keep out of sight, but he'd hugged me for a long time before he'd been willing to let me go.

Still, I couldn't help hesitating now, watching the beady-eyed man. Whatever his attitudes and opinions, he was one of the ten figures who'd decided my fate on the Day of Letters. He'd agreed, or at least been badgered into agreeing, that I should have most of my magic Dampered rather than be allowed to take my place as a full mage at the college.

My mother had suggested that the Confed made decisions like that because they were afraid of powerful new-magic mages who had no family history to establish their loyalty. I'd gone into the Exam determined to prove that I wasn't any kind of threat. And yet here I was, a special ops soldier gone AWOL, responsible for leaking the Confed's biggest secret to the Dull government…

Was this man going to look at me and think they'd been right about me all along?

I hadn't wanted any of this. All I'd wanted was to study at the college and foster more appreciation for magic in those who were scared of it. I'd only gone astray when I'd tried to protect the magic itself. I just wasn't sure any member of the Circle would see it that way.

I *had* to take this moment, though. Even if Leron didn't get the agreement of the rest of the Circle, his word alone, vouching for how the military attacks damaged the magic, might be enough to change what happened next. If we couldn't convince the whole Circle to listen, one member would do.

With a murmur, I dropped the magic around me. As I

walked over to his table, Leron looked up. I couldn't tell from the twitch of his expression whether he recognized me or he was simply surprised to find anyone approaching him.

"I just want to talk," I said, taking the chair across from him. "I hope you'll be willing to listen before *you* talk to the president."

His gaze flicked to the window that faced the college and then back to me. "I'm not sure why I should listen to someone who's blatantly thrown away her opportunities as Champion."

So the Circle had been brought up to date on the latest National Defense difficulties. I winced inwardly and resisted the urge to glower at him. "I think you know that those 'opportunities' aren't anything most mages would want. I did the duty I was forced into as well as I could for as long as I could. I couldn't just stand by when I knew a storm like we're facing now was on the horizon."

He wet his lips in a nervous gesture, but he didn't argue that point. Maybe I had an opening here after all.

"Is this really what you want?" I asked, nodding toward the street, where the awning of nearby store flapped in a gust of magical furor. "For the magic to flinch away from us, flailing every which way because of what we've forced *it* to do? You know why this is happening. I can't believe the examiners haven't shared their observations with the Circle. We can't ignore it now, and I have to think it'll only get worse if you don't call off the National Defense operations."

Leron turned his cup of tea between his hands. "What makes you think I'll give you a different answer than we've given others who've made this argument?"

I let my mouth form a grim smile. "I don't actually think you will, but I'm hoping you might. Because I'm coming to you personally. Because I took a risk, knowing what you must think of me, but also knowing how important this is. If I can stick out my neck, is it really so much to ask one of the leaders of all the mages in the country to do the same?"

I didn't have Finn's easy way with words, but I had plenty of conviction. At least some of it must have gotten across. Leron fiddled with his teacup again, but when his jaw worked, he looked more thoughtful than defiant.

"The situation is far more complex than you realize," he said.

"And you don't think it'll get a hell of a lot *more* complex if we reach the point where we can barely cast at all?" I asked. "How much leverage will you have with the Dull authorities then?"

"We do have to defend our country."

"Fine. Then defend it. Just don't go launching attacks in retaliation. It's the destructive spells that damage the magic. Even if you could convince the president to take a more cautious approach... I'm not stupid. I know you'd have to be strategic in how much you ask for to start with."

He rubbed his mouth, his gaze going distant. He really *was* thinking about it. The faint hope I'd been holding onto stirred into a brighter spark. If we had someone in the Circle on our side, everything would be so much easier. Please, Dios mio, if this one thing would just go my way...

Leron's eyes narrowed abruptly, focusing on something beyond the front window. I swiveled in my chair, and my stomach plummeted.

A crowd was marching by on the street outside, the magic whipping over their hair and jerking at the collars of their coats even more erratically than before. The rippling of their poster-board signs didn't stop me from reading the messages printed in thick lettering. *Our home, our country, no magic!* one nearby said.

The anti-magic protesters had decided to voice their opinions during the president's visit. Maybe they were pissed off that he was consulting with the leading mages in the first place.

My teeth set on edge. Of course they'd blame us, when most of the international tensions that had caused the insurgent attack had nothing to do with the Confederation at all. We were just a convenient, obvious target.

When I turned back to Leron, I could tell the demonstration had soured any progress I'd made with him. He took one last gulp of his tea and stood up.

"That's why this isn't the right time to renegotiate our stance with the Dulls," he said with a sharp wave of his hand. "One step wrong and they'll accuse us of being traitors to the country. And then where will we be, when we can't even fully count on our magic and there are thousands of them for every one of us?"

I scrambled to my feet. "If you explained to them about the effects on the magic—that they'd be sacrificing the abilities they could be tapping into too—"

His face stiffened at my reference to that one huge secret. "Then we'll be traitors for keeping that information from them. There is no winning here. We're doing our best to survive. Now, I need to get back to work before the streets are completely flooded with people who'd like to see my head on a stick."

He didn't realize that the Dull government had already heard that secret from me, however much they believed it at this point. The thought of revealing just how far I'd compromised the Confed froze me in place for a second, and that was long enough for Leron to hustle out the side door with a quickly muttered casting. His form blurred as he slunk along the sidewalk, keeping as much distance between him and the growing mass of protesters as he could.

There was nothing else I could do now. Me lleva. Of course, Leron might never have agreed to anything anyway. How could he believe he had the right to lead the Confederation if he wasn't even willing to defend the magic that made us who we were?

The chants were rising in volume, filtering through the glass. "No mages in our city! Fight with magic someplace else!"

I eased over to the front window to peer out at the scene. The main thrust of the crowd had come to a stop by the college building, blocking the intersection there. At least a couple hundred Dulls had joined the protest. More trickled down the street to join them—latecomers to the rally, or maybe newcomers to the anti-magic contingent who'd been roused by the display to join them. I swallowed hard.

Why did people have to be like this? Why couldn't the Bonded Worthy's attack have brought us together to protect the city side-by-side instead of provoking more fights?

For the same reason the kids at the Dull schools where I'd had my tutorials had either harassed me or flinched away from me, I guessed.

Would they really rather the mages decades ago had kept their society secret instead of coming forward? Did they even think about how 'chantments sped up their trains and protected the banks where they kept their money? I'd *fought* for these people on the other side of the ocean without even wanting to, and they all just wanted me to disappear.

A few cop cars were pulling up at the edges of the crowd. When the presidential cavalcade arrived, it'd have plenty of security too, but the last thing Dull-mage relations needed right now was for him to see hundreds of his constituents calling for him to shut all of us out of the decision-making. I'd failed with Leron, but the metaphorical storm brewing outside could set us back even more.

My shoulders tensed. I wavered on my feet for a second and then marched out toward the protest.

The wind gusted around me with the dissonant thrum of the

magic that propelled it. The chill stung my eyes. I skirted the edges of the denser crowd and made for one of the police cars. Controlling these people was *their* job.

A woman in uniform was just getting out of the car. I strode up to her, hugging myself through my coat. She met my eyes with a tightening of her lips. I didn't think she liked the look of this situation either, though I couldn't tell whether it was because she disagreed with their shouts or she dreaded policing a crowd that could turn unruly.

"Can't you make them leave?" I asked her.

"We'll maintain control as well as we can, miss," the cop said. "Don't worry. We're keeping an eye on things."

I swept my arm toward the still-expanding crowd. "So what they're doing right *now* is okay? Don't I have the right to feel safe in my own city without people yelling at me to get out?"

Something shifted in the woman's gaze. She hadn't known I was a mage until I'd defined myself as the target to the protesters' message. The magic-driven wind chose just that moment to slap her ponytail across her cheek, and she swept it back with a frown.

"Considering recent events, it's natural that people are upset. When we stop seeing magic storming all over, I'm sure tempers will calm down."

She looked expectant, as if waiting for me to get on with calming it down right now. If only she knew I was one of the few mages actually attempting that.

"It's hard to make that happen with people ranting about any of us using magic at all," I said. "The president is supposed to be here soon. Can't you make them leave?"

My voice had risen a little too loud. Someone on the fringe of the protest glanced over. His face flushed an angry red.

"They're trying to tell us we can't be here!" he hollered to the protesters around him. "The witch assholes think they can order the cops to arrest us just for saying what's true!"

My legs went rigid. A bunch of the protesters turned my way, their expressions tightening with similar rage… and in some cases what looked more like panic. An elderly woman several feet away cowered deeper into the crowd. Did some of them actually think *I* was going to attack them?

"This young lady is allowed to raise a complaint just as you all are," the cop said.

Before I had a chance to feel grateful or say anything myself, another voice rang out farther away. "And we have just as much a right to live in this city as you do. There've been mages here longer than some of your families. You're the assholes for trying to blame everything on us!"

The crowd shifted toward the new speaker, who I couldn't even make out. Obviously another mage had noticed the protest and had a bone to pick, maybe even someone from the League.

"Yeah," a higher-pitched voice joined in. "How many things have you Dulls ruined around this place, anyway? We should be telling *you* to get the hell out."

Curses and shouted insults volleyed back. The protesters weren't paying attention to me anymore, but I couldn't take any comfort from that. The tension vibrated through the wind and raised goosebumps on my arms, even under my coat sleeves. I wasn't sure if the other mages were using some kind of hostile castings or if the distressed magic was simply responding to all the emotion in the crowd.

More mages were yelling back—the first two must have come with friends, or maybe others had been passing by and heard the confrontation. A few of the police officers stepped forward. "Hey!" one of them called out. "Let's keep this peaceful—"

"The terrorists should have crushed *all* of you!" one of the protesters barked over him.

"You keep talking like that, and you'd deserve it if we rained hell down on you!" a mage retorted.

At the same moment, the wind lurched again, slamming into the protesters hard enough to send several of them stumbling. Driven by a casting or just a random fluctuation? I had no idea.

My pulse lurched with the screams that rang out from the Dulls. The police officers, including the woman I'd been talking to, charged toward the other mages, and from somewhere in the fray came a screech so choked with rage I couldn't make out the words.

*Bang.*

A shot crackled through the air. One of the mages who'd been exchanging insults crumpled near the edge of the crowd. The cops ran faster.

I spun around, my throat choking up. Where was the gun? I scrambled onto the hood of the police car next to me so I could get a better view.

"Get off of there!" someone snapped at me, but I'd spotted the shooter. The guy with the pistol was raising it again.

A line I'd used in the field spilled from my lips. The gun jumped from the guy's hand. With a flick of my arm, I sent it flying up onto a nearby rooftop where no one else could grab it.

One of the police officers was running at *me* now. I scrambled off the car with the whirling of the wind. My efforts hadn't been enough anyway. Another shot rang out from somewhere else in the crowd, followed by a pained cry. Somewhere near me, a cop raised his radio to his face.

"Gunfire exchanged outside the College of Mages. Alert the cavalcade."

Another officer was still rushing at me, not satisfied that I'd moved away from the car. I scrambled backward with a stutter of my heartbeat. The crowd churned, so many of the faces pale with fright now.

Would the protest have taken this turn if I hadn't tried to get the police to clear them out? That exchange seemed to have started everything. I'd been angry… just like some of them were angry. We were all viewing each other as the enemy, and it wasn't helping any of us.

I didn't know what else to do. Before the cop could catch up with me, I turned on my heel and fled.

# CHAPTER NINE

*Finn*

I was developing a sort of love-hate relationship with the news. I couldn't help having it on almost the whole time I was in the hotel room, keeping track of the outside world that way since I couldn't step out and observe it in person. But that also meant I could glance up and find myself staring at the ghoulish mask of a member of the Bonded Worthy.

Like in the video broadcast that had run while my granduncle was in the hospital, the central masked figure was flanked by others, their faces simply covered by scarlet cloth. Maybe they were the same group who'd claimed responsibility for Granduncle Raymond's injuries, or maybe they were another faction entirely —it was impossible to tell. My fingers clenched around the remote, but I left the TV on.

Rocío came out of the bathroom, rubbing her damp hair with a towel. "What's going on?" she asked when she saw me.

I tipped my head toward the TV. Behind the mask, the figure must have been speaking, but not in a language I knew. A translation slid by beneath the recording as a newscaster added her commentary.

"The Bonded Worthy sent another video," I said. "Threatening that they're not done with us. It doesn't sound like they're hinting at anything specific, but I'm sure they're pleased that we're at each other's throats over this."

The meeting between the Circle and the president yesterday hadn't even happened. The president's security team had steered clear of the area when violence had broken out, and I couldn't blame them. I was just glad Rocío had made it back without any bullets in her.

"They might not be planning anything at all," she said, coming up beside me. "Just like they hadn't really hurt your granduncle." She set a gentle hand on my shoulder. "Security all over the country must be ten times as tight right now. It'd be difficult for them to get away with anything. They just want us to stay scared."

"Hence the term 'terrorist,'" I noted, but flippancy didn't shake the uneasiness crawling through my body. Outside, the wind was howling even louder than before, periodically rattling the window in its frame. I'd seen Rocío wince this morning when she'd tried to cast a basic shielding spell. On top of all that, somewhere on the other side of the ocean, my best friend had been sent to fight these insurgents where they lived. I had no idea what was happening there.

I glanced at my prepaid phone where I'd left it charging on the bedside table. I'd wanted to check in with Prisha's parents as soon as we'd realized National Defense had launched their big assault, but I'd been too nervous after the alerts had gone out. They'd always tolerated me as Prisha's friend because of my family's standing, even though as Dulls they viewed mages—including Prisha—with a kind of impressed wariness. What would they think of me now?

That didn't matter nearly as much as finding out if they'd gotten any news from her. Since I'd left home and abandoned my usual phone, she'd had no way to reach out to me… if she was even well enough to do that.

"I can't keep worrying," I said. "I've got to see if Prisha's parents know whether she's all right."

Rocio's touch tightened to a squeeze. "They should know you're not a criminal," she said, picking up on my worry. "I can go pick up lunch, give you some privacy. What do you want me to get?"

"Let's try that Chinese place down the street," I said. "I'm sure they do takeout. You've got enough cash?" It felt strange handing over money to my girlfriend as if she were on a payroll, but I was the only one in the League with pockets that ran at all deep. I hoped the big withdrawal I'd made right after we'd fled the meeting with the Circle would tide us over long enough. I wouldn't be surprised to find a hold on my account if I tried again.

"Yep." Rocío patted her hip pocket where she had her wallet and shot me a sympathetic smile. "Text me as soon as you know anything, okay?"

"Of course."

When the door clicked shut behind her, I forced myself to pick up the phone and tapped in the number. My chest clenched as the line rang. It was a little after one, but the family worked out of their brownstone. If the Mathurs were following the same schedule they had for as long as I'd known Prisha, they'd just be finishing their own lunch. I could picture her grandmother puttering around to clear the table while whichever of Prisha's siblings had kitchen duty loaded the dishwasher.

"Hello?" Prisha's dad said.

I had to untangle my tongue before I could get any words out. "Hi, Mr. Mathur. It's Finn. I was just wondering if you've heard from Prisha in the last few days. With everything that's going on, it's hard not to worry."

"Finn." He paused, and I made out the clinking of dishes in the background. My free hand balled in my lap. He might decide not to talk to me even if he had heard from Prisha.

"You don't have to tell me any details," I added quickly. "I just want to know if she's all right."

He sighed. "I have been rather concerned by the recent… publicity you've been getting. But Prisha did give us a call yesterday. I mentioned the news alerts to her, and she said we shouldn't trust them—that she was sure it was Confederation politics we wouldn't understand and not any 'real' crime."

She'd called yesterday—well after the main assault overseas. My shoulders sagged as the tension washed out of me. "Yes," I said. "It's something like that. I'm sorry to have bothered you. It's good to hear that nothing's happened to her. I guess you can understand why I haven't been able to get in touch with her myself."

"I appreciate you keeping her out of whatever trouble you may have found yourself in," her father said, somewhat loftily. Clearly, the conversation was over. That was fine. I'd gotten the information I really needed. It was probably too much to ask him to pass on so much as a hello from me.

Prisha would know I'd be thinking about her. She'd probably tried to call me too, but even if I'd had my usual phone, talking to her now would get her into all kinds of trouble.

"She's not involved in that at all," I said. "I was just worried about her as a friend. Thank you, and have a good afternoon."

I'd only just put the phone down when it rang again. I recognized Rocío's number on the call display.

"Hey," I said when I picked up, expecting that she needed my opinion of the lunch offerings.

"Finn," she said in a whisper, "can you turn on Channel Four?"

"What?" I said, but I was already reaching for the remote. The fear in her voice made my chest constrict. Something was wrong.

The second the TV flicked to the channel, I didn't need her to say any more. A photograph of Rocío—it must have been her school picture from her last year in her tutorial class; she looked a little younger but just as intent as the girl I knew—filled a quarter of the screen.

"The Department of Defense asks that anyone with information about her or her whereabouts come forward," the newscaster was saying. "Details are sparse, but the press secretary confirmed that Lopez may have used magic to interfere with recent military maneuvers overseas. Could this local mage be partly responsible for the terrorist attack in Manhattan just days ago? More as we know it."

A wave of nausea washed over me. Rocío had gone to the Secretary of Defense, had trusted at least that small part of the Dull government to work with her—and not only had they turned on her, they were framing her as the enemy.

Why were they putting out the alert themselves instead of reporting Rocío to the Circle and letting the Confed handle their own? This move disturbed me a lot more than seeing my own face on the news.

"Is it bad?" Rocío asked, her voice still low. "I saw my picture come up on the TV behind the restaurant counter right after I placed our order—I'm hiding out in the bathroom now. I don't know if anyone was paying attention, but it didn't seem smart to stand there and give them time to realize it was me."

"It's… pretty bad," I admitted.

She swore in Spanish under her breath. "Why would the Circle be coming after me right now? Zacher or his people must have said something to them even though they didn't have the in-person meeting with the president. I—"

I gripped the phone harder. "Rocío, it wasn't the Circle. It was the Department of Defense—the Dull government is asking for information on you. Making it sound like *you're* a terrorist, or allied with them, anyway. They're saying you interfered with 'recent military maneuvers overseas' somehow."

"What?" That startled question burst out as if she couldn't stop it. After a hitch of breath, her voice came quietly again. "That doesn't make any sense. I haven't even *been* outside the country all week."

"Maybe they're pissed off that you gave them the slip and they've finally decided to bring you in this way," I said. "They're making up the interference thing to justify it."

"I guess. It seems so specific. And the way people are feeling right now... if someone spots me after hearing I'm associated with the terrorists, I'll be lucky if they don't shoot me outright, forget about delivering me to the government."

My jaw tightened. "We're not going to let that happen."

Her hair rustled as if she'd shaken her head. "It doesn't matter right now. The food is going to be ready in a few minutes. Can you come down and pick it up—and distract everyone while I get out of here? Just in case they did catch that part of the broadcast. I didn't even bring my scarf, it was such a short walk. I... I'd try to disguise my face or something, but the magic is really acting up right now. I don't trust a 'chantment to hold."

I jumped up. "I'll be right there. You hang tight. Why don't we stay on the phone so you'll know when I'm there?"

All I needed was my hat and my own scarf, well-placed, to ensure *I* wouldn't be recognized. Thank Zeus we'd found ourselves wanted citizens during the winter.

I hurried down the hotel's dim hallway and took the stairs to make sure the call wouldn't cut out in the elevator, rehearsing the order number Rocío gave me. People could say what they wanted about my Academy education—it had given me a lot of practice at memorization.

The street outside was bright and whipped by the fierce blasts of frigid wind. A building nearby groaned with the pressure of the air—and the magic churning through it. I walked faster, the skin around my eyes tingling. It was already going numb by the time I finished the brief trip. My words puffed condensation into the scarf as I said, "I'm about to head in. When you hear me talking loudly, make your escape."

I stepped inside the restaurant, met with a comfortable warmth and a savory ginger smell. A couple was sitting at a table in the corner, sharing a big plate of fried noodles. A woman stood behind the cash register, and a guy in a white apron was wiping down a table someone must have recently vacated.

Only four people to distract. I should be able to manage that.

I restrained myself from glancing at the little TV mounted on the wall and walked up to the counter with my most winning smile. "Hi! My girlfriend placed an order for takeout and had to, well, take off unexpectedly, so she asked me to pick it up. Number 1395?"

The woman bobbed her head and turned toward the kitchen door that stood partway open—right next to the short hall that must have led to the restrooms. "Hey, where are we at with order 1395?"

"Five more minutes!" someone called back.

"No problem," I said easily. My gaze slid over the wall behind the counter and settled on what looked like a poster from a movie. Most of the writing was in Chinese characters around a wide-eyed woman in a dramatic pose. It was at the far end of the room from the restaurant's side door, too. I had to find a way to use that.

I jerked my gaze away and raised my phone as if to catch up

on my texting while I waited. Surreptitiously, I snapped a picture of the poster and popped it into an image search. The movie name came up, along with the main actress's name. Bingo!

Meandering in front of the counter, I tapped in a couple of searches. Then I shoved my phone back in my pocket and gazed around the space again. This time when my eyes came to rest on the movie poster again, I stopped and blatantly stared at it.

"Oh my God!" I said, pointing at it. "I know her. What's that from?"

Both the woman at the cash register and the guy at the tables turned to look. "You know her?" the woman said skeptically. "She's a big star in Hong Kong. That's one of her movies from a few years ago. A good one, but…" She looked me up and down as if weighing whether a guy as white as me could possibly follow a movie entirely in Cantonese.

"No, seriously," I said, talking even louder with over-eager gestures. Even the couple eating lunch had swiveled to watch me. "I went with my dad on a business trip to Hong Kong last year. We ended up talking with her in a restaurant for, like, half an hour. I had no idea she was anyone famous! I thought she was just bored and friendly. She had all these crazy stories about her childhood, like how she spent a year living on a houseboat going all over Asia, and—wow."

That detail had come up in one of the first articles about her, so it must have been well-known, and most of the woman's skepticism faded. Now I really had their attention.

The side door squeaked like Rocío had just slipped out. I kept my gaze on the poster.

"Really?" the woman said, leaning closer as she studied the picture too. "What else did she tell you?"

I opened my mouth as if to launch into another excited story and hesitated. "Well, I probably shouldn't say. I mean, maybe she only talked to us because she could tell we didn't recognize her. I've got to respect her privacy."

The guy who'd been wiping tables let out an audible sound of protest. The woman motioned to me. "Oh, come on. You can share just one more thing."

I grimaced. "I shouldn't have mentioned anything. I'm sorry. I'd feel awful if I said something she didn't want shared widely."

She wheedled me a couple more times, and then the bag with our food came out of the kitchen. I paid and took off for the hotel as if the hounds of Hades were at my heels.

When I reached our room, Rocío was braced in the middle of the bed we'd been sharing, her knees drawn up to her chest, one arm hugging them and the other extended as she flipped through the TV channels. Her back was rigid.

"I want to see it," she said. "I want to know exactly what they're saying."

I left our lunch on the desk and climbed onto the bed next to her. She leaned into me as she kept clicking through the channels, but her muscles stayed tensed. I tucked my arm around her and rubbed her side in what I hoped was a reassuring way.

"I've had alerts about me running for days, and we've been okay," I pointed out.

"I know. I just didn't expect the government to go this far. I was trying to *help* all of us by talking to them." She inhaled sharply. "Maybe it's because I broke the guys out of their custody. It didn't feel like I had a lot of choice, with the way Zacher was talking. And that had nothing to do with the Bonded Worthy attack. I don't know what other crime they think I've committed, if they really believe I have. Has that examiner—Khalil—reached out to you again?

"No, not yet. She's got one of the League members' phone numbers, and he'll let Luis know if she has another message. Why?"

"She's our closest contact to either of the governments. Maybe the Circle has some idea what the Department of Defense is freaking out about—and maybe she's caught on from them. I don't know. It's a long shot."

The distress I'd heard over the phone was back. My stomach wound into one big knot as I hugged her close. In that moment, I had the sense of the walls closing in, the Confed authorities on one side and the Dulls on the other, with us and the League squeezed between them no matter what we did.

Khalil *had* reached out to us in the midst of the conflict, though. She'd shared information with me even though she knew nothing about me except what she'd observed in the Exam. People in the Confed might take our side if they believed we meant to set the current chaos right.

There might be others who'd support us if I gave them the chance.

"She isn't," I said.

Rocío glanced up at me. "Isn't what?"

"Our closest contact with the governments. Either of them." The thought of seeing my parents again, of facing their reactions to my disappearance and the Confed's alerts, of admitting all the lies I'd told, closed my throat, but only for a second. "My dad could only be closer to the Circle if he were in it. And my sister works in the Department of Defense." My older brother Hugh had never had much time for me anyway. I could leave him out of this.

"But they're not exactly contacts we can use."

"Not yet."

She blinked at me. "You're saying— Are you sure you want to risk it? Talking to them—telling them all of this? When we told your sister some of what we knew, she wasn't really on board."

Margo hadn't been—and then we'd stolen her security

clearance so that Rocío could get to Zacher's office. Facing her wasn't going to be enjoyable either. Nevertheless…

"It's so hard trying to do this on our own, just us and the League," I said. "Appealing to the authorities directly hasn't gotten us any traction. We're no one to them." Just an AWOL Champion and a teenage boy. "If we could convince even a handful of the important people in the Confed to see what's at stake and to support our cause, they would have far more influence than we ever could. It could buy us time to get your plan with the Dulls up to speed before the magic breaks down completely. It may even give us an avenue toward healing the magic openly."

"Do you think your family will listen?"

"I don't know, but I've at least got to try."

I hadn't really before. I hadn't trusted my parents or Margo enough to say very much. Perhaps I owed them the opportunity to prove my doubts wrong. That mattered more than my reluctance to face their disapproval.

By the time the conversation was over, we'd either have new allies… or I'd have lost the last people from my old life who saw me as anything other than a failure.

I dragged in a breath and took out my phone. "That thing you did when you were calling me from overseas—to make sure no one could listen in on the call—can you cast that for me now? Just a quick 'chantment?"

"I think I should be able to convince the magic to do that much." Rocío laced her fingers with mine. She moved her other hand in the air in time with her intoned words. Her hair rustled with a restless current of magic, but after a few moments, she nodded.

I dialed my dad's number without giving myself any more time to second-guess my decision. He picked up and answered in a harried voice. "Hello?"

"Dad," I said quickly, aware that the casting keeping this conversation private might not last. "It's Finn. I—I'm sorry for taking off on you. Can we talk? I want to explain everything—to you and Mom and Margo. I don't think it'd be safe for me to come around the house, but... I could meet you at Grandaunt Phyllis's tonight if you go over for dinner? She should probably hear this too."

"Finn?" Dad said raggedly, as if he hadn't heard anything except for the fact that it was me. "Are you okay?"

Guilt punched me right through the chest. I closed my eyes, trying to block it out. "Yeah. As good as I can be. So... will you trust me?"

# CHAPTER TEN

*Rocío*

Snow started to fall as Finn and I slunk the last few blocks to his grandaunt's house. Or maybe "fall" was the wrong word. The flakes careened with the rising howl of the wind and the crackle of magical energy that ran through the storm. At least they hid our passage as much as the concealing 'chantment that I was having to refresh every couple minutes as the erratic energy wore it away.

We walked through the lengthening shadows cast by the houses to the west. When we reached Finn's grandaunt's block, we ducked down a driveway. The brownstones were so tightly packed that our only access to her back door, which we'd agreed would be safer than coming in off the street, was through the yards of the houses around it.

I boosted us over the four fences between their yards and hers. Each casting took a little more force in my voice and left my breath a little shorter. The cold stung my throat.

The sound of our landing on the patio was lost in the wind. I studied the back door, which was up three stone steps and across a little deck.

"I can unlock it for you, so you can slip right in," I said, leaning close so Finn could hear me.

He nodded, his gloved hand still tight around mine. The chill had turned the tops of his pale cheeks pink. He squared his shoulders, but I could see the worry in his bright green eyes.

"No time like the present," he said. "You have to get going to teach those lessons."

"I *can* stay." I had to say it, even though we'd already had this argument.

He looked at me, and I watched his nerves fall away behind steely determination. "No. It's enough of a risk that you came with me this far, when the Circle probably has security on the lookout in this neighborhood. It's too dangerous for you to stick around. If this goes well, my parents will help me get out of here safely. If it doesn't, there won't be anything you could do to help anyway."

He was probably right. My main strength was my magic, and there were four talented mages in that house waiting for him. If *they* decided to take him into Confed custody, I wasn't so overconfident as to think I could stop them.

All the same, the thought of abandoning him here with uncertain allies left a hollow feeling in my gut. It had only been days ago that I'd told him I loved him, and that emotion had gotten more intense with every moment we spent together. The one good thing in this horrible week had been Finn and the closeness we shared. If something happened to him…

My mind shied away from even imagining it, but that didn't stop a deeper pang from spreading through my heart.

My hesitation must have shown. Finn gave me my favorite of his smiles—not wry or sheepish or cheerfully bright, but softly fond and just for me—and tipped his head to speak right by my ear.

"You made me hang back while you went off to meet the head of the Dull military and a whole lot of people with guns," he reminded me. "Compared to that, this is nothing."

"I know," I said. "But you can't blame me for worrying."

"I don't." He tugged his scarf down to kiss me quickly, a flash of heat in the winter chill. Then he stepped away. "I'll text you as soon as I'm leaving. Are we ready?"

"Just a second." I focused on the door. With a murmured lyric, I tested the magic against the shape of the lock as I had many times during missions overseas. This one was pretty simple, with just a minor protective 'chantment lying over it, either because Finn's grandaunt wasn't all that concerned about security at the back or the magic's turmoil had leached away some of its energy.

I gathered more energy with a shift in the tempo of my casting, straining against its shifting currents, and prodded it against the simple mechanism. A ripple passed over my skin as the lock flipped over.

"There," I said. "It's open."

"Perfect. Now you get on with saving the world."

He winked at me as if that comment had been a joke, but I knew he meant it. As if he wasn't doing his part by putting himself out there with this visit right now. I opened my mouth to say as much, but he was already loping up the steps to the door.

I waited in silence as he eased inside. When he'd crossed the threshold, I released the concealing 'chantment I'd cast over him with a quick intonation. The magic shuddered away from him with a tremor through the spinning snowflakes. Resisting the urge to sneak in there after him and watch over this meeting, I turned away from the house.

It should have been easier vaulting just myself over the fences between the yards, but the magic seemed to be getting even more irritable with each casting. Maybe there'd been more fighting overseas that had disturbed it today. I had to repeat one casting three times before it caught hold of the magic enough to lift me over the fence and set me down on my feet. The final time, the cushion of energy I'd conjured tossed me off at the last second. I sprawled on my hands and knees in the driveway, biting back a gasp of pain from my jarred knees and palms.

My gloves had protected my skin, but my knees throbbed as I hurried down the street. I sang a quiet healing lyric to soothe the joints. The pain faded, and a bubble of magic around me steadied just for a second. Then a fresh wave of distress whipped through it.

It was too broken for anything I cast on my own to offer a real fix.

I hustled to the nearest subway station, trying not to fret about how Finn was doing. My thoughts veered to my own parents.

Had they seen *my* alert on the newscasts? Even if they hadn't happened to, someone must have told them by now. News passed around the neighborhood quickly, and either one of the few Dull families who was a little friendly with ours would have passed on a warning or, more likely, one of the many who were unnerved by the mages in their midst would have rubbed it in their faces.

Hell, the Department of Defense had probably sent someone to interrogate them by now, not that Mom and Dad would have been able to reveal anything other than that they believed I'd been studying intensively at the college for the last few months.

Regret over all the things I hadn't been able to tell them gripped my chest. I *still* couldn't tell them anything, not without making them more of a target, but I couldn't leave them in total uncertainty.

When the nearest subway station came into sight, I ducked

into the sheltered doorway of a shop that'd closed for the night and fumbled for my phone.

Mom picked up with a tentative "Hello?" that socked me in the heart all over again.

I swallowed thickly. "Hi, Mom. It's me. I can't really talk. I just—I wanted you to know that I'm okay, and I haven't done anything wrong, and I'll explain everything as soon as I can."

"Rocío! Mija, where are you? What's going on? If you need help, you know—"

"I know," I said, blinking hard as I cut her off. "It's better if you stay out of it. I don't want anything happening to you. I'm hoping this will all be over soon. Te quiero."

I hung up before I could get any closer to tears. The bit of moisture that had crept out stung against my skin in the icy air. I gathered myself with a couple swipes at my eyes. Then, my jaw tight but chin high, I jogged down the stairs to the subway station.

When I got to the storage room turned classroom, several of our Dull students had already shown up. With time seeming tighter every day, I'd given Luis the okay to invite fifteen people who'd already learned the basics tonight. We'd run through the initial exercises with some newbies this afternoon.

As I slipped inside, Luis and Tamara were just reminding the dozen students currently in the room of how important it was that they kept this training a secret. Something about the League leader's emphatic voice and the wide-eyed nods of the students set off a fresh ache in my gut.

Sam and Desmond were helping Eduard lay out the mats. Brandt apparently thought he was above manual labor. He was leaning against the shelving unit near the door. His gaze slid to me as I came to a stop there to wait for Luis and Tamara to finish their talk.

"I'm not so sure about this big plan of yours anymore,"

Brandt said in his usual blunt tone. "Dulls are shooting mages in the streets, and now we're teaching them magic on top of that? We should be putting them in their places, not lifting them up to new ones."

I restrained myself from glaring at him. Brandt had revealed some of his family history on our stealthy trip to the Pentagon: parents who'd died when he was little, grandparents who'd made him feel like he was nothing but an imposition in their lives. I didn't *enjoy* being around him, but it was a little easier to understand why he was such a bitter jerk now.

"The people we're teaching aren't the same people doing the shooting," I pointed out.

"But that's the idea, isn't it? Spread the word until all the Dulls are on board?" He cracked his knuckles. "I'd like to show those anti-magic assholes what *real* magic can do—to them."

I gave his arm a light knock with my fist. "That'll only make our problems worse, both politically and for the magic. Anyway…" My mind slipped back to yesterday in the protest, the genuine fear I'd seen on so many of those faces. "Maybe they're not just assholes. Maybe if we talked to them and figured out why they're so scared, we'd be able to show them they don't need to be. Beating them up with a bunch of castings definitely isn't going to get them on board."

"It'll get them to shut up and stay away," Brandt muttered. "Better than teaching goons how to use magic."

"The Dulls have been policing themselves for centuries. I'm pretty sure they can figure out how to adapt to this change. It's not like someone who registered that low on the tests is going to be able to cause any major damage with magic."

Brandt made a skeptical sound. "It doesn't take much of a casting to kill a person."

That was a reassuring comment. I grimaced as I turned back to the students. They needed my attention more than he did. I just hoped he found his way back out of that sour mood before too long.

Noemi bounded in with the last few students, her eyes lit with her usual excitement. "What are we going to work on today, teach?" she asked me with a grin. I could see why she and Finn got along well. They both had the same easy humor.

I glanced toward Eduard instinctively and caught myself, remembering what Finn had said to me the other night. This *was* my plan. I understood what the magic was going through better than anyone here. At some point, doubts or not, I was going to need to take the lead or our efforts would fall apart.

"We'll keep going with those mending castings we started last time," I said. Working on the concrete walls had proved a little difficult for many of the students. My gaze slid to the boxes of paper on the supply shelves. I looked to Eduard, not wanting to presume too far. "A casting to seal a tear in a piece of paper shouldn't be too complicated, right?"

He cocked his head as he considered. "I don't know if we'll be able to get them casting perfectly in the time we have, but we should be able to make some progress."

Eduard and I started with the warm-up exercises we used every lesson. Afterward, he drew back to let me explain the next step. His Dampered talent wouldn't let him do even this small work, since it didn't fit the small range of skill he'd been left with.

I tore a piece of paper halfway down the middle and melded the material back together with a soft lyric so the surface looked as whole and unmarred as it'd been before. Our students stared.

"We're going to do *that?*" one girl asked, testing the paper I'd fixed.

"With practice," I said. "And then we'll work up to even bigger mendings. Let's get started. First you'll need to think of a lyric that captures the idea of sealing or fixing something for you."

We split off into smaller groups, two students to each "teacher," but before the others got started, I led one of the novices who'd ended up with me through the casting while the others watched, so we'd all approach it the same way. With a halting verse from a rap song, the guy I was teaching managed to join a few fibers here and there along the tear, leaving gaps in between. He made a face at the result.

"That's *really* good for a first try," I told him, channeling Finn's hope-filled smile the best I could.

The girl with me struggled even more. With her first couple castings, I couldn't see any change to the paper at all. It didn't help that the magic was twitching and twisting every which way even in here. She sat back with a frustrated huff.

"We'll get there," I promised, but I wasn't sure how much she believed me. "Why don't you take a few minutes to get back in tune with the magic and just practice shifting it around without a focused purpose?"

I took a moment to check on Brandt, but while he didn't look all that enthusiastic tonight, he didn't seem to be discouraging his students either. The guy he was talking to had just managed to seal an inch of his tear.

As I worked on improving my other student's progress, Luis's phone rang. He stepped away from his pair with an apologetic bob of his head.

The space was so small I couldn't help overhearing his side of the conversation. "Hey, what's up? Wait, what? How bad is it?"

When I glanced over at his tone, his face had grayed.

"What?" I said. Anyone who hadn't already been watching looked over.

"Just a second," Luis said to whoever had called, and held the phone to his chest to talk to us. "Someone's set fire to the Manhattan Academy building. It looks really bad. A few mages have already shown up to try to hold the fire back along with the firefighters who've made it there, but they're having trouble getting it under control."

A fire at the Academy. In my mind's eye, I saw all the books I'd browsed through in the library. I hadn't been able to afford to attend classes there, but the texts had helped me develop my talent. At the thought of them eaten away by flames, queasiness shot through me.

"Is it a magical fire?" I asked. Had the Bonded Worthy launched another attack already?

Luis shook his head. "Regular, but there's gas or something in the mix to punch it up, and with the windstorm raising the flames and interfering with the castings, it's harder than usual to handle it. No one's around taking credit for starting it, but it could have been the anti-magic protesters."

"The Confed building and then the Manhattan Academy in less than a week," Desmond said with a twist of his mouth. He closed his eyes for a second and said as if reminding himself, "Even darkness must pass."

His words stirred a resolve I hadn't known I had in me. "We can't let it burn down. There's so much history, so much information about magic in that place... I don't think it could all be replaced."

If the Circle hadn't held onto their secrets so tightly, if all the Dulls in the area could have contributed to the efforts as well—

Inspiration sparked alongside a sliver of fear. What I'd just thought of doing was reckless. But... since the Circle *wouldn't* reveal their secret... maybe this was our first chance to show just how much the Dulls could do after all. And at the same time, we could prove to our students that what they were doing here was a heck of a lot more important and more real than playing with paper.

"Every bit of help might make the difference between losing the building and not," I said, pitching my voice to carry through the room. My hands balled at my sides. "I say we all go out there and contribute what we can. There are simple techniques that should help the firefighting efforts—just pushing the wind away from the flames, or pushing magic against the fire to smother it. We can channel our efforts together. I'll show you how."

I looked at the faces around me, ignoring the stutter of my pulse. Our students exchanged uncertain glances.

"I'm not going to lie," I added. "It isn't going to be easy, and we could get in trouble if the Confed authorities notice while we're there. But sometime we have to start showing the world what they've been keeping from you. I think it's worth the risk to see just how much power you can summon and how you can use it—and let other people see that too. Who's willing to come with me and try?"

Noemi stepped up next to me with a determined expression. "I'm in. Let's do this. I'm not letting the library in there burn when I haven't gotten the chance to read anything in it. Maybe we're all new at this, but there's strength in numbers, right?"

At her statement, the novices stood a little straighter. Determination overcame the anxiety on their faces. "Yeah," the girl I'd been helping earlier said. "Let's show them we're not just Dulls."

Luis nodded to me. "Let me see who's nearby that I can call to get us over there."

As we gathered by the door, a weird rush of exhilaration and nerves swept through me.

My brother had always told me that I'd end up doing great things with my magic. Please, let Javi have been right—and let this be one of those times.

# CHAPTER ELEVEN

*Finn*

It was amazing how just one whiff of a familiar smell could recalibrate your emotions so completely. The second I stepped into Grandaunt Phyllis's house, the mingled scents of her sage candles and the piney furniture polish the cleaning service used washed over me. In an instant, I was back at the broad dining table with Granduncle Raymond presiding from the head, keeping up my smile while my heart sank farther with each sharp look and critical remark he aimed at me.

I'd dreaded our family's monthly dinners here. At least when they'd come over to our house, I'd had avenues for escape if I needed to catch my breath.

Of course, I would never have to face that steely gaze or judgmental tone again. Granduncle Raymond was gone. Even if he'd still been here, I wasn't the mezzo talent of a mage at whom he'd directed that disappointment. Somehow I'd become both less and more.

It was the more I needed to focus on tonight.

Voices carried from the dining room. I recognized Dad's and Mom's and then Margo's, all of them rather frazzled. Halfway through the kitchen, I hesitated, the understanding of what I was going to do and how much it might change their opinion of me hitting me again at full force.

I squared my shoulders and pushed myself onward.

"—doesn't matter in the—" Dad was saying when I reached the dining room doorway. At the sight of me, his mouth snapped shut. The three of them standing next to the table froze for an instant.

Mom broke from her shock first. She grabbed me and pulled me into a hug so tight I could barely breathe, although the constricting of my throat might have been partly to blame for that.

"We have been so *worried*," she said, sounding choked up herself. "Where have you been? What's happened? You can't just vanish like that."

I hugged her back, fighting for my composure. *She* smelled familiar too, with that light citrusy perfume she'd worn since I was a little kid. I dragged in a breath and forced myself to ease back so I could look at all of them.

"Where's Grandaunt Phyllis?" I found myself saying first. I'd been dreading looking her in the face now that she must have seen the footage from the protest, known I'd been an accessory to Granduncle Raymond's death, but she deserved to be part of this conversation for that exact reason.

Dad rubbed his mouth. "She's been very anxious for the last few days, for obvious reasons. I suggested she take a nap before dinner, and it wasn't difficult to encourage her to accept a calming 'chantment to help her sleep. I felt it would be best if we kept this meeting between immediate family—for both her sake and for yours."

Guilt and relief twisted together in my chest. I'd always gotten along all right with my grandaunt—she would make sure to tug me aside and give me a few encouraging words after Granduncle Raymond had been needling me—and I didn't like the idea of the suffering she must be going through. At the same time, she'd agreed with many of his traditionalist views. Of everyone here, I'd been least sure of whether she'd report my visit to the Circle.

Clearly, Dad hadn't been sure of her loyalties either. He'd chosen my safety over any penance I owed her.

"Okay," I said. I was going to have to face her eventually, but this conversation would be hard enough already. "I want to start out by saying how sorry I am for making you worry, and for keeping so much from you—and also that whatever the Circle is claiming I did, I haven't hurt anyone. I did everything I could to make sure no one would get hurt. Granduncle Raymond… I had no idea that was going to happen. I just wanted the Circle to talk with us."

"Of course you weren't expecting anyone to attack him," Mom said. "We hardly imagined you'd been associating with international terrorists." She paused. "By 'us,' I assume you mean this Freedom of Magic League, if that's what they're still calling themselves."

International terrorists—so, the Confed still believed the Bonded Worthy's claim that they'd been responsible for that first minor assault on the Circle. How would my family react when they discovered the real culprit had been a member of the same League? Mom's voice had held a hint of derision when she'd mentioned them.

My gut clenched, but I went on. "Yes. I've been—I've been a part of the League for a while now. There's so much that's happened. Will you let me explain it all my way, and when I'm done you can ask me whatever you want about it?"

"I'm definitely curious to hear this story," Margo said, her tone slightly wry although her expression was serious. "Somehow my little brother became a revolutionary."

That label didn't sit quite right… but maybe it should have. At least my sister didn't seem angry, even though she must have realized how Rocío and I had tricked her.

"Maybe we should sit down," I said. "This is going to take a little while."

I ended up at the head of the table with my parents on one side and Margo on the other. I shrugged off my coat and braced my elbows against the mahogany surface.

"If I were going to be really thorough, I'd have to say everything I've been involved in started with the Exam… but I can't really get into that. It's difficult to explain."

"For you." Margo glanced across the table at my parents. "The Exam staff puts silencing 'chantments on all the examinees before they leave. He literally can't talk about anything he saw, did, or found out there."

I blinked at her. "How do you know that?" She hadn't indicated she was aware of the 'chantment when we'd talked before.

Her lips pursed in a grimace. She ran a hand through her messy, ash-brown hair, free from its usual loose braid. "There've been quite a lot of meetings in Washington in the last few days, as I'm sure you can imagine. A number of them focused on the Confed's policies. Apparently someone on our side mentioned those… precautions to someone in the Dull government. I'm not sure of the exact context."

As the mage advisor to the Director of the Joint Staff, Margo would be in the loop on almost anything to do with the relationship between the Confed and the White House. How much else had the Circle been willing to reveal since the insurgents' attack? The Department of Defense must have had plenty of questions about our National Defense operations.

Mom let out an irritated sound. Dad's expression had stiffened, but he didn't exactly look surprised. He'd suspected the conditions of the Exam were more fraught than the public knew—that was why he'd tried to stop me from declaring.

Before we got further off topic, I barreled ahead. "Anyway, you know I was feeling a little unmoored after I came back. And there were things I knew… I wasn't comfortable standing back and letting everything continue as it was. I saw a flyer for the League meetings—for Dampered mages and Burnouts who weren't happy with the status quo—and I thought I might as well see what they were doing."

Mom's eyes had widened. "How long ago was that?"

"Three months ago," I admitted, wincing inwardly. Three months of lies and obfuscation. "I told you I was going out to see friends, which wasn't entirely untrue, but… I didn't think you'd like the idea, and I couldn't explain all my reasons for going. It was easier to avoid the subject. I realize that wasn't the most honorable move ever."

Dad pressed his hand to his temple as if he had a headache. "And what have you been *doing* with these Freedom of Magic people for the last three months?"

I laid it all out, from the early meetings when I'd hidden my family name through to that final protest when I'd provoked one of the security officers into hitting me to get the Circle's attention. Dad's face turned sallow when I admitted to sneaking a look at his work files to direct one of the League's earlier protests.

"If you'd just talked to me," he said. "Finn, I expected more of you than for you to go behind my back like that."

From the look on Mom's face, she was thinking the same thing. The guilt I'd already been carrying curdled in my stomach into something ten times as sour. Still, something in me balked at hanging my head more than I already had.

"I *tried* to talk to you," I said. "I brought up my concerns about the Exam and how the Circle runs things, and you dismissed all of it. If you wouldn't even admit something needed to change, how could I go to you for help making that change? Of course I *wanted* to."

Dad's jaw worked. "I didn't know—if I'd had any idea how involved you already were with those people—"

I held up my hand. "Let's be clear. 'Those people' are just like me—mages who lost most or all of their magic because the Confed authorities decided they weren't worthy. The only difference is that they didn't have an old-magic name that would pave all kinds of roads for them regardless."

"They had choices, and so did you. I've never denied that there are problems with how things are run, but there are ways to tackle them that don't undermine our security."

The rush of shame I'd have expected that authoritative tone and the disapproval in his eyes to provoke didn't come. Instead, anger flared through me.

"How much were you worrying about the Confed's security when you ran off to save people from the Mount St. Helens, like you told us about?" I demanded. "You were hardly any older than I am. How much did you consult *your* parents before you took matters into your own hands? You saw where something needed to be done, and you did it—and, unlike me, you didn't have a whole group of people with more experience to help you figure things out."

"Finn," Mom said, staring at me as if she couldn't believe how I was acting. Dad's face had gone from sallow to blotchy, half pale and half flushed.

My throat tightened, but I forced myself to keep going. "I think it's a valid point. Delaying a meeting of world leaders is a lot less risky than revealing magic to the entire Dull world. Don't you think all the people who are being stripped of their magic deserve to be saved too?"

Dad opened his mouth and closed it again as if he were struggling to find the right response. Margo spoke up before he could.

"Finn's right," she said quietly. "We weren't ready to listen. I wasn't either. We've all gotten too comfortable with our jobs and the way things are… What he's been doing isn't foolhardy. It's brave. He was trying to stop the mess that's going on out there." She flicked her hand toward the window, where the snow had let up but the leaves of the hedge were spasming in the wind.

After how Rocío and I had compromised her job, I hadn't expected her to go as far as to come to my defense. "I'm sorry about the other day," I had to say. "Taking your pass, and—"

She shook her head. "I should have seen how urgent the situation was from the way you were talking. If you'd waited for me to get comfortable speaking up, Hades only knows how much worse things might be. *I'm* sorry. I thought I'd broken away from all that old-magic complacency…" Her mouth twisted. "And here you were the real rebel all along. Are you going to tell them the rest? The really important parts?"

"The rest?" Mom said. Her tone suggested she wasn't entirely sure she wanted to know.

I glanced at Dad. He dropped his gaze for a second before meeting my eyes again. "All right," he said, his voice strained. "You have a point. Maybe… maybe I haven't given you enough credit for your judgment. If there's more, I'm ready to hear it."

I wet my lips. "It's going to be hard to believe, but you have to understand that I've seen the evidence of both of these things."

He nodded.

I laid out as well as I could what I understood about how the magic was affected by different sorts of castings. My parents held their tongues, listening as promised, until I got to the second of the Circle's big secrets. When I mentioned the Dulls' capacity for magic, Mom's jaw dropped.

"That can't—surely that can't be possible."

"I've watched one of my friends cast spells after being told her whole life she was Dull," I said. "And some of her friends, the same. Rocío found a whole database that lists people's scores. Doesn't it make more sense that the talent would work that way, on a broad scale, considering how much variation there is in ability between mages? Why would there be a sudden cut-off point where you go from having obvious potential to none at all?"

"And the Circle knows that you've discovered this," Dad said.

"Yes. They're not happy about it. Hence the news alerts." I related how the Circle had reacted when I'd gone with Luis and Tamara to talk with them.

"I've been scared to talk to you about any of this, especially after what happened to Granduncle Raymond," I finished. "But I came here tonight and faced that fear because I'm even more afraid of what will happen if we can't pull together and start mending those conflicts, for the magic's sake if nothing else. I'm just a seventeen-year-old Burnout. Hardly anyone on our side has their full talent. We need people the Circle will listen to—people the Dull government will listen to—to speak up. I need your help."

"I don't know how much I can influence things." Margo made a queasy face. "I think I may have already made your situation worse. But I can at least verify that from the discussions I've been a part of, what you're saying makes sense to me." She looked to our parents. "The second wave of instability in the magic did happen right after National Defense launched a major assault against insurgent targets overseas. And I know Rocío was able to teach the Secretary of Defense to cast, just a little, even though he should be Dull."

"What do you mean about making things worse?" I asked, my stomach sinking.

She turned back to me with something pleading in her eyes. "My boss brought me to a meeting—they asked me about the whole situation with the Dulls and magic... and I didn't know yet how bad things were going to get. I didn't have any information other than what you'd told me, and I could tell it'd set off a backlash against the Confed. So I told them I didn't know anything about a cover-up. From the things they've said since, they've decided Rocío was lying to Zacher so he'd stop the assault, that she 'chanted him somehow to be able to hearken the little bit he could."

My blood ran cold. Rocío had mentioned something about one of Zacher's colleagues suggesting he'd been tricked. No wonder they saw her as some kind of terrorist accomplice if they believed she'd deliberately deceived Zacher to stop attacks on the Bonded Worthy. Gods take me.

"That's why they put out the alerts for her," I said. "You've got to tell them she never would have wanted to help the terrorists."

"I can give it a shot, but I don't think they'll listen to me, not when I've already told them the opposite. Not everyone there trusts *me*, because I'm a mage too. When they lost Rocío and her colleagues, they pressed the Circle about the issue, and of course the Circle denied everything. The Dull government has never had to deal with problems like this before—mage insurgents attacking their cities, the magic raging around of its own accord. They're overwhelmed and not thinking all that straight."

No doubt they preferred to believe one young, AWOL mage had screwed them over rather than think the entire leadership of the Confederation had been pulling the wool over their eyes for decades. Just like that, all the effort Rocío had put into convincing Zacher had backfired on her.

Throughout my exchanges with my sister, Dad had drawn his posture straighter. He stepped in with a new firmness in his voice. "Then maybe it's time we see if my years of service to the Confederation will mean enough to sway the Circle to take some kind of stand. What exactly were you hoping for, Finn?"

The fact that he was offering at all diffused most of the tension inside me with a glow of joy. I couldn't stop a smile from curling my lips.

"Appeal to the Circle that they at least admit how certain castings are harming the magic and stop further magical attacks by National Defense until we've calmed the magic. That's the most urgent concern. If they won't even do that much, the League is preparing to spread the word with a much more public demonstration. The Circle can control how the information comes out if they act quickly enough."

"I'll speak with the members I know best first thing tomorrow," Dad said. "And I'll reach out to the friends who worked with us to push forward the Unveiling for additional voices of support. We both will, won't we?"

He turned to Mom, who still looked a little shell-shocked. She gave me another of those glances as if she didn't quite recognize me, and my skin itched under her gaze, but she tipped her head in agreement. Perhaps she wasn't quite ready to accept who I'd become, but she'd support me all the same. That was enough, even if it dampened my sense of victory.

"I have to apologize for my initial response—and the way I reacted when you brought up subjects like this before," Dad went on. "We *have* tried to teach all of you to stand up for what you believe in and treat everyone in this country as your equal, but still… I know I shied away from some hard conversations with you after your burning out. I told myself it was because I didn't want you dwelling on your loss, but maybe it was more that *I* found dwelling on it hard. I should have been there for you."

I choked up as much as I had when Mom had first hugged me. "I get it. I'm sorry for how much I hid from you. And—you know I can't come home, right? If the Circle is going to lay down sanctions on me, I can't give them the chance until I'm finished with all the work I need to do."

Mom's shoulders stiffened, but she didn't argue. "You grew up an awful lot in the last few months, and somehow I didn't notice it nearly enough," she said roughly. "All that really matters is that if you need *anything*, I want you to come to us first."

"Thank you." It took me a second to master my emotions, heat coming into the back of my eyes.

"For now," she added, "can I at least get a proper dinner into you?"

I wavered. The thought of a family meal for the first time in what felt like forever was so very tempting. Rocío wouldn't be expecting to find me back at the hotel for at least another couple hours.

"I shouldn't stay very long," I said. "I don't know how closely the Circle has Confed security watching for me in the area."

"We'll make it a quick one, then. The food is already ready."

We didn't talk much during the hasty meal, with so many revelations hanging over us, but the atmosphere felt more companionable than fraught. When I pushed back my chair to go, the rest of my family got up too. Mom and Dad pulled me into a round of hugs.

Margo squeezed my arm. "Let me help you get out of here safely. It's the least I can do."

She called for a taxi and cast a concealing 'chantment to shield me before we headed out into the night. The cab had just pulled up to the sidewalk when my phone vibrated with an incoming text—and then another. Margo opened the back door and then paused for a moment to chat with the driver, giving me a chance to slip onto the seat without it being obvious to anyone watching that she wasn't the only passenger.

As she slid in beside me, I fished out my phone. My stomach flipped over when I read what Luis had sent. I tapped out a quick message on my screen and set my phone on Margo's lap so she could read it.

*Change of plans. Have the driver drop me off a block from the Academy.*

# CHAPTER TWELVE

*Rocío*

The magic flung the smell of smoke into our faces as we closed the last short distance to the Academy, a current of warmth breaking the winter chill along with it. Night had fully fallen while we'd been teaching, but the clouds reflected a faint, eerie light.

Next to me, Luis was on his phone again. Then he dropped his hand to his side with a weary expression.

"It's all the academies," he said. "A coordinated effort. We've gotten word from Houston, Seattle, and San Francisco—fires at all of them."

"Shouldn't they have some kind of magical protections on them?" Noemi asked.

"One of the guys I talked to figured that, with the way the magic has been behaving, even long-standing 'chantments could have been weakened."

That theory was far too easy to believe. I hugged myself. "Have they seen any indication of who was responsible?"

Luis made a face. "No one's claimed responsibility, but anti-magic protesters have already turned up to 'celebrate', so I think we can reasonably assume they were involved."

Even as he said that, shouts reached our ears. We rounded the corner and came into view of the old stone building. Flames raged over its roof and lashed out of smashed windows. Three firetrucks were parked out front, the uniformed men spraying water that clearly wasn't enough to douse the fire. Mages stood in their midst, chanting verses that couldn't quite control it either. Across the street from them, a group of protesters were waving their signs and hollering.

"Let it burn!" one of them yelled. "There's no place for magic here."

"Destroy the mages, and their enemies will leave!" someone else called out.

As if it would be that simple. As if the Bonded Worthy wouldn't wipe out every part of this country that they felt opposed their interests, magical or not. Didn't these people understand that the enemy mages worked alongside the Dull insurgents just as much as the Confed's National Defense helped the Dull military?

Obviously not. And they didn't care at all about the resources they would destroy, magical texts that might help *them* wield magic themselves.

The angry flare of the fire against the darkness, the creak as a section of roof started to crumple, made my stomach ache. There were times when I'd resented the mages who got to attend the Academy so much—but I'd also loved those shelves upon shelves of old books, offering knowledge to any mage who wanted it. Our Dull students deserved to have the same chance.

They'd stopped with the rest of us, staring at the fire and then the demonstration. I urged them onward with a sweep of my arm.

"Ignore them. We'll show them how wrong they are about

magic. Magic is going to help save this building—and anyone who might still be inside it."

The idea that there might be lives at stake spurred the Dulls on. I led them past the official firefighting efforts, farther down the building. The heat snapped against my face. I tugged my scarf as high as I could without muffling my mouth, but in the chaos and the fractured light, I didn't think anyone would get a close enough look to connect me to the recent news alerts.

My special ops colleagues and the few Dampered mages from the League who'd been with us gathered around the cluster of Dulls. Luis had sent messages to other League members, and unfamiliar figures joined us from the sidelines, as well as one I recognized. Callum peered up at the burning building, the firelight turning his hair even starker red while yellowing his face. Or maybe he'd gone pale out of horror. He might have reveled in destruction during the Exam, but he'd have learned most of his magical skills in this building, and taking in the attack, he looked only sick.

The warbling of the flames filled my ears. I dragged in a breath and nearly choked on a waft of smoke. My hand came up to grasp my sunburst necklace along with a flash of memory of the magical fire that had singed it.

Those attackers *had* been insurgents—but they'd also been defending themselves from an attack that we'd launched on them. To them, we'd been the enemies, just like all mages were to the furious but frightened people ranting on the sidelines now.

I couldn't let myself be distracted by my own frustration. The anti-magic contingent's motives, good or bad, understandable or not, didn't change what we needed to do.

In the minivan we'd come over in, Desmond and I had coached a bunch of the Dull students through the basic technique I thought would work, and Sam and Brandt should have been doing the same in theirs. Now we just had to put those strategies to work.

I turned to my students. "Reach out to the magic as much as you can and guide it with the lyrics you've picked, focusing on conjuring a solid surface to smother the flames. It doesn't have to be a lot. Every little bit helps. Those of us who have more casting experience will pull all the pieces together. Just give it all the power you can."

The eyes that met mine were wide with nervousness, but one of the guys set his jaw and stepped forward. He waved his hands toward the building as he murmured his verse. Noemi took a spot beside him, her chin high and her voice pealing out. The others joined in, their different words and rhythms melding together in a weird sort of harmony through the roar of wind and flame.

My former teammates raised their voices as well, consolidating and pushing forward the shreds of magic the Dulls had summoned to their will. I was about to join them when Luis touched my arm.

"What do you want me to do, Rocío?" he asked, as if I were the leader here and not him. As if he was perfectly happy to hand that authority over to me.

Watching my students' faces glow not just with the wavering light but with the pride of accomplishment, the last of my hesitation fell away. The magic still thrashed through the air around us, but each added voice increased its vibrancy. I hadn't felt that kind of energy since before the Bonded Worthy's attack. I thought of the wanted ads the Confed and the military had plastered all over the news, and an idea clicked into place.

"We can make this a *real* public demonstration," I told Luis. "Show everyone what magic is about—healing, not destroying. Prove how much the Dulls can contribute, too. Will you record us on your phone?" I paused. "I mean, if you're okay with that.

We'd be risking someone recognizing members of the League, and it could mean more trouble for you. They're your people—that's your call."

Luis gave me a small smile as he pulled his phone back out. "You know, Rocío, I never meant to set myself up as some kind of authority figure. I just wanted things that weren't happening, so I reached out to see who else felt the same way… and somehow, I ended up calling most of the shots. It's not because I think I have all the answers."

I grimaced. "I don't have all the answers either. I'm figuring out the best strategy as I go."

"I think that's how this works. The person in charge isn't the one who's the most right. It's who's willing to step up and put those ideas into motion." He waved his phone. "From what I've seen, you've got the ideas and the guts. A lot of people have trusted me based on a lot less. I think you deserve at least as much from me. Let's see how much farther you can take us."

His vote of confidence sent a quiver through me, giddy and anxious at the same time. I turned toward the fire.

A steady hum was penetrating the magic's jittering as my colleagues directed their attention and the Dulls' sparse conjuring toward the section of roof above us. The flames there wavered, dipping lower under the weight of the joint casting. All around me, murmurs carried to my ears. I started to intone my own lyric under my breath, reaching out to the magic and guiding its rhythms to twine around the tendrils of energy even more tightly.

With a lift of my voice, I conducted the conjured smothering blanket faster toward the roof. Lay it over the fire, press down the flames, and snuff them out.

More heat and smoke washed over us. The protesters must have noticed our group and guessed what we were doing, because a few of the shouts rang out louder. A bottle careened toward us to smash near my feet, and I flinched.

What if one of them had a gun like at the college the other day?

"Keep helping them," I said to my colleagues, and called up a separate conjuring all my own. The magic jerked away from me and then settled down at my crooning. I wove it together into a transparent barrier that shielded our group, just in time to deflect another projectile the protesters hurled our way.

I swiveled to focus on the Dull students again. A wave of magic from somewhere beside us brought the flames even lower. A few of the other mages who'd arrived to help must have been adding their strength to ours. One small patch of roof was only smoldering now. The Dulls' eyes were still wide, but they all looked awed now instead of worried.

They were seeing how much power they could really offer. Maybe they'd needed more experienced mages to guide that power along, but they'd contributed. They'd made a difference.

A spray of water from the firefighters' hoses made the worst of the flames near us sputter out. One of the firefighters motioned to us and pointed to a particularly fierce line of flame by one of the chimneys. "Can you tackle that part near the top?"

"Let it burn! Let it burn!" the cry went up from the anti-magic protesters, but we trained our attention higher in spite of them. In the shifting light, Desmond's face was tense with concentration, Sam's determined. Brandt, to my surprise, laughed and raised his hands as if he could push the magic faster with them. Maybe he was simply happy to be pissing off the protesters with our success.

A rock and another bottle thumped into my conjured shield. I gritted my teeth for a second before continuing with my casting. Whether it was fear or anger driving the people behind us, they made the insurgents of the Bonded Worthy feel very far away. Between the Confed's authorities on one side and Dulls from government to civilians on the other, we faced so many enemies and so much potential for destruction here at home even without any outside interference. How could we ever protect ourselves if people within our own country were constantly squabbling for domination?

Working together was what had gotten Finn and me—and Desmond and Prisha—through the Exam. We'd been from all different backgrounds with all different histories and abilities. Right now, the Dull firefighters were working alongside mages both full and Dampered and Dulls just discovering they were more than that. Why did it have to be so hard to manage this kind of cooperation on a larger scale?

Because people were messy and confusing and too many of them were insecure or greedy or both. But we still had to try. I was here, fighting the best I could for what was good about magic, because I couldn't bear to do anything less.

The flames at the peak of the roof were dwindling. I propelled the energy forward with a surge of resolve and a renewed casting of my own. Black patches marked the shingles, and here and there an entire hole had opened up. The frames of the broken windows were scorched. I hated to think of what might have become of the rooms inside and their contents, but it looked as if we'd gotten the fire under control before the flames ate absolutely everything.

Police cars had pulled up near the protesters. Angry voices volleyed back and forth, but they didn't throw anything else our way. I doubted the cops wanted a repeat of the president's attempted visit. I wiped the sheen of sweat from my forehead and pulled my scarf higher in case they took a closer look our way.

Luis lowered his phone. "Do you think the recording will show enough?" I asked.

"It's hard to know with the lighting, but I got as much as I could," he said. "What do you want to do with the footage?"

"If we want to boost the video quality and edit it for

maximum impact, my son could lend a hand," Tamara said. "He's always putting together zany videos with his friends on the computer."

"We want as many people as possible to see this," I said. "The Circle wouldn't listen to us, and the Dull government wouldn't believe me just talking to them, so we'll show them our proof." I glanced at Desmond, who was a whiz on computers in other ways. "Is there an easy method for getting lots of people watching if we post it online?"

He grinned. "I know optimization tricks and the best places to post it."

"Then maybe…" I bit my lip. "People might still not believe the Dulls were helping—or that the people with us even are Dull. We should do more than send it out to stand on its own. Add in a little message."

Luis dipped his head to me. "You tell them whatever you want. Just let me know when you're ready."

For a second, my chest tightened around my heart. But the Pentagon was already after me. Why should anyone else become a target?

The magic had chosen me as its champion. I could take that mantle and run with it.

"Okay," I said, ideas of what I wanted to say spinning through my head. "Start recording."

Luis lifted his phone again. I tugged down my scarf and focused on the thrum of magic around me—the thrum that tugged at me a little less frantically now that we'd conducted it toward preventing disaster rather than causing it.

"I want everyone to listen to this," I said. "Whether you're a mage or consider yourself nonmagical, whether you think magic is amazing or scary—you need to hear it. I think we're all scared right now. But we can't lash out at each other. Then we're just doing our enemies' work for them."

Sam gave me an encouraging thumbs-up from where he'd come to stand near Luis. I inhaled deeply and kept going.

"We do have plenty of enemies from outside this country. But after everything I've seen since the attack on the Confederation building, I believe that before we can protect ourselves from any of them, we need to fix things here. We need to deal with the problems we have with each other—find a common ground, accept each other, recognize the rights we all have—before we're going to be able to fix anything anywhere else."

Someone let out a little cheer behind me. "That's right!"

I couldn't keep a smile from twitching at my lips even though a weight settled in my gut, knowing how many minds we were going to have to change.

This video was a start. We had to begin somewhere, just like with everything else we'd done.

"Every one of you watching this has the capacity to hearken and conduct magic," I said. "More than a dozen people we'd have thought of as Dulls were with us helping put out the fire tonight. If you give us a chance, if you give *magic* a chance, it can be part of your life too. Tell the Confederation leaders you're ready to learn. If they won't listen, seek out the mages who will. We're here."

"And to everyone who can already conduct the magic— you've all felt how erratic it's become since the first attack. We can restore it. Every time you work with the magic to mend something, to heal someone, to build something or prevent it from being knocked down, we bring stability back to the energy we're working with. So let's do that—all of us. Find whatever you can, big or small, that you can fix, and do it. If you want to help even more, record yourself doing it and share how you've pitched in too."

I raised my hand over my head with a spike of adrenaline.

"Magic is music. It's beauty. No matter what anyone throws at you, let's show the whole country how true that is. If you remember anything, remember this: We defend; we don't attack."

As I dropped my hand, Desmond caught my arm. Luis jabbed his thumb to stop the recording.

"I'm picking up some movements I don't like the feeling of heading this way," Desmond said by my ear. With his limited sight, he'd been in the habit of using castings to test his surroundings even before we'd been forced into the special ops division. Our time in the field had only perfected his scanning techniques. "I think we'd better get out of here if we want the chance to share that video—or do anything else."

# CHAPTER THIRTEEN

*Finn*

Whoever had set the Manhattan Academy on fire, I doubted they'd intended to unite the magical and nonmagical communities. More likely, their motivation had been the opposite. Yet for minutes after I arrived while I relayed suggestions between the Dull firefighters and League members who'd congregated by the west end of the building, watching the flames dwindle, that was exactly what the situation felt like. We were a united front, battling a fresh threat.

As the last of the flames sputtered out, Mark coughed next to me. I tugged him farther from the lingering smoke and turned to find myself face-to-face with the last person who could ever make me think of unity.

"Lockwood," Ary said. The flashing lights of the police cruiser down the street made the streaks in her hair flicker in the darkness like a different sort of flames. Her gaze skimmed me up and down as if she took issue even with the scarf partly covering my face and the clothes I was wearing, most of which weren't even mine. Those of us dodging the authorities had been relying on what other League members could lend us while we kept clear of our homes.

"What are you doing here?" I blurted out. I hadn't even seen Luis or Rocío since I'd arrived, though I assumed they were around the building somewhere. The situation had seemed so urgent I'd jumped right in where the cab had dropped me off rather than taking time to circle the block.

I'd spent so many years in the building beside me, making what little magical progress I could. I might not have lived up to the Lockwood name, but my teachers here had always encouraged me—even more than I really deserved. The meager talent I had developed, I owed a great deal to them. Even now that the fire had been quelled, seeing pieces of the place ravaged, and injured staff ushered out to the waiting ambulances, sent an ache straight through my gut.

Ary wrinkled her nose at me. "I'm still part of the League. I heard the news. I might not like the airs all you Academy mages put on, but that doesn't mean I want the Dulls screwing us over." She glanced up at the building. "Looks like the bunch of you took care of everything already, though."

I wasn't sure how much I believed her explanation. She'd once proposed that the League should burn the Academy to the ground ourselves. Did it really make that much difference to her that Dulls had been behind the attack? I wouldn't be surprised if she was simply looking for a way to insinuate herself into Luis's good graces, to show she could be a team player—conveniently without doing any actual work.

Clenching my teeth, I searched for the politest way to tell her to take a hike. Between the talk with my family and the fight against the fire, my composure wasn't at its best. As I struggled, her gaze shifted to a point behind me.

"Who's *that?*" she asked, her eyes narrowing.

A hand came to rest on my shoulder. Margo studied Ary with

a warily impassive expression. My sister had insisted on staying—she was as much an Academy kid as I was—and she'd certainly been able to pitch in more than I had, considering she still had all the ability the school had trained her to use. A bit of soot smudged her cheek, and flyaway strands of her hair floated around her face where they'd escaped from her hasty braid.

Hades take me. I already knew this meeting wasn't going to go well before I spoke, but Margo wasn't going to let me get away with lying, even if I could have convinced Ary. The family resemblance had likely already tipped her off to the truth.

"This is my sister, Margo," I said. "She didn't want anyone getting 'screwed over' either."

Margo's grip on my shoulder tightened at the slight edge in my voice. How many of the pieces could *she* put together from the stories I'd told her and our parents about my time in the League? She knew at least a few of the other members had been openly hostile.

"Pleased to meet you," she said in a perfectly even tone that must have served her well in her work at the Pentagon.

"I'm sure," Ary said with a sharp little smile I didn't trust at all.

"I'd better talk to the official emergency force before I go," Margo said to me. "Are you…" She trailed off as if not entirely sure how to ask after my well-being or perhaps whether she should at all in this company.

"I'll keep going as I have been," I said quickly.

"You know how to get in touch if you or your friends need any help I might be able to give," she said. "We'll figure this out, Finn."

O gods, I hoped that was true.

As Margo headed toward the fire trucks, a bunch of familiar figures—and some unfamiliar ones—streamed past the massive vehicles. From the look of them, they must have been fighting the fire at the other end of the building. In the hazy light offered by the streetlamps, Rocío's exhausted but smiling face lifted my spirits. Luis and Tamara were talking with each other just behind her. Her special ops colleagues eyed the surroundings as they all approached, Desmond drumming his fingers against his thigh to supplement his vision.

With them came several other League members and perhaps a dozen people I only vaguely recognized. At the sight of Noemi, understanding clicked into place. These were our current Dull students, the ones Rocío and the others would have been teaching when they'd heard about the fire. They'd brought their novice sort-of mages with them.

Clashing emotions collided in my chest. Had the Dulls actually managed to contribute to the firefighting with whatever magic Rocío had brought out in them in just a few days? We were making so much progress already. *Nil mortalibus ardui est.*

It was progress we wouldn't necessarily have wanted certain people here finding out about, though.

Ary was still standing in front of me. Her eyes narrowed even more as she took in the newcomers. She didn't know about this part of our plan. She didn't even know about Rocío.

Rocío grabbed my hand without appearing to notice the other girl's simmering hostility. "Hey. I didn't realize you'd made it here. We have to get going. Desmond thinks trouble is on the way—either Confed security or Dull military. Maybe both."

I was inclined to trust the guy's instincts—and it wasn't as if *I* could contribute anything more here.

If I'd hoped we might lose Ary as we hurried away from the scene, I wasn't so lucky. She tagged along with our expanded group as we took a roundabout route away from the scene of the fire.

Rocío leaned close as we hustled along, pitching her voice so only I would hear it with the wind still warbling around us. "How did your visit go?"

"About as well as I could have hoped," I said with a renewed wave of relief. "We had to hash some things out, but they said they'd try to help, right away. If their efforts work, we should see a response from the Circle within the next couple of days."

She squeezed my hand. "It's a good thing you reached out, then. We have other options for putting pressure on the Circle now, too, so maybe the combination will convince them to stop covering everything up."

After a few blocks, Luis sent off the Dull novices, who'd been murmuring to each other with suppressed excitement. A little farther on, he turned to face the rest of us—twenty or so League members and Rocío's little squad.

"I think it'd be best if we split up now," he said. "If the Confed or the Dull government are investigating the area around the Academy, we'll be more noticeable as a large group. Those of you who haven't already been targeted by one or the other, head home and say nothing."

"Hold on," Ary said before anyone had the chance to move. "I've got a few questions that no one else seems to want to ask." She spun on me. "What the hell were you doing bringing your sister along like this was some kind of family field trip? How much have you told her about what we're planning?"

*More than we've told you,* I thought but knew better than to say. "There were plenty of mages tackling the fire who aren't part of the League," I said. "She was in the area. Why shouldn't she have helped too?" I wasn't going to admit I'd just had dinner with her.

A glint of triumph lit in Ary's eyes. "You didn't just happen to run into her here. I saw you get out of a cab with her. Why are you lying about it if you haven't been talking with her about things you shouldn't have?"

Luis stepped up next to me. "Ary, this isn't a good time."

"When is a good time, then? You've been having meetings without telling a bunch of us about them, haven't you? And you've been letting some mage the Dull government thinks is involved with the *terrorists* pitch in?" She lifted her chin toward Rocío. "I thought we were supposed to discuss anything risky, all together."

Rocío stiffened at my other side. A few of the other League members who hadn't been part of our Dull training sessions stirred.

"*Has* Finn been telling his family about the League's plans?" one of the guys demanded. "I could accept him coming back, but we all know what the Lockwoods are like. You can't get closer to the Circle than them. They're the ones we're supposed to be up against."

Callum's gaze darted from Ary to me and back again. My former classmate didn't look all that pleased with either of us. "He never got along with his granduncle in the Circle," he put in. "But he *was* a total suck-up when it came to his parents, as far as I saw."

I reined in my temper. Snapping at Ary or anyone else would only make me look less trustworthy. The League members watching needed to know my judgment was sound.

"I've gone against my parents' interests more than once for the sake of the League," I said with all the calm I could summon. "I picked my side."

"I'm sure Finn has been discreet, even if he's in contact with his family," Tamara said. "He's proven his loyalty to our cause. I watched him stand up to the Circle with my own eyes. Why do you think they've been putting out alerts about him?"

"He's too prominent, too easy a target," Ary said smoothly. "That's what it proves. And now he's going running to his big sister for help?"

My stomach knotted, but I squared my shoulders. I'd made my choice. I'd made it for a good reason. I just had to make sure I sounded like the reasonable one here.

"I *have* talked with my family—not about the League's plans, but about the problems we can all see are happening and what every mage needs to be doing to help settle down the magic. I talked to them because it's the best thing I can do for the League. I don't have any magic to offer. I don't have any sway within the Circle. I *do* have a connection to people who might be able to make the Circle listen, so that's what I'm using."

"Sure." Ary waved her hand toward me as if I'd just proved her point. "He's going to lead the Confed right to us. Is that what we want?"

I forced my voice to stay dry rather than annoyed. "We're a lot more likely to be caught because you insisted on stopping us to make a big deal out of this than because of anything I said."

At the discontented muttering that rose up at my words, Ary whipped back toward Rocío. "And why are you so cozy with a terrorist? How does that help the cause?"

"I'm not a terrorist," Rocío said before I had to defend her. "I tried to prevent the attack on the Confed building, and the Dull government is making up stories because they're looking for someone to blame. I'm doing everything I can to make sure we don't lose the magic we have completely."

Callum spoke up again and partly redeemed himself after being an ass a few minutes ago. "It's not like they've been hiding her. She was there at the first meeting after the attack, talking like this then too. Way before the Dull government started looking for her. You'd have seen her there if you'd turned up."

Ary's face flushed at the insinuation that she hadn't been committed enough. "Well, I don't see why you're all taking your cues from some girl who wasn't even in the League a week ago."

Instead of her, she meant. I fought the urge to grit my teeth.

"She'd have been with us from the start if she could have, Ary. You have no idea what she's been through fighting for the same cause we have."

"And you should believe me because I know way more about this situation than the Confed wants any of us to know." Rocío gestured back toward the Academy. "I just led a bunch of *Dulls* in using castings to put out that fire. I understand what's happening to the magic. I'm not going to keep quiet when I can use that knowledge."

Oh, no. I swallowed thickly as Ary's eyes widened. Quite possibly she'd have put the pieces together about our work with the Dulls once she'd asked more questions, but now she didn't even need to do that.

"You did *what* with the Dulls?" she spat out, her face etched with horror.

"Leave it, Ary," Luis said, more firmly than before.

Her gaze jerked to him. "Is she serious? She's teaching Dulls to use magic somehow? You're letting her—helping her?"

Rocío's colleague Sam cleared his throat behind us. "Not that this doesn't seem to be a really important discussion, but I'm going to suggest you pick it up another time. Because if we keep it up here and now, chances are we'll all end up in one prison or another. Whoever was sniffing around the Academy, they're heading this way."

Luis clapped his hands. "You all heard him. Our safety has to come first. We'll discuss the rest later—I'll call a meeting soon. Get going!"

Ary's shoulders came up, but after a tense second, she whirled and stalked off, beckoning to a cab that cruised by. Luis tipped his head to me and Rocío and took off as the other League members scattered.

"If they're actively hunting us down like this, I think we're safer in numbers," Desmond said to Rocío. "Between the four of us, two could keep watch while the other two sleep."

I clearly wasn't included in that metric, but it made sense. Part of me might balk at giving up a night's privacy with Rocío, but I wasn't risking *her* safety over that.

"It's late," I said. "If you don't mind squeezing onto a bed together or taking the floor, you three could come back to the room we've got. We can work out better arrangements in the morning."

"Sounds good to me," Sam said. "Let's move."

Farther down the street, we managed to hail a couple of cabs for ourselves. As I sank into the one I was sharing with Rocío, the whir of the motor seemed to carry us far away from our most immediate worries. I'd almost relaxed, as much as I ever did these days, by the time we climbed out at the hotel.

"It's ridiculous," Brandt muttered as we tramped up the stairs to our floor. "Now that everyone's pissed at us, they're not going to let up until they've crushed us. Are we just going to keep running from the Dulls and whoever else for the rest of our lives?"

Rocío shot him a stern look. "Don't go talking like that again. We're going to get the whole mess sorted out—but it'll take a lot longer if we start taking pot-shots back at them instead of just steering clear."

He let out a huff. "Who says I'm only talking about pot-shots? I'm tired of being kicked around."

"Brandt." Sam said his name like a warning, and the other guy shut up. Still, his sentiments set me on edge all over again.

How long *would* we have to keep running—and how long could we feasibly stay ahead of the forces that wanted to stop us?

# CHAPTER FOURTEEN

*Rocío*

"Up!" An urgent voice penetrated my sleep. "Everyone, up! Move it!"

I was already scrambling out of the bed I'd shared with Finn —chastely, since we had company. Adrenaline thrummed through my body, even more potent than the magic whirling around me. Three and a half months of military training and service meant that my mind could snap from asleep to alert in seconds.

"What's going on?" I asked.

It'd been Sam and Desmond's watch. Sam was standing by the window, the whites of his eyes gleaming in the faint light seeping from the street outside. The clock on the table between the two beds told me it was one in the morning.

Finn fumbled out from under the blanket and swiped his hand across his eyes. Brandt was shoving out of the other bed. Sam nodded to the window.

"We've got some kind of company—at least ten soldiers coming around the building."

"They don't feel like mages," Desmond added from where he stood farther along the outer wall. "I haven't caught any castings."

"Zacher's people." My stomach sank. How had they found us? I guessed it didn't really matter right now. All that mattered was getting out of this place before they closed in on us. We'd slept in our clothes in case we needed to make a hasty exit, gracias a Dios.

"Seems like we picked the wrong place to crash," Brandt muttered.

I ignored him. "What's our best option for getting out of here?"

Sam frowned. "I'm not sure. They came so fast, I think they'll already have the entrances covered. I'd rather slip out unseen than mess around trying to make a distraction…" He pointed at something on the other side of the glass. "I think we'd be safe in the alley there. We can get a good enough look at it to teleport, and it's not that far. I know the magic isn't very stable right now —do you all think you can handle it?"

Brandt nodded with a jerk of his head. Finn paled, but I caught his hand. "I can get both Finn and me over there."

Desmond's mouth had flattened. "I can't go by sight. To teleport, I need other impressions of the spot. We weren't outside this place long enough to give me a clear sense of anywhere I've got the power to reach."

I dragged in a breath, testing the tremor of energy in the air. The magic had calmed a tiny bit when we'd fought the fire at the Academy, but that effect had only been temporary. Now, it jerked away when I focused on it. But I hadn't done any major castings in the last few days. I should be able to manage two teleports across a relatively short distance.

"I don't think I can carry two at once, but I can bring Finn and then come back for you," I said to Desmond.

"No." Finn squeezed my hand and then let go. "Take

Desmond first. They're looking for the four of you. The Dull military has nothing against me. If you end up having to leave me behind, I'll be fine."

Resistance to the idea of abandoning him gripped my lungs. He *wouldn't* be fine. At the very least, they'd question him, and I didn't know how harsh they'd be about it. They might take him into custody for helping us, or hand him over to the Circle for the mages to deal out their justice.

But I could tell from the set of Finn's jaw that he was determined to have his way, and there was no time to argue about it. Sam had continued his casting to monitor the soldiers, and now he grabbed the shoulder bag he'd left on the floor nearby.

"They're heading up through the building," he said. "We've got to go now."

Brandt hustled to the window to take a look at the alley. I peered over the two guys' shoulders and reached over to grasp Desmond's arm.

"I'll help direct the magic to your casting," he said. "Less work for you, at least."

"Thanks." That would help. I took in the spot: the dip in the pavement right at the alley's edge, the sheen of ice within that hollow, the brick wall on one side and the concrete one on the other, the streetlamp casting its yellow glow just a few feet away. In the back of my mind, I could sense the chill and the way the uneven pavement would feel under my feet. My fingers clutched Desmond's arm harder, and I murmured the lyric that had carried me from danger before.

"Como veían que resistía."

The magic shuddered as it wrenched around us. Desmond's voice rose alongside mine, with an extra rush of energy. Sam and Brandt blinked out of sight with a tingle like a passing breeze. I was just training my mind on the alley to complete the casting when heavy footsteps thumped in the hall outside.

¡Mierda! I closed my eyes and sang the lyric once more with all the concentration I had in me. The magic slammed into us, and my body flinched with the sudden jolt.

The winter cold closed against my skin. I opened my eyes to the shadowy alley, Desmond beside me, the other guys waiting farther down it.

"I have to go back for Finn," I gasped out, and focused on the hotel room. If the soldiers had already made it there…

I threw myself into the casting as quickly as I could. The magic seared through my mind, aching inside my skull. It seemed to scrape over my skin as it heaved me back into the room.

Finn stood where we'd left him at the side of the bed, his body rigid. A bang came from the hall—someone ramming the door. I snatched at his elbow just as the dead bolt snapped.

"Halt right there!" a figure in a dark uniform shouted.

He could forget about that. I yanked Finn to me, slinging my other arm around his waist, and drank in his warm scent as I sang the words to cast us away one more time. The magic vibrated in my throat and gnawed up my arms. Then it swallowed us up with a thunderclap right inside my ears.

I landed in the alley, dizzy and queasy. The casting had left me so off-balance I stumbled into the brick wall with a smack of my shoulder. Finn tugged me into his arms before I hit my head too.

"Are you okay?" he asked quietly. "We're out. You got us out." A tremor ran through him.

"I'll be all right," I said. For a second the ache in my head felt as if it were trying to snap my skull right in half, but then it started to dull, the magic twining around my limbs with a quaking that felt almost apologetic.

"We're not all the way out," Desmond said, his voice rough. A second later, shouts rang out from down the street. Boots thudded over the pavement. The soldiers were spreading out their search.

"Come on!" Sam beckoned us farther down the alley. The growl of an engine reverberated somewhere in the distance. As we swerved around the back of the apartment building, more footsteps pounded toward us, way too close for comfort. The squad that had stormed the hotel had brought company to patrol the surrounding streets.

I intoned a few lines under my breath to draw the shadows closer around us, hoping to conceal at least Finn and me from view. The ache in my head jabbed deeper, and most of the strands of magic slipped away from me. An icy spear of panic ran through my chest.

I'd worn myself out with the repeated teleportation. I might not have enough strength left to conduct the energy around us in any useful way right now.

Brandt mumbled something low in a halting rhythm. Darkness wavered around his form but didn't totally conceal him. My former teammates were much weaker mages than I was. Just teleporting themselves once must have taken a lot out of them.

A holler carried from ahead of us. We stopped in our tracks near the end of the alley. Did the soldiers have us surrounded? Understanding clamped around my gut: our chances of making it out of this situation with our freedom were slipping away from us fast.

"Here!" Desmond whispered, motioning us to the back door of a shop. He was the freshest of us, since he hadn't needed to cast a full teleportation spell, so he sang softly at the lock, and it popped open. We dashed inside and yanked the door closed behind us.

A thick boozy smell filled my nose, turning my stomach. Muffled voices and laughter filtered through the wall across from us, followed by the clinking of glasses.

We weren't in a shop after all. This was the back room of a bar. As my eyes adjusted to the dark, I made out the shapes of liquor and wine bottles along the shelves.

"Sorry," Desmond murmured. "I only had time to check the doors closest to us. The other places nearby had alarm systems."

I edged closer to the inner door. Light and warmth seeped from beneath it. "Do you think we can go through the bar without causing a commotion that'll bring the soldiers this way?" They might be patrolling the street beyond the bar's front door, too.

"All five of us?" Sam looked doubtful. He pressed the heel of his hand to his temple. "All it'd take is one person recognizing either of you, and we might not even make it out of the bar. The magic is so hard to work with right now… I'm not sure I can cast much of anything to help us."

"We could wait it out," Finn said tentatively. "The soldiers can't know we've come in here. We'll just hold our ground until they go by and the coast is clear—right?"

That sounded like a good enough plan for the minute or so that passed before a much more unsettling noise reached our ears: the distant rattle of a doorknob.

"Try them all," a voice ordered from down the alley. "We can't leave until we've checked every possible route."

Another scuffing sound came as a soldier tested a door even closer to us. My gaze jerked to the entrance we'd come through and then to Desmond. "Did you relock it?"

He shook his head with a grimace. I eased over, my pulse booming so loud it amplified my headache. With a swift twist of my fingers, I slid the deadbolt back into place.

Not quite discreetly enough. "Over here!" someone yelled, almost right outside. I hadn't realized anyone was that close.

I leapt back from the door as more soldiers stomped across the alley to join him. Any second now they were going to break that lock and charge in at us. We *had* to take the gamble of going through the bar—we had to run for it.

I caught Finn's eyes in the dimness. He tipped his head in silent acknowledgment, his expression taut. Just as I stepped toward the other door, Brandt held up his hand.

"Stay here," he murmured. "Keep hidden as well as you can. I'll deal with this."

I stared at him.

"What are you *doing*, Brandt?" Sam said, but the more junior operative walked over to the back door without answering.

Here, now, we weren't soldiers ourselves anymore. Our team leader had no hold over any of us—and Brandt had never seemed to respond well to authority anyway.

"I *said* keep hidden," he said, as brusquely as he could under his breath. The door rattled. He jabbed his hand toward the other side of the room.

We didn't have much choice. I couldn't see him suddenly siding with the Dulls and turning us in, so whatever he was planning, I had to trust it was for our benefit, not theirs.

We flattened ourselves against the shelves at the farthest, darkest end of the room. The soldiers outside bashed at the door handle. Clenching his jaw, Brandt flipped the lock. He threw the door open and held up his hands.

I couldn't see the soldiers, but there was no mistaking the rustle of their uniforms as their gun hands came up.

"Hey," Brandt said. "Easy there. It's just me, and I'm done running. The others took off on me. You want a mage, right? Let me come peacefully, and I'll do whatever Zacher and the rest of them want."

"Come out," one of the men barked. "Keep your hands up."

Desmond started crooning in the barest thread of a whisper, his fingers pattering faintly against his thigh at the same time. I braced myself against the pain in my head and sang out a brief lyric to match his.

The magic shivered and thickened in front of us. Here, in the near-complete darkness of the room, with a few minutes' rest after teleporting, we had a hope of disguising ourselves.

A couple soldiers stepped into the room, guns ready. My heart hiccupped, but their gazes slid right over the wall where we were standing. Brandt had told them not to expect to see anyone, and between that and our hasty casting, we'd convinced them the room was empty.

They stalked through the space and then tramped outside. "It's clear."

The door thumped shut. The voices faded as the squad must have ushered Brandt down the alley. More handles rattled as they went, but they had no reason to come back and check this one again.

I released the spell with a sag of my shoulders. My gaze caught Sam's. The slant of his mouth showed the same confusion I felt.

What was Brandt up to? I couldn't believe he'd sacrificed himself for the rest of us out of the goodness of his heart. That wasn't the guy I knew. I also couldn't believe he'd decide surrender was better than being on the run.

Brandt had come up with plenty of plans on his own in the past... and the one thing I could say about them was that I hadn't liked the intended results at all.

# CHAPTER FIFTEEN

*Finn*

I'd never have thought I'd miss the dingy hotel room where I'd spent most of the last few days. It turned out, though, that there were even less cheerful accommodations.

The plastic folding chair wobbled under me next to the makeshift desk in a corner of the basement apartment, where Desmond was working his internet skills. It was mid-afternoon, and the sky was clear outside, but only a thin steam of sunlight slanted through one small, low window. A damp chill seeped through the garbage bag taped over the other, broken one. The place smelled faintly of mildew and corn chips, a combination I hadn't noticed the one time I'd been here before, when the League had gathered after the attack on the Confed building.

I couldn't complain, though. Luis's friend who rented this apartment had offered it to the four of us in the middle of the night after we'd fled our hotel. No one had come around to question him since that first meeting, so it seemed his neighbors weren't particularly nosy. That didn't stop my pulse from stuttering at the scrape of shoes outside the door, but it was only a couple of League members dropping in early for the meeting Luis had arranged to start in about an hour.

Desmond had glanced over at my anxious jerk toward the door. As the newcomers flopped onto the couch in tense conversation, I turned back to him. My face wouldn't have been much more than a blur to him, but his distant gaze appeared to see plenty all the same.

"Last the soldiers knew, we were in New Jersey," he said. "Even if they figure we came back to New York, it's a big city to search."

"I know," I said. We also had the reassurance that Rocío and Sam were taking turns checking the streets outside for any sign of military movement—as well as they could with the magic's current state. The wind outside had risen again, making the basement windows rattle and creak. When we'd watched the noon news, the reporters on every channel had given concerned commentary on the "unruly" weather.

What they *hadn't* been talking about was the video Desmond had uploaded this morning or any revised statement of intentions from the Circle. We'd been tracking down an explanation for the first omission, and it looked like Desmond had found it.

He leaned forward to squint at the enlarged text on his laptop's screen and let out a frustrated huff. "There's no sign we ever uploaded the thing—either time. The Confed must have been watching for content with related keywords. That's the only way they could have found the video and shut it down so quickly."

"*Some* people must have seen it, right?" I said. "It was up for a little while."

He nodded. "Not very many, though, I don't think. It takes time to gain that viral momentum we were hoping for. And even the people who did see it can't show it as proof that the Dulls are magical, so I don't know if anyone else would believe them. I'm just lucky I made the backup before I shared the link."

When he and Rocío had discovered the database of magical capacity ratings in their base wherever they'd been stationed overseas, he'd managed to copy a portion of that over to a private server of his. He'd offered a link to it with the video for viewers to confirm Rocío's comments about the Dulls having magic. Confed security had shut that down so completely he couldn't even access the server anymore.

I sat back in the chair, tensing my legs as it wobbled again. "What can we do, then? Could we send the video around privately and hope people will pass it on? The Circle can't pick up that with a search, right?"

"They can't," Desmond agreed, "but I'd still need to host the video somewhere. An attachment that big would either bounce or get sent into spam on most email servers. I'll need to see what I can get set up. The last thing we need is them tracing the activity back to our location, and I'm sure they're calling in all the internet security gurus they can reach now that we've shown our hand." He rubbed his face. "Maybe we should wait until we have a clearer demonstration of the Dulls casting magic so we can be sure of making an impact."

The video Luis had recorded of the Dulls working to subdue the fire was clear enough to anyone who knew what they were looking at, but between the darkness and the erratic light from the flames, it'd be incredibly easy to cast doubt. You could barely see anyone's faces except Rocío at the end, which protected the Dulls but also meant no one could confirm they were Dulls in the first place.

I frowned. "Any video we make, if the Circle doesn't shut it down right away, they can claim we faked the evidence with magic or edited effects." Zacher barely believed he'd really been able to cast after Rocío had walked him through the process.

How in Hades' name were we going to convince the hundreds of millions of Dulls we couldn't even talk to directly?

"True. We'll just have to find the right combination of things so they can't deny it." Desmond gave me a crooked smile. "We keep trying new strategies until we find one that gets us where we want to go, just like in—"

He cut himself off with an abruptness that was familiar. He'd been going to say *in the Exam* but the silencing 'chantment had cut him off.

"I guess we did all right there," I said, keeping my own comments vague. "We made it out, anyway, even if none of us got the outcome we'd have wanted."

Desmond guffawed under his breath. "No kidding. Although…" He trailed off, but this time he sounded more purposefully hesitant than forced. I waited without prodding him as he gathered his words.

"I'm never going to thank the Confed for how they handled that whole situation," he said, quiet and careful with his phrasing. "But honestly, taking on that role as Champion—I'm not sure I ever felt that competent with my magic before. In the tutorials, I always seemed to be a step or two behind because I was focusing part of my attention on compensating for my sight. What we were doing, after the Exam, let me use *those* skills for something useful."

His mouth twisted. I couldn't blame him for feeling conflicted about that admission.

"I think that just shows that you're good at making the best of a bad situation," I said lightly. "Let's hope for better situations ahead."

He tipped his head in acknowledgment. "That's what I'm counting on. There's got to be another place where I can contribute just as much, but at something I'll actually want to do. Someplace I won't be treated like a second-class mage. In the words of the great Tyrion Lannister, 'Never forget what you are. Make it your strength.' So, I'll keep trying things until I find that spot where I'm meant to be. Assuming I get the chance."

My gut pinched. "I'm sorry," I said. "The Confed really should do better by every mage, not just the ones from the 'right' families. I wish I'd never been a part of that whole system."

Desmond turned his vague gaze on me again. "You didn't pick that any more than I picked where I was born. You make the best of that like I do with the lot I have, yeah? You'll always be a part of the system, but it sounds like you've managed to spin that to other people's advantage a couple times."

Looking at it that way was both reassuring and depressing, especially when the guys on the sofa had just turned the news back on. I swiveled in my chair to watch the broadcast, but the only mention they made of the Circle was of "continuing efforts by the National Defense division to bring to justice the culprits of last week's attack on New York City."

"They don't seem to have made much progress so far," the other reporter at the desk said with a disapproving frown. "You'd think with magic it'd be a piece of cake to track down these criminals."

Wonderful. Even the Dull media was becoming skeptical of the Confederation.

The reporters barely touched on the Manhattan Academy fire, which I supposed was less newsworthy with the building still standing—and with only local civilians to blame. They definitely gave no sign that anything shocking had happened during the fire-fighting efforts.

Rocío came over behind the sofa to watch. Desmond dove back into his work, and I couldn't really help much, so I got up to join her.

"Emergency services and the mages who jumped in managed to save at least part of the other academies too," Rocío said as the clip on the fire finished. "But a couple people who went to help in Houston were shot by the protesters there. They just want us *gone*."

"It'll be different when they know they can work with magic too," I said, but that reassurance felt hollow when we had no idea how we'd get there. I didn't have any good news to offer from Desmond's end. I made a face at the TV. "I guess my dad wasn't able to convince the Circle to change their tune. I'd expect they'd act quickly if they were going to listen to him."

"There's still time," Rocío said, but her face fell in a way that tugged at my heart. "Maybe we should have waited with the video. They probably saw that as an attack—not a great way to encourage them to cooperate."

"Hey." I set my hand on her shoulder. "They'd already shown they were going to be incredibly stubborn about this. For all we knew, the video could have had the opposite effect, forcing them to get ahead of the story. We couldn't have realized they'd be able to shut it down that quickly and effectively."

She didn't look all that comforted by my point, but then, neither was I. I slipped my hand around her waist, and she leaned into me a little as we waited to see if the news would offer anything else of interest.

It was almost time for the meeting anyway. The guy who owned the apartment returned from work and promptly nabbed the last spot on the sofa. Luis, Tamara, Mark, and Noemi turned up along with other League members who trickled in by pairs or trios. As the room filled, I turned to check on Desmond's progress, just as the apartment door opened yet again. Ary froze on the threshold, staring at me and Rocío.

For the first few seconds, I simply stared back at her, unable to make sense of her obvious shock. Why the hell would she be surprised to see us here when she'd accused Luis of arranging exclusive meetings with us as part of a special inner echelon?

Then her expression hardened as she mastered her reaction, with a flicker of what I could only call disappointment.

A suspicion prickled my brain. We *wouldn't* have made it to this meeting if the Dull military had successfully taken us in last night. The only way someone could know we'd been ambushed but not that we'd escaped… was if they'd tipped the soldiers to our location in the first place.

Normally, I would have given Ary a wide berth. With that suspicion rattling around in my head, though, I moved toward her.

"You made it," I said evenly. "I guess that was easier for you than it was for us."

The tightening of her jaw confirmed it. She didn't look remotely confused, only defensive. "I'm not sure what you're talking about," she said in a haughty tone, but her hands had balled nervously at her sides. "I'm here to have my say, just like you are."

"But you were hoping we wouldn't be here." The wheels in my head spun. She'd gotten into her cab before us—she could have told her driver to follow us and found out where we were staying. It wouldn't have been hard for her to call in the tip after that. She hadn't liked Rocío's sudden appearance in the League or the plans we were carrying out, and she'd known the Dull government was searching for her.

Nausea swelled in my stomach. Any of us could have been killed in that confrontation. She'd sicced soldiers with assault weapons on us for the chance to steer the League the way she wanted. Rocío was the best equipped to salvage this catastrophe, and Ary would have ripped her away, not just from me but from the entire movement.

Ary shrugged with forced nonchalance. "Maybe I was. There isn't much you can do about that, is there? Are you going to make a big fuss and throw around more accusations you can't prove?

Who do you think most of the people here will side with? You need the League to get what you want just as much as I do."

She sauntered off, her hands still clenched. Perhaps I could have turned the League against her with an air-tight argument, but she was right. I couldn't prove what she'd done to Rocío and her colleagues any more than I could prove her role in my granduncle's death.

Regardless, she was a danger to everyone in the League. She'd made it clear that she would throw any of us under the bus if our goals didn't align with hers. If she had her way, the truth about the Dulls would never come out, the magic might never be healed…

We had no way to control her, though—no security officers or prisons—

The Confed did. The thought rose up with a chill I couldn't blame on the basement air. Desmond was right—I was still a part of that world. I knew how they thought.

The Circle wanted me so badly they were publicizing it all over the news. How much more would they want the murderer of one of their own? Hell, what might they offer us in exchange for delivering her?

Rocío was watching me curiously. "What's going on?" she asked.

"I'm just… thinking we might have another way to sway the Circle," I said quietly, with another lurch of my stomach at the ruthlessness of the thought. Was I willing to go that far? Could I treat a person like a bargaining chip?

If it protected Rocío and everyone else I cared about… Yes, I believed I could.

# CHAPTER SIXTEEN

*Rocío*

Murmurs filled the basement apartment, but Luis kept off to the side, waiting until the official meeting time to get started. Next to me, Finn looked tense, but he hadn't wanted to say any more about his idea in front of everyone here. That girl who'd laid into him and then me last night—Ary, that was her name—was eyeing him from across the room, so it made sense that he was being cautious.

Desmond was still typing away on his laptop. Sam left his post near the windows to say something to him, and after a moment Desmond closed the computer. The solemn look on Sam's face when they both made their way over to me made my pulse skitter.

"Did you sense some kind of trouble outside?" I asked, keeping my voice low so I wouldn't cause unnecessary panic.

"Not exactly." Sam patted the shoulder bag he'd been carrying since we'd run from the hotel room last night. "There's something I think we should talk about alone—it doesn't affect the rest of the group."

Finn glanced between us. "People here will pitch in if you need help with something."

Sam gave him a small smile. "I appreciate that. I'll let you know if I think more hands on deck would be a good thing."

He motioned me and Desmond out to the basement landing. A couple newcomers squeezed past us, and then we were alone. I rubbed my arms in the dank air, chilled despite my coat. "What's going on?"

Sam scratched the back of his head, ruffling his short dark hair. His smile had disappeared as quickly as it'd come, leaving him looking way too serious again.

"I don't know for sure. It might not be anything. It's not as if Brandt didn't enjoy grandstanding. But I don't like how easily he went off with those soldiers last night."

"Neither did I. I know he was all for solidarity among Champions, but I didn't think he saw the three of us as worthy of that much loyalty. Are you just nervous about his motives, or did something new happen?" I couldn't imagine Sam making a big deal of this all of a sudden if there *hadn't* been a new development.

He patted the shoulder bag. "The three of us have been keeping all our things, including the new phones we picked up, in one bag so that if we have to leave fast, we're not scrambling for our stuff. I had it last night because I was on watch. Brandt took off without asking me for anything from it."

"He might have thought he didn't have time," Desmond pointed out. "The soldiers were about to break the door down."

"Yeah, that's not the part I'm concerned about. A few texts popped up on his phone a little while ago. They're from one of the guys he worked with a lot on the special ops team—someone he probably did see as a close friend. Apparently, Brandt emailed him sometime yesterday. He might not have expected his friend to get the message so soon, but the guy was already home on leave. He's asking if Brandt's okay and telling him not to do anything too crazy."

My chest tightened. "Can you find out what he said to the guy?"

"I talked to him just now," Sam said. "He forwarded the email on to me, because he's worried about Brandt. It's all pretty vague, but Brandt was going on about how no one here knew how to take action after the easy plan failed, we were letting the Dulls push us around and telling him that was how it had to be, so he was going to go all-in his way as soon as he had the opportunity. He signed off saying to remember him well, however it turned out."

The constriction in my chest traveled down to grip my gut as well. "As far as we could tell before, 'his' way was killing every important person he could reach in the White House."

"He might not mean that," Sam said. "We did talk him down."

"But he's right that my plan of just talking things through didn't work. Not enough to stop the attack or all the problems afterward." I'd promised him *my* way was the answer, and so far, it hadn't solved much of anything.

Brandt had disliked a lot of people, but he'd hated the Dull government most of all. They'd insisted that the Confed's National Defense division stay as active as possible overseas— they'd fired the one superior officer who had cared about our well-being while we were stationed there. As far as Brandt was concerned, they were the enemy, a danger to the special ops colleagues he saw as his only real family.

He'd complained about our refusal to engage with the Dulls yesterday, and I'd dismissed him without really discussing it. Maybe if I'd taken the time to really listen to him... But it was too late for that now.

"He was surrounded by soldiers," Desmond said. "How much could he get away with, wherever they took him?"

"Not much, I hope." I looked at Sam. "Do you think he's going to try to follow through on his original plan?"

Sam grimaced. "The email he sent sounds an awful lot like a suicide note to me. The way someone would write if they don't expect to come back. It obviously struck his friend the same way. From the way Brandt phrased it, it wasn't about the danger he was already in, but what he expected to do next."

Desmond's fingers twitched against his side. "He can't have hurt anyone yet. We'd have heard about it."

"He could have changed his plan somehow," I said, although it could still involve people getting hurt. "Or he might be looking for a chance to make the biggest impact. Do the major government figures have public appearances soon that he might be able to get to?"

Sam consulted his phone. "This might take a little while. My data has been on the fritz in the last few hours." He skimmed through the search results he eventually brought up and clicked through to a couple of links. His expression turned even more pained.

"The president is holding a big press conference this evening," he said. "It sounds like Zacher will be there too, to talk about the threat from magical terrorist groups. I don't know if Brandt would be able to talk his way into getting access…"

"But he couldn't dream up a bigger statement than an assassination in front of all the White House reporters." I pulled out my own phone. "We've got to call and warn them. Even if that's not his plan, we can't take that chance."

The two guys waited in tense silence as I placed the call. The first ring broke apart with a burst of static. Reception wasn't going to be great down here. I hurried up the steps to the main floor.

The wind outside was howling even more harshly than before, making the hinges on the outer door groan. The magic careening through it rushed inside to yank at my hair and coat. Had something upset it all over again, or was it just getting worse on its own now? I couldn't tell. Who knew what magical attacks the Confed might still be ordering on the other side of the ocean?

I dialed the number again and waited with my back braced against the wall and the phone pressed to my ear. The line on the other end rang with a fractured tone once, twice—and then cut out again.

All the warped energy in the air was interfering with the cellular waves. Maybe I could have gotten a text through, but I didn't think the official White House phones had that capability.

I spun toward the others as they came up the stairs. "I can't get through. The magic is acting up too much. Can one of you try?"

Sam tapped in the number I showed him and waited with a grim expression. Relief crossed his face just for an instant. "Hell —" he started, but before he'd even gotten the first word out, the connection must have snapped. He swore, scowling at the phone.

Desmond peered toward the street. "We can keep trying. Maybe it'll settle down enough that we can get through soon."

"But maybe not soon enough." I paced from one end of the tiny foyer to the other. "If Brandt does something awful, it's our fault. We're the ones who agreed to bring him along. *I* agreed to bring him along, knowing how he was thinking." It was on me to make sure he didn't carry out whatever violence he intended. The resolve I'd found at the fire held me steady under my uneasy nerves. "We might be able to make it to DC in time for the press conference if the trains are running. We'll keep calling on the way there, but if we can't get through to them that way, we'll warn them in person."

Sam nodded slowly. Desmond rubbed his hands together. "We've decided, then. We leave now?"

"The sooner the better." I hesitated with a skip of my pulse. "I have to tell Finn we're leaving."

I scrambled back down the stairs just as Finn poked his head out to check on us. "The meeting is about to start," he said, and then took in my face. His eyes darkened. "What's wrong?"

"We think Brandt might be planning something catastrophic, and we can't get through to the White House," I said. "We're going to take the train down there to warn them. I'll get back as soon as possible for whatever else we need to do here."

He studied me. "I shouldn't offer to come along, should I?"

An instinctive protest sprang to my lips, but his wry smile stopped me. He wasn't being down on himself, only realistic.

"I don't have any magic," he added matter-of-factly. "I can't help out with any stealthy maneuvering you need to do—or with stopping this guy. I'll just be deadwood you have to spend energy to keep hidden. It's okay. Hopefully I can get something good done here in the meantime, for when you get back. And you'd *better* get back."

"Finn," I said, not knowing what to say to make this separation easier.

"It really is okay." He drew me closer to him. "We've always accomplished the most when I work on my end of things and you work on yours. Just... be careful out there. You're the one they want the most."

"I'm not going to forget that," I said. "Hopefully I'll be able to at least text you if there's any news."

He smiled again, sad but fond, and leaned in for a quick kiss. "If anyone can stop this disaster from getting even more immense, it's you, Dragon-Tamer."

My cheeks flushed at the words and the nickname I'd come to love as much as the boy who'd given it to me. "I'll see you soon."

I stepped away from him with a pang and hustled up the stairs to rejoin my colleagues. A taxi Desmond had arranged had just pulled up outside.

I tried calling the Pentagon a few more times on the ride to the train station, but only got dead air and once, weirdly, a busy signal. Maybe some major military offensive was going on right now. Desmond tried the White House's public number with no more success than I'd had.

The wind roared around us as we got out of the cab, but the train operators must have decided they could keep going as long as they didn't have to contend with snow or rain as well. We dropped into our seats on the next train to DC with sighs that were more ragged than relieved.

As Desmond and I kept up our periodic calls, Sam looked for more information on the press conference, with long pauses as he waited for the data to come through. Just as a particularly shrill blast of wind shrieked past our window, he stiffened.

"There's been a Bonded Worthy attack on an American embassy in Romania," he said. "The reports are just starting to come in. They don't say, but I'd bet National Defense was called in to fight back."

Freaking out the magic even more in the process. I sucked a frustrated breath through my teeth. "And because of that, the Dulls could be screwing over their own safety back home."

Sam's head drooped. In that moment he looked so young, not at all old enough to have been leading squads of special soldiers all over eastern Europe.

"*I* screwed up," he said. "I knew what a loose cannon Brandt is. I should have kept him under control and not running off to carry out some wild plan."

My hackles rose in his defense. "No way. Keeping him from causing trouble should *never* have been your responsibility. You didn't ask for that job. And it was doubly not your responsibility as soon as we left those jobs behind. You always looked out for us —you made sure I didn't get myself killed. Anything Brandt decides to do is on him."

"I could have given myself up to let the rest of you get away. That's what a real leader would have done."

"If you expect me to blame you for hoping we could get out of the situation without any of us giving ourselves up, I'm not going to." I looked down at my hands. "I helped him come home, knowing what he's like. I'm the one who brought the Dull government down on us in the first place. If we're going to blame anyone, it should be me."

Sam made a sound so dismissive he didn't need to say how much he disagreed with that idea. "If none of this is my responsibility, it definitely shouldn't be yours."

The weight I'd been carrying since the magic had first reached out to me shifted in my chest, but I found I could still breathe around it. "It is what it is. I'm in this position now because of my connection to the magic. The best thing I can do is own it—and see if we can't stop Brandt from going ahead with this private mission of his."

We spent the rest of the train ride hashing out our approach —how we could quickly let someone relevant know of the danger without getting rounded up by the security around the building. Desmond brought up a map of the area, and we agreed on a spot where we'd regather if we had to scatter to avoid the guards. The train started to slow, coming up on our station.

I tucked my scarf more firmly into place as we hurried through the station to get a cab for the last short distance. We were just coming up on the doors when the magic flailed around me with a sudden flinch.

The surge of energy smacked into me, knocking me into the door frame. Pain shot through my shoulder. A crack split through the glass beside me, and the waiting vehicles outside rocked on their wheels.

Oh, no. I shoved myself upright with a wince. Desmond's head jerked around, the whites of his eyes gleaming starkly.

Over the tops of the buildings outside, a streak of smoke streamed up against the darkening sky. It flickered with currents of residual magic. My stomach plummeted.

"What's going on?" someone wailed.

"This goddamn magic won't leave us alone," another bystander muttered.

I pushed at the door, but two police officers were already charging toward the station from the other side. They motioned us all back in.

"Everyone stay here until the situation is under control," the first one ordered. "There's been an attack at the White House."

My throat closed so tight that for a second I couldn't speak. We'd tried everything we could and still been too late.

"Please," I said to the officer in a raw voice. "Do you know if everyone's all right? The president, and the other staff…?"

His eyes were full of worry and regret as he waved us further back into the station. "I don't know."

# CHAPTER SEVENTEEN

*Finn*

As much as I generally disagreed with Ary, she'd been right about one thing: I needed the League. When it'd come to taking her down, the first person I'd turned to was Luis.

He and I stood at the edge of another department store promenade. The shoppers out today looked more nervous than before, many hanging close to the artificial Christmas tree with its twinkling lights as if in search of comfort. The big tree at Rockefeller Square had toppled in the magical wind yesterday. At least in here we had a little shelter—and Christmas was only five days away, as hard as it was for me to summon much holiday cheer.

"Are you sure we can trust them to keep their end of the deal?" Luis asked as we watched for Ary among the people streaming through the broad front doors.

"My father performed a conditional casting in coordination with the Circle," I said. "If I can give them the person responsible for my granduncle's death—and proof of their culpability—they'll retract news alerts and re-open discussions with the

League. They'll also make a public statement asking mages to focus on constructive castings."

I hadn't been able to insist on more than that, plus safety for Rocío and her colleagues with the Confed. The Circle members who'd agreed to meet with Dad and me had eyed me suspiciously at first and demanded to know why the League hadn't come to them with our information sooner. I'd lied through my teeth that we'd only just discovered the culprit in our midst.

Remembering the conversation and the haggling over what amounted to a person's freedom made my stomach churn all over again. *Why shouldn't we pursue this criminal on our own?* Cunningham had asked, her tone only slightly less patronizing because of my father's presence, and I'd had to say, *Because the Dulls are starting to think you can't manage any of our enemies at all. In just a few hours, you could announce that you have the person behind the first attack on the Confed building in custody.*

I'd felt slimy making that kind of negotiation, but it had started the Circle murmuring together more intently—and ended with the deal I'd just told Luis about.

His expression stayed skeptical. Most new-magic mages wouldn't have participated in conditional castings before to know how effective they were. "As long as I fulfill my end, they have to keep theirs," I said. "It's as solid as..."

As the 'chantment preventing me from talking about the Exam, which included talking about the fact that I'd been 'chanted at all. "As any casting," I finished, without quite the punch I'd have liked.

"It'd be nice to go home without fear of being arrested," Luis acknowledged. His brow knit as he considered the crowd. After the League's meeting, while I'd intruded on my father's office and then the Circle, he'd managed to get a few texts to Ary telling her someone had proposed an idea for undermining the Circle that he thought she'd want to be involved in. She'd agreed to meet him here, most likely coming with allies in tow.

We weren't alone in watching for her. Several Confed security officers, as well as Leron and Cunningham, had concealed themselves around the edges of the promenade, ready to close in when they saw me talking to, as they put it, "our target." Neither Ary nor her League friends had the magical ability to detect a full mage who didn't want to be noticed. All I had to do was get her to admit to her role in Granduncle Raymond's death, and they'd arrest her.

Luis shifted on his feet. It was about time for Ary to show up. "If the rest of the League finds out how this went down, without really understanding how harmful her actions have been… there may be some backlash, you know."

I'd been prepared for even *him* to recoil when I'd suggested this tactic—and he had until I'd laid it all out in detail. I swallowed thickly. "I know. I take full responsibility. No one will know you were in on it."

Luis shot me a startled glance. "I don't expect you to lie on my behalf."

I'd already done an awful lot of lying in the last several weeks. Why not a little more for a good cause?

"I don't matter as much," I said. "They need you—and trust you—more than they need me. So if they're going to be angry at anyone, better it's me than you."

Luis didn't look entirely happy, but just then we caught sight of Ary slipping past the front doors with a few of her friends. He nodded to me and eased away to vanish out the back doors as planned.

My pulse thrummed as I waited for Ary to reach the Christmas tree, where she and Luis had agreed to meet. Then I pushed myself forward.

With the Confed security forces already here watching this

entire exchange, I'd let my scarf fall loose around my coat collar rather than keeping my face disguised. Ary spotted me when I was still some ten feet away. Her eyebrows jumped up, and she backpedaled a few steps. Thank the gods her pride made her hold her ground there.

"What are you doing here?" she asked, her stance rigid.

I held up my hands in an appeal for peace—possibly the biggest lie I would tell today, without any words at all. "I heard Luis talking about meeting you here. He's on his way but a little delayed. I was hoping the two of us could talk first. Clear the air."

"Who says I want to do that?" she asked, without any pretense of diplomacy.

"We've been at odds pretty much since I joined the League. I still don't agree with everything you've done, but I think we need to find some compromise if we're going to get through this disaster."

Her lip curled with a sneer. "Because you're worried about saving your own skin. Meanwhile, the Circle and the Dulls and everyone else are monumentally screwing up the whole world out there." She waved toward the blustering weather outside, with a shiver she couldn't quite hide. "I think I'll continue looking after my own, and you can look after yours, and we'll see how that works out for both of us."

She turned on her heel, grabbing her phone, presumably to text Luis. "Wait," I said, scrambling for the right approach, but she kept walking. I hadn't expected this conversation to be easy, but somehow I hadn't expected her to be quite this resistant to my olive branch.

With a lurch of my insides, I hit on the one thing I knew would stop her in her tracks—if I could stomach it. There was lying, and then there was outright brutal manipulation.

I didn't have much choice. In another second, she'd be out of my reach, causing more chaos and making it twice as hard to fix the very problems she was complaining about.

"You don't know everything," I said, catching up to her with a few hasty steps. I pitched my voice low enough that I didn't think our spectators would overhear. "There's a way to reverse the burning out. To get our connection to the magic back."

"What?" Ary whipped around with a flash of her streaked hair, so much hope behind the wariness in her eyes that it might as well have stabbed me in the gut. All the anger she had stewing under the surface came from that one place—the magic the Confed had stolen from her. I'd seen it clearly in her horror at the idea of the Dulls getting that opportunity in her place.

Even if Rocío was right, even if we could convince the Circle to get their magimedics to conduct the reversal, Ary would never benefit from it. Even a Chosen mage who committed a major criminal act would have their abilities stripped. It was something Ary had never dared to so much as dream of, and I was dangling it as a lure, knowing I would fling it impossibly far out of her reach.

Perhaps I shouldn't be so offended by her sneers. Why shouldn't she sneer at me when I was willing to resort to these tactics to hand her over to the people she hated? I'd already committed myself now, though. All I could do was ignore the shame prickling through me and plow onward.

"It's true," I said. "When everything has settled down, we're going to campaign for it. I can put in a word for you—I will—as long as you don't send anyone else after Rocío and me. I think that's a fair trade."

I cringed inwardly at the implied promise of the words, but I managed to keep my expression earnest. Ary studied me. "Why should I believe you'd do that?"

"Because I realize you had a right to be nervous last night, and I shouldn't have dismissed your concerns the way I did. You should know by now that tackling the big problems is more important to me than differences of opinion." The thing was, she'd made herself one of the big problems when she'd called in the military on us.

Perhaps my usual candidness had bought me a little trust from her after all. I didn't know whether to feel more guilty or triumphant when she swiveled to face me completely.

"And all you want is for me to leave you and your girlfriend alone?" she said.

"Well, I also…" I pushed my mouth into a sheepish smile. "We can talk honestly, can't we? I understand why you wanted to strike out at the Circle. But if I'm going to speak up for you, the truth about what happened to my granduncle can never come out afterward. Are you sure the mage you had 'chant the doorway on the Confed building won't start talking?"

Ary folded her arms over her chest with a lift of her chin. I'd suspected she wouldn't let a question of her competency go unanswered. "He knows if he says anything, it'd be his word against mine, and I've got people who'll say I've got nothing to do with it. No way he'd take the risk of admitting his part in the death of a Circle member, even if for some bizarre reason he decides he's unhappy about what went down."

That was close, but I wanted to be sure the Confed authorities had heard enough to make their charges stick.

"You're sure that when you gave him the orders, you didn't give away anything that could incriminate you?"

"I told him the point was to shake things up. Give the Circle something to think about if they tried to go back on any agreement with the League. Just put a few cracks in the stone and nudge it loose while they were under it—that's all. I don't see how any of that could tie back specifically to me."

That was a full admission. The discomfort that had soured

my mouth took away any sense of victory. I had one more thing I wanted to be sure was perfectly clear.

"I'll want to vouch for other people in the League too. Who else did you get involved that I don't know about? I can't have any surprises."

Ary rolled her eyes. "After the fuss you made the first time you caught me, I figured it was better to go low key. Luis made it clear he didn't approve. At least, not if he had to sign off beforehand. Don't worry yourself, Academy boy. I took care of everything. I knew what the hell I was doing." Her lips formed a thin smile. "And if you don't follow through on this reversal thing, I'll just have to tell the Confed that you knew someone was going to mess with the doorway and didn't stop them. Who do you think they'll believe when you're already a wanted man?"

That threat might have mattered if I didn't already have Confed security waiting in the wings. I tipped my head. "Understood," I said, my voice gone raw. "Thank you. I'm glad we could have this conversation."

Ary glanced around. "Now just how big a delay did you get Luis wrapped up in?"

I never had to answer. At that moment, two Confed security officers materialized out of the crowd on either side of her. More appeared around the friends she'd brought. Ary jerked as if to bolt, but one of the mages by her had already snapped out a casting. Her legs froze in the grip of an invisible conjured vice.

"Ary Huon, you're under arrest by the order of the North American Confederation of Mages," the officer said. "You'll come with us now. If you try to run, I'll have to lock you back down for the rest of the trip."

Ary's gaze snapped to me, so fierce it practically burned. I took a step back, even though I knew she couldn't hurt me any way now.

"It wasn't just for me," I said. "You put everything the League has worked for in danger."

Of course, that didn't change the fact that I'd trapped her in a way that felt even more slimy than my bargain with the Circle.

Ary sucked in a sharp breath but caught herself before she said anything. She must have realized any harsh words she threw at me would only reflect badly on her at this point. Mouth tight, she let the security officers haul her away.

Leron came up behind me. "That'll be more than enough to prove the case," he said. "Your end of the casting is satisfied."

I glanced around, but Cunningham apparently wasn't interested in chatting just yet. "You'll arrange for those retractions to be broadcast tonight?"

He nodded. "And the statement on constructive castings that we agreed on. As for meeting with your League—"

A phone alert went off before he could continue. He checked it, and the color leached from his face in an instant.

"We'll discuss that as soon as we can," he said, already turning away.

Apprehension sliced through me. "What—" I started, but he'd already dashed into the crowd.

I scanned the people around me, but none of them gave any sign of a potential emergency. When I made my way to the front doors, the howl of the wind sounded no better but no worse than it had been when I'd arrived. I shifted my weight from one foot to the other.

The Circle *had* to keep to the agreement of the casting. He couldn't have just been making excuses.

I wandered the store for several more minutes, hoping I'd overhear something illuminating, but the people around me were too focused on finding their last-minute presents. Finally, I braced myself and ducked out into the wrenching windstorm to hail a cab.

There weren't many running in this weather, even in the evening. The man who picked me up, after my face was already aching with the cold, looked harried. I dove into the back seat and sat there without much to do other than worry the whole drive into Harlem.

When I burst into the basement apartment, the guy who owned it and a couple of other League members were sitting rigidly on the sofa, their eyes glued to the news. All I had to see was the image of the White House and smoke rising above it for the bottom to drop out of my stomach.

One of the guys glanced back at me. "They're saying a mage terrorist attacked during a press conference at the White House. A bunch of people are dead, the president in the hospital—no one knows if he's going to live."

O gods. My legs wobbled. I managed to make it to the armchair in the corner and collapsed there in shocked horror. For a stretch of time that passed in a blur, none of us spoke or moved, just followed the news reports for the vague details they were offering.

Rocío had been heading down there. Had *she* gotten caught in the attack?

I went to text her, and at the same moment, my phone rang. I didn't recognize the number. When I raised it to my ear, my sister's voice crackled from the speaker in fits and starts.

"Finn? Thank the g— —had to warn you. It's— —get bad."

"What? I can hardly hear you." I sprinted for the door to climb the steps, praying for better reception.

The line stayed staticky, but I caught every word this time. "The government is going to declare a state of emergency," Margo said. "They didn't consult anyone in the Confed first. They're going to take every mage they can find into custody as a threat to national security."

# CHAPTER EIGHTEEN

*Rocío*

The bus depot smelled like stale sweat and dirty slush. Sam, Desmond, and I had ended up crammed together on one of the benches next to a woman who was eating from a bag of chips with horrified smacks of her lips, but even though it was nearly morning now and my head was spinning with grogginess, I had no intention of moving. Like everyone in the building around us, our eyes were glued to the TV mounted over the windows.

The volume had been off when we'd gotten here, nabbing a ride on an Uber Desmond had summoned after we'd realized the trains weren't going to be running from DC anytime soon. After enough frightened complaints, one of the staff at the depot had turned the TV up so we could make out the reporters' voices as long as everyone kept to their state of quiet shock.

"Doctors report that the president's condition is serious but stable," the current newscaster said with a matter-of-fact voice, as if the leader of the country were nearly killed by mages every other day. "They're optimistic for a full recovery, although it may be several days, if not weeks, before he returns to the Oval Office. After the first emergency medical treatment, all magimedics have been asked to remove themselves from his case."

"Shooting themselves in the foot to spite their face," Sam mumbled through his scarf, but he sounded more exhausted than irritated. After all the pain mages had caused in the last couple weeks, I didn't know that I could blame the Dull government for taking that precaution. They couldn't be sure of Brandt's motivation or that he'd been acting alone.

For all we knew, there *would* be other mages angry with the government who'd be inspired by his statement to make one of their own.

That thought made my stomach list. I clasped my hands on my lap as a picture of Zacher appeared on the screen.

"Secretary of Defense John Zacher emerges as the primary hero in this tragedy," the reporter went on. "Eyewitness accounts confirm that he shielded the president at the expense of his own life."

*I'd* been pretty angry with Zacher after the way he'd tried to force my cooperation, but I didn't take any joy from his death. He'd trusted me more than maybe anyone else in the White House would have. He'd trusted Brandt enough to let him get too close.

In that last moment before he'd died, how much had he regretted his open-mindedness?

I couldn't stand to sit in silence any longer. With a few soft words I murmured under my breath, I managed to draw enough of the still-jittering magic around us to cover our voices for a few minutes. Still, I kept mine low when I spoke around the lump in my throat. "We should have realized sooner that this might happen—soon enough to warn them."

Sam turned to me. "Before we heard from his friend, we didn't have any reason to think Brandt was still considering going that far. If he *hadn't* been planning something like that, and we'd gotten him in trouble anyway, we might have provoked him rather than preventing a disaster."

It was hard to take comfort in that fact when I couldn't imagine how this disaster could be much worse. I rubbed my eyes. "I thought I had everyone on the right track, that I could get people to see—that I could lead the way—" In my fatigue, I couldn't even string my words together coherently. Maybe I'd taken on too much after all, and that was why it'd all gone wrong.

"Neither of us realized what he was up to either," Desmond reminded me.

I was the one who'd kept brushing off Brandt's objections to the Dulls, though. I'd dismissed his restlessness as his usual irritability and not something bigger.

The newscast switched to a story about some corporate merger I couldn't have cared less about. I adjusted my position, but my butt seemed to have melded to the bench. It was still another half an hour before the first bus to New York City was due to arrive. I checked my phone, not really expecting to see any further messages from Finn at this hour.

I'd texted him after we'd snuck away from the train station to reassure him that I was okay, and he'd told us to come to the college as soon as we got back to the city—that something big was going on with the Dull government in the wake of the attacks, and we should take extra care to keep our faces covered up. Not that I'd wanted to tempt fate by letting myself get recognized after one of my colleagues had tried to assassinate the president.

If the Dull authorities hadn't been sure I was allied with terrorists before, I'd guess they were now.

Sam risked getting up to grab us some food from the vending machine. Desmond tapped a subtle rhythm on his thigh.

"No sign of soldiers out there?" I asked.

He shook his head. "Not that I can pick up. They're probably still focused on combing DC." We'd put about an hour between us and the capitol to get here. He glanced toward me. "You know you can't blame yourself for what happened, right? Even if we could have figured it out sooner, Brandt's still the one who launched the attack. That's on him."

"But if I'd done something differently, maybe he'd never have had the chance. Or maybe I could have talked him out of it again."

"There must be dozens of other people who could say that too. That's not—" He paused as if groping for the right words. "You know, even in books and movies where everything's made up and the characters could be completely perfect, heroes make mistakes all the time. Luke Skywalker screws up all over the place. It's basically his defining trait. And let's not even get started on Bilbo Baggins."

"I only have a vague idea of who those people are," I had to tell him.

He clucked his tongue. "Blasphemy. If the world ever goes back to normal, we need to work on your education in speculative fiction. You get the gist, though, don't you? Even when you look at the most iconic heroes, what makes them heroic isn't that they always had the perfect solution. It's that they keep pushing for what's right and don't give up even after they realize they made mistakes."

"Is that supposed to make me feel better?"

"I was kind of hoping it would. Did it work at all?"

I tested the jagged bits of anxiety and guilt inside me. "Maybe a little."

Desmond gave me a wry smile. "Look, I don't expect you to have it all figured out. But I've seen enough to trust you to know what the magic needs way more than I'd trust anyone else. And if we lose the magic, I don't know if we could ever fix the rest. A whole dimension of the world just gone... The main reason I'm not assuming we're all screwed is that you're still defending it. So I'd really appreciate it if you kept going."

That did more to quiet the churning of my gut than the bit he'd said before. I sucked in a breath. "Okay," I said. "Thank you for saying that. And—I hope I can get everyone from overseas back here safely too. You haven't heard from Leonie since we went AWOL, have you?"

His smile slanted into a frown. I didn't know if he and the girl we'd met in the Exam and then worked with overseas had been in an official relationship, but they'd been close enough that the distance and the uncertainty were clearly eating at him.

"Nope," he said. "No pressure, but if you can manage that too, I'll make sure you get a trophy or something."

I couldn't help a ragged laugh I instinctively muffled with my hand to my scarf despite the bubble of semi-privacy I'd conjured for us.

When the bus arrived, we piled in, taking three seats at the very back. I was so tired I managed to drift off for part of the drive. The jerk of the vehicle at the Port Authority terminal jolted me back into awareness.

The wind blasted our faces as we stepped outside. Farther down the street, a store's sign had crashed onto the sidewalk. A roof groaned as the magic clenched around me and then ripped itself away again. The few cars on the road this early drove by at half the speed limit.

We opted to walk to the college, hugging the sides of the buildings for as much shelter as we could get. When we reached the stone façade of the Academy, my legs locked.

I'd given up everything for the chance of enrolling there. Whatever Finn said, the people who ruled that place were the same people who'd approved of the Exam's tortures, who'd agreed to send the Champions overseas to fight their battles unwillingly. I didn't think they'd be any happier to see their special operatives gone AWOL than the Dull government would.

*We're here*, I texted to Finn. *I'm not sure about walking right in.*

He answered within a few seconds. *I'll be right there.*

The front door eased open less than a minute later. From the flush in Finn's cheeks, he'd run. At the sight of him, my body moved forward as if drawn by a gravitational pull. We crossed the street and hurried up the steps to let him usher us in.

The second the door creaked shut, Finn tugged me to him. His embrace felt as fraught as when I'd teleported us away from the soldiers in our hotel room. I hugged him back hard, not really wanting to let go but knowing that clinging to him for the rest of the eternity wasn't actually an option.

When I drew back, my gaze slid past him to the wide front hall with its posh décor. The space was empty, but contrasting murmurs carried from rooms farther down.

"What's going on?" I asked. "Why are we here?" The Circle had obviously changed its mind about arresting Finn, anyway.

The flush in his cheeks deepened with a duck of his head. "I —I made a deal with the Circle. To get Ary to confess and turn her in for my granduncle's death in exchange for an armistice between the Confed and the League. She's the one who tipped the Dull military off on where to find you, and it seemed too dangerous to risk her interfering with what you're trying to accomplish more than that. Then we heard about the president and everything…"

His head jerked up again, his gaze searching my face and then Sam's and Desmond's. "I don't know if you've seen anything yet. Margo called to warm me that the Dull government is going to move against mages somehow, but she couldn't stay on the line to explain much."

Move against mages? An icy prickling cut through my

exhaustion. "I haven't noticed anything except them being extra cautious about the president's medical care."

"Well, just in case, a few of us have holed up here. My parents and some of their friends convinced the Circle that they need to be ready to provide a haven to *all* mages if we need it. Luis and Tamara and a few others from the League came around early this morning. We're hoping to talk with the Circle later about other matters if the situation doesn't escalate after all."

"Did your sister—" Desmond started, and a head poked from a doorway down the hall.

"Hey, Lockwood," the guy called. "It's happening. You need to see this."

My pulse hiccupped. The four of us hurried over to the classroom.

Luis and Tamara were sitting at desks there, along with a handful of League members whose names I didn't know. Someone had set up a laptop with a streaming newsfeed on what would normally have been the professor's desk at the front of the room. A yellow bar at the bottom of the video announced that the current broadcast was a Special Alert.

Behind the reporter sitting at his desk, a smaller image at the top right corner showed a man in a suit speaking behind a podium on a stage I could now recognize as the White House press room.

"The White House is declaring a state of national emergency," the reporter was saying. "All mages in the country are required to present themselves at local checkpoints to be assessed for potential threat. Press Secretary McClure assured those at the conference that for most citizens registered with the Confederation, this will be a mere formality."

The image zoomed in on the press secretary.

"Over the last several days, it has become increasingly clear that a group of mages operating within the Confederation is seeking to undermine and even destroy the very foundation of our country," McClure said in a sternly clipped voice. "We have not yet determined to what extent these actions are in conjunction with terrorist forces from abroad, but for the safety of all our citizens, we intend to address this menace swiftly and thoroughly."

The chill collected in my gut.

"A *group* of mages undermining national security?" Desmond said. "What the hell is he talking about?"

"They think I lied to Zacher about Dulls having magical ability," I reminded him. "And that I did it to hold off the strikes against insurgent targets, theoretically to help them. I guess Brandt didn't do anything to change their minds about that, unsurprisingly."

"And then we took off on them, and then Brandt launched a literal attack on the president." Sam winced. "They've got to realize people are helping us stay hidden—they'll see those mages as complicit too."

The broadcast cut back to the reporter. "To speed along the security measures, soldiers have been dispatched to the cities with the largest mage presence: New York, Houston, San Francisco, and Portland. They will escort registered mages to assigned facilities for interviewing."

There were going to be soldiers all over this city then. They must have access to the Confed records, which included addresses —would they just go from door to door bringing people in? Would they come here? I couldn't imagine the haughty mages of the Circle submitting to any kind of imprisonment, no matter how temporary.

"Should we turn ourselves in and explain?" Desmond asked. "Rocío can prove that she wasn't lying."

"If they're willing to listen. If they don't shoot us on sight at this point. I can't prove anything *quickly*." It'd taken me a while to get Zacher to where he could cast, and that proof hadn't been blatant enough to stop him from explaining it away when he'd started to doubt.

"I think it's gone too far for that," Sam said grimly.

The newscast showed a shot of a big army-green van parked outside a house on a residential street that didn't look so different from the one where I'd grown up. Two figures in military uniforms strode up to the door, one knocking and the other consulting a tablet.

A puzzled looking woman opened the door. After a brief exchange the news camera's audio didn't pick up, one of the soldiers took her by the arm and ushered her down the steps to the van. The other marched inside and emerged a minute later with a man I assumed was her husband and a boy who looked to be about ten.

My heart lurched. "It'll be the Dampered mages and the Burnouts they grab the easiest," I said. People like my parents. "They won't have enough magic to really resist."

I fumbled for my phone, and Finn exchanged a glance with Luis.

"We've got to talk to the Circle and confirm that they'll continue to offer shelter here," the League's leader said. "If they will, we contact every member of the League we can reach and let them know they can join us."

As they hustled out of the room, I dialed my mom's number. The line fizzed but held its connection as the other end rang, but no one picked up. I bit my lip.

It was early. Dad would be sleeping off his night shift and Mom could be in the shower or still sleeping too.

"I've got to go get my parents," I said, whirling around.

Sam straightened up in an instant, even though he must have been as tired as I was. "Do you need help?"

"I…" I very well might if the soldiers got there ahead of me. "I'll take it if you're offering."

He nodded, and Desmond moved to join us like the cohesive unit we'd become back in Estonia. A pang of gratitude shot through me, but my panic blared louder.

"Tell Finn where we went," I said to Tamara. "And if it isn't safe to come back to the college after all, text us as soon as you know that."

"You've got it," she said.

Out in the howl of the wind, my spirits sank. How the hell were we going to get all the way to Brooklyn at any kind of speed?

Sam marched up to a blue Toyota parked a little way down the street. "They already think we're criminals," he said. "And we'll just borrow, not steal."

Part of me balked, but a much larger part of me couldn't stand to delay any longer than I had to. "All right," I said.

He unlocked the doors with a forceful casting, and Desmond and I jumped inside. With another brisk lyric, the engine rumbled to life.

I gripped the edges of the seat, wrinkling my nose against the smoky nicotine smell that saturated the leather. Sam pulled away from the curb into the roar of the wind. "Where are we going?" he asked as the car swayed.

"Brooklyn," I said. "Keep going this way to Park Ave, and that'll take us most of the way to the bridge."

My pulse raced as I directed him to my parents' neighborhood, skipping a beat every time a particularly fierce surge of wind and magic threatened to tip the car over. My heart outright halted for a second when we zoomed past one of those green army vans. "Right turn here," I said. "Left… Stop!"

Another van was parked right outside my walk-up. Dios mio, ayúdame.

"We're with you," Sam said. "If you want to get them out of here, we can manage it against a few soldiers."

Every bone in my body screamed to do just that—to burst into the apartment and carry Mom and Dad away from these people like I had Desmond and Finn from the hotel. But… "And then what? If they openly flee, they'll be fugitives too. Criminals." Would that be better in the long run? What would Javi have said?

I couldn't conjure any imagining of my older brother who could tell me how to tackle this impasse.

As I wavered, the soldiers strode out of the doorway, nudging my parents ahead of them. Dad was still wearing his dotted flannel pajamas. They were both handcuffed—because of their association with me? I jerked forward in my seat, but the thought of how much worse I could make this situation for them held me in the car.

The soldiers guided them into the van and slammed the back doors.

"We've got to at least find out where they're taking people," I said, my mind glomming onto the one useful thing we could do that wouldn't make things worse for those detained. The van was already pulling away.

Sam waited until it was nearly a block ahead of us and then started up the engine again. I glanced from him to Desmond as he drove after the van.

"What about your families? Will they be okay?"

"If they're only rounding up people in the Academy cities right now, my parents will have a chance to lay low," Desmond said. "Not too big a mage community in Chicago."

"Mine are in San Francisco," Sam said. His brown skin had paled around his knuckles where he gripped the wheel. "But there isn't much I can do for them all the way over here."

"Not much we can do even for the people who *are* here," I said with a growing ache in my chest.

The van took the next left turn, and we followed it several seconds later. It was heading back the way we'd come, over the bridge into the south end of Manhattan. A few minutes later, it took a right toward a squat brick building that covered an entire block. A school, I realized—vacant for the winter holidays.

A crowd was starting to gather around the building, more people joining it as we approached. Even with the wind whipping at their hair and clothes, they sent up a volley of cheers as the van pulled into the parking lot. The soldiers led the mages they'd taken into custody toward the building accompanied by more shouts of encouragement.

Sam parked farther down the street. "Anti-magickers," Desmond observed. "They're obviously overjoyed by this development."

"Yeah, and keep them in there!" someone hollered, putting even more proof to his comment.

By rushing to my house, by following the van, I'd managed to hold on to an illusion that I was accomplishing something. Now, faced with the brick walls that imprisoned my parents and the growing crowd of people who wanted to see me and everyone like me locked away, a wave of hopelessness rolled over me.

My fingers closed around the sunburst necklace that my mother had given me. I could hand myself over, like Desmond had said. I could present myself at that building and accept whatever treatment they'd give me, and maybe they'd go easier on my parents once they had me in custody. That was what a good daughter would do, wasn't it?

But I was more than just their daughter now. I was the magic's champion. I was the leader of a small but expanding group of Dulls discovering their own talents. There was so much more I wanted to do—*needed* to do.

The ache crept right up to the base of my throat. If I gave up my freedom trying to protect my parents, there were vastly more people I would leave unprotected. How could I make that trade? Even if the refusal stabbed at my conscience like a dagger.

Por favor, Dios, let them be all right. Let them understand.

"Take us back to the college," I said roughly.

Sam considered me for a moment, his mouth set at an awkward angle. Then he turned the car toward whatever fate might be waiting for us there.

# CHAPTER NINETEEN

*Finn*

There had to be something very, very wrong with our world that my current reality presented greater horrors to me than the Exam ever had. The girl I loved was being hunted by soldiers. The highest authority in the country was demanding we submit ourselves to some sort of threat assessment. The fact that mages existed at all had turned into a national emergency.

I'd wanted change, but this was definitely the wrong direction.

At least Rocío was safe for now. I took some comfort from the steady rise and fall of her breath as she slept on one of the infirmary cots. Most of us were going to make do with the floors and the extra sleeping bags and blankets some of the mages had brought with them to the college, but I'd convinced the magimedics to give up the cots for Rocío and her colleagues for the time being. From the looks of them, they'd been running on empty. She'd barely stirred since she'd fallen asleep hours ago.

It'd taken a while to convince her to take that rest. Even after I'd explained that the Circle was refusing to cooperate with the

Dull government's commands and had warded the entire building, she'd argued that we needed to push them to do more —argued with her eyelids drooping and her head listing with exhaustion. It was only after I'd pointed out that she'd be able to make her case a lot more coherently after she gave herself a break that she'd capitulated.

Tamara came up to the doorway as I stepped out. "Do you figure the Circle will leave them be, not hand them over to make the Dulls happy?" she asked quietly.

"They agreed not to place any sanctions," I said. "I don't think they care very much about keeping the Dull government happy at this point. We've helped them in all sorts of ways for decades, and they still distrust the Confederation so much that they'd subject us to this kind of treatment? We've cooperated a lot, but volunteering to be incarcerated until *they* determine we're 'safe' is ridiculous."

So far there hadn't been any reports of mages released from the "assessment facilities" the army had set up, even though most of the day had passed since they'd started rounding up people this morning. The soldiers had taken in so many mages that they'd started moving some of the New Yorkers to another building outside of the city.

"Well, I hope they keep thinking that way." Tamara nodded to the hallway. "We just had another group of League members make it here, some of them pretty shaken up. It's almost a full house."

More than a hundred people from the League had already arrived, many of them bringing Dampered or burned out family members. Several of the old-magic families, including my own, had opted to stick it out here for safety in numbers, although many were taking a stand in their homes.

"You'd think even the military would realize how ridiculous this situation is," I said as we meandered away. "They've mostly ended up taking in mages with little or no magical ability left, since those are the ones who can't defend themselves—but they're also the ones least likely to do any damage." I gestured to my burnout mark. "I'm no more of a threat to the powers that be than any Dull is."

The corners of Tamara's lips quirked up. "I don't know. I think you've proven you can make plenty of impact with talents other than magic."

A group drifted out of a room up ahead. From their clothes and general impression of being overwhelmed by the college's grandeur, they were obviously League members, not old-magic refugees. One of the guys caught sight of me, and his posture went rigid. He made a sharp gesture toward me as he muttered something to the others. Their expressions hardened as well.

That didn't bode well. My own shoulders tensed as we reached them, but I kept my demeanor friendly. "Settling in okay?"

"Like you care, Lockwood," the guy shot back. "You're probably waiting for the chance to throw the rest of us under the bus like you did Ary."

Every inch of my skin went cold. I'd been expecting a reckoning over that decision, but in the midst of the chaos, I'd almost forgotten it hadn't come yet.

His raised voice brought several more League members into the doorways and the hall to see what the commotion was about. Luis emerged from one of the classrooms farther down with a frown. I held tight to my resolve even as a fresh rush of shame shot through me.

I might not like how far I'd stooped to achieve my ends, but they'd been the *right* ends. Rocío's experience with Brandt had only proven that extending too much trust to someone who'd already proven themselves willing to take extreme measures could end in horrific disaster.

"She was taking matters into her own hands, dealing out justice based on what she wanted rather than what's actually for everyone's good," I said in the calmest tone I could summon. "She was responsible for at least one *death*. I didn't turn her into a criminal. She did that to herself. I only turned her in."

"And of course you and your old-magic friends are the ones who get to decide what makes someone a criminal. She was right about you the whole time, that you'd go running back to your family and the rest of them when the going got tough. Didn't take long for you to prove her point, did it?"

I didn't know how to answer that. As I hesitated, a girl nearby spoke up, her brow furrowed. "Wait, Finn had Ary arrested?"

The guy, who must have been one of Ary's friends, nodded emphatically. "I saw the whole thing. She was already nervous, so she asked me to keep an eye out by the door where they met up. He pretended it was all some friendly chat, and then, *boom*, there's Confed security all over the place ready to haul her off."

"Because she admitted that she ordered the casting that killed a member of the Circle," I said. "She said it in her own words."

"I'm sure you weaseled it out of her somehow. What the hell does it matter? He deserved to go down."

A spark of anger joined the hot flush spreading through my body. I reined my emotions in as well as I could. "That's not how we'd see it if someone important to the League was killed because the Confed decided to harass us."

Callum had joined the growing mass of spectators. "Why'd you have to go running to them, though?" he asked, his eyes narrowed with suspicion. "Couldn't they have sorted *their* justice out themselves?"

"I was trying to help all of us," I protested. "It was a show of good faith, proving that we weren't going to harbor people overtly harmful to the Circle and the rest of the Confed. Do you think they'd be letting the League hide out here otherwise?"

"He's right," Tamara said beside me. "Sometimes we have to make tough decisions to support the larger cause. We'd all probably be in detention centers if Finn hadn't stepped up for us."

"Stepped up by crushing one of *us* under his feet," someone muttered. My gaze darted over the figures around me and caught on Mark with a lurch. He wasn't the one who'd spoken, but he was eyeing me with a wary twist of his mouth that made my stomach knot in turn.

Luis made his way through the small crowd. "I can confirm that Ary was behind Mr. Lockwood's injury at the Confed building," he said. "Unless any of you have arranged someone's death, I don't think you should consider yourselves in the same position. This one time, it wasn't about the Confed vs. the League."

His declaration only set off more uneasy muttering. I didn't think telling them that Ary had threatened Rocío, too, would win me any points. Most of these people barely knew her other than from the alerts the Dull military had sent out. They might see her as a threat just as much as Ary had rather than as the invaluable ally she was.

"Say what you want," Ary's friend announced, "I'm not joining any plans *he's* helping set up. Who knows what he'll decide is crossing a line next, or how else he can get in good with the snobs around here?"

Several of the murmurs that followed sounded like agreement. A protest wriggled up my throat, but I shut my mouth against it. I'd given them the best explanations I could, and those hadn't been enough to change their minds. If I kept harping on the subject, I'd look like a bully.

Most of the League members drew away from me, Mark among them. As always, Luis had his ways of taking charge. He waved them over to one of the classrooms. "We have a more immediate concern, don't we? Let's work out a contingency plan if the wards fail or the Circle changes their mind and we need to get out of the college fast."

Tamara gave me a sympathetic smile and followed them. I shifted my weight from one foot to the other, wanting to be a part of that conversation and afraid it'd make half the group scatter if I joined them. The determination that had gotten me through my confrontation with Ary settled like a heavy stone on my gut.

No matter what I'd given them, the Circle didn't have any more respect for me than they had before. Leron hadn't even deigned to tell me about the attack on the president that had sent him running yesterday. They'd only dealt with me at all then and this morning because my parents had spoken alongside me. Now a significant part of the League saw my motives as suspect too.

I'd tried to find a strategy that would benefit both sides… and in the end, I might have lost my place with both.

I closed my eyes. Quam bene vivas referre, non quam diu. That was only a small comfort.

Footsteps rapped on the floor behind me. I turned to find Examiner Khalil—well, Salma Khalil now that we were out of the Exam—coming up to me. A fresh flush of shame shot through me at the thought of how much of that conversation she might have overheard.

If she realized how much condemnation I'd just faced, she acknowledged it only with a soft smile. "Sometimes we do things because we care what happens to people, whether they're going to appreciate the gesture or not. I'm glad you made it here."

I exhaled slowly. "So am I," I had to admit, even if I wasn't entirely pleased with the method I'd used to get here.

"I might have some good news for you," she said, and tipped her head back the way she'd come. "In preparation for this morning's announcement, the Dull government demanded that all National Defense teams stationed internationally return to American soil. We've just brought in a few special squads, one of which I believe includes a friend of yours."

My heart leapt. "Where?"

Her smile widened. "Come this way."

She led me to the stairs at the end of the hall and then up. The second we came out into the upper hallway, my gaze locked onto the one person I'd been hoping she meant. My legs locked and then launched me forward.

"Prisha!"

My best friend spun around and rushed to meet me halfway, a grin splitting her face.

It'd been weeks since I'd last seen her, and I couldn't help noticing the brisk efficiency of her stride, the precision of her movements, honed by all that military training and fieldwork. She had a new scar too, a slash of paler skin along her jaw and down her neck where the magimedics hadn't been able to fully heal her in time. For a second, she hardly looked like herself. Then she grabbed me in the tightest of hugs, and she was Prisha again.

I kept staring at her as she pulled back, willing myself not to linger on the scar. I grasped her hands and asked, "Are you okay? I've been so worried ever since we realized… I talked to your dad, but he didn't want to tell me much."

She laughed. "He mentioned that. All indignant about it for some weird reason, like your criminal status might have rubbed off on him over the phone. The rest, what we had to do…" She trailed off around all the things she couldn't say but that I understood, and her humor faded. "It was awful. That sums it up pretty well."

"I'm just glad you made it through, and that you're here now instead of wherever they sent you." I squeezed her hands.

I wished I could tell her everything would be okay now, but

the reason she'd been called back was exactly why it wasn't. She might have flown from the frying pan right into the fire.

Prisha must have caught something of my inner turmoil in my expression. She nudged me off to the side, away from the other newly returned Champions who were talking in hushed voices amongst themselves. "Have *you* been holding up all right? I gather it hasn't exactly been a picnic around here."

I waved off her concern. "Nothing compared to what you've had to face."

"That doesn't answer my question." She gave me a firm look. "What crusade have you taken up now?"

I looked at the floor. The admission came out haltingly. "I'm… not totally sure I have one anymore. Or that the crusaders want me to stand with them. But at least I accomplished something that seems to be for the best in the meantime."

Prisha gave a harrumph. "That group you've been working with is giving you the cold shoulder all of a sudden?"

"It's my own fault." I swiped my hand over my face. "And it's my own problem to deal with. It's just—it's difficult, being caught between where I grew up—a side of myself I can't totally throw away—and the people who need help the most… but maybe don't want it from me."

"Hey." She gave my shoulder a light punch. "Anyone who shuts you out, it's their loss." At my grimace, she went on more insistently. "Look, I know a few things about being stuck in the middle. Between mage society and a Dull family; being new magic in the middle of a bunch of old-magic novices and teachers. It's never *fun*, but after a certain point, you have to either focus on what people don't accept or on what they will, and then you make the best of it. Even if what you make is sometimes a total hash."

The tightening of her mouth told me she was thinking of her choices in the Exam: the way she'd agreed to spy on our fellow examinees to ensure she came out a Champion. I didn't know any way to tell her how thankful I was for her faith in me, even if it couldn't fix the bonds I might have already shattered, and how little I cared about what felt like the distant past now. The best I could manage was pulling her into another hug.

After, she glanced at her colleagues, and a shadow crossed her face. When she turned back to me, she looked twice as haunted as before. "What do we do now, Finn? The Dulls are treating us like traitors, after everything we put ourselves through for them… I'm not sure there's any 'best' to make of that. How are any of us going to come back from this mess?"

My throat closed up, but I couldn't lie to her. The most honest answer I could give her was, "I don't know."

# CHAPTER TWENTY

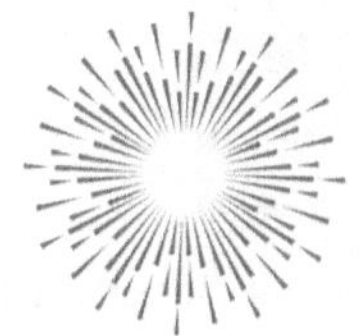

*Rocío*

I woke up still feeling groggy, like I could have slept another day or two before I was totally rested. But the second I registered my surroundings, my awareness of all the trouble we were facing smacked me in the head. I sat up on the cot with a jolt, swallowing a yawn.

Sam and Desmond were still out cold. Beyond the college infirmary window, the sunlight was dwindling. I guessed it was late afternoon. I couldn't see much else other than the thrashing of the branches of a nearby tree. The magic rippled through the room around me with jerks and shudders that brought me more full awake.

My stomach balled. I couldn't afford to spend any more time conked out if I wanted to be champion of anything at all.

When I peeked into the hall, Finn was just heading toward the infirmary—from the way he perked up, I thought it might be to check on me. "Feeling better?" he asked when he reached me.

"As good as I think I can afford to get." I swiped the final bits of bleariness from my eyes. My thoughts leapt back to my last clear memory before I'd crashed here. "What's the news from the assessment facilities? How many people have they cleared?"

He grimaced. "Ah, no one, as far as we know. That's part of the reason we're still holed up here. It's looking more and more as though the whole 'just a formality' line was a load of bull."

My parents were still shut away in that school building, then. How were the soldiers treating them—worse than the other mages, trying to harass them into giving up some information about me they didn't even have?

"As far as we know, they haven't hurt anyone either," Finn said quickly at my expression. "They're just… taking their time with the whole threat assessment thing. There's good news too. Because the Dull government apparently doesn't trust any mage now, they recalled all the National Defense forces from abroad. Prisha and Leonie made it here."

That *was* good, both because it was a relief to know the operatives I'd left behind were still okay and because it meant no more magical assaults overseas. I glanced toward the wall as if I could see through it to outside.

"Maybe the magic will start calming down now that those teams aren't active," I said. "It still feels pretty riled up at the moment."

Finn's grimace deepened. "I don't know about that. The squads were recalled last night, and if anything, things out there have gotten worse. At least, as far as I can tell. Come here and see what you think."

He motioned me over to a small office that was currently unoccupied, but which had a large window filling the narrow wall at the far end. I set my hands against the cold glass. The view beyond the pane made me stiffen.

At first glance, the windstorm looked less intense than before. The sapling trees on the wall outside waved this way and that. A door on a business across the street had come unlocked and was swinging wildly, and a faint rattling built louder… only to fade away again. The tenor of the magic felt more worn out than fierce. But it didn't take long for me to notice the more blatant signs of outright destruction.

Halfway down the block, an electrical pole had been shoved right over. The snapped wire crackled, and sparks sputtered on the pavement. In the other direction, one of the few cars left on the street had been flipped over onto its side.

As I stared, the magic bunched around me and spasmed. The swinging door across the street blasted right off its hinges and flew several feet, the frame bowing in with a massive dent.

"That's mostly what we've been seeing," Finn said. "It's like the magic is wearing itself thin, but that disturbs it so much that it's lashing out even harder whenever it finds the energy."

"How long has it been acting up this badly?" I asked, dread wrapping around my lungs.

"It knocked the pole down a couple of hours ago. Hit the car sometime in the last half hour. I think the outbursts are happening more and more often."

I cursed under my breath. I hadn't gotten anywhere near as much sleep as my body needed, but all the same, it looked like I'd slept too long.

"We need to talk to the Circle," I said. "They might not be able to protect this building soon, even with all of us here. And seeing the magic go wild like this is only going to make the Dulls even more scared of us. The Circle can't keep standing back— they have to admit that the Dulls can do magic, that I wasn't lying to Zacher, and we need to get everyone working on those constructive castings *now*."

The castings to quell the fire had calmed the magic a little bit, for a little while. That'd been with just a few dozen people working on it. If we could get the whole city casting even minor efforts to heal or mend, we might manage to calm the magic permanently in a matter of hours.

"The Circle has been shut away in one of the larger rooms for ages, consulting with my parents and other old-magic families," Finn said. "All that talking doesn't seem to have gotten them anywhere. If you want to crash that meeting, I'll be right there with you."

"Do you want to get Luis and Tamara—or anyone else—so they can say their bit?" I asked.

He shook his head with a wince I could tell he'd tried to hide. "The League is getting their own business in order. You're the one who can really speak to what's happening with the magic anyway. At this point, I don't think we should bring up any issues that could distract from that."

I nodded. "All right. Lead the way."

A couple of security guards stood outside the heavy wooden door where Finn stopped. He looked at them with a clench of his jaw. "We need to talk with the Circle. It's urgent."

One guard gave him a skeptical look.

"Tell them Rocío Lopez knows how to get us out of this mess," I added. I didn't know if that statement would carry much weight, but the Circle must have some idea who I was by now, and that I'd been more closely involved in the current crisis than any of them had.

My name didn't appear to have any impact on the guard, but he ducked into the room all the same. The door stayed open a crack—not a wide enough gap for me to see anything inside, but enough to let voices filter out faintly. I couldn't make out the whole conversation, but there was obviously a bit of an argument. Finn's mouth twisted into a grim smile.

"My dad and some other people are arguing for them to hear us out," he said, managing to sound both proud and embarrassed at the same time.

I took his hand, and he gripped mine tightly. A minute later, the door swung open wider.

"All right," the guard said. "In with you."

I let go of Finn as we stepped inside, wanting to look more like an authority figure than like a nervous teenager, but I might have undermined that impression with my first startled reaction to the room. I'd been expecting another office or classroom. This space was more like the gym at my old high school, though without any of the sports equipment and with a long table set up at one end. Maybe, like my tutorial class had used that other gym, the college students came here to practice larger scale conjurings and things like that.

Not only was the room big, it was also nearly *full*. The seven remaining members of the Circle sat around the table, and around them stood a crowd of maybe a hundred old-magic figures, including Finn's family. They might have been facing the Circle a moment ago, but now most of them had turned to eye the two of us. Even Finn looked taken aback.

He stepped forward anyway, and I followed him, weaving through the crowd until we reached the opposite end of the table from the Circle. Leron sat at the far left, his pinched expression giving nothing away even though *he* definitely knew who I was and what I was here to talk about. The woman who'd been on the news the first day—I thought Finn had called her Cunningham—was poised next to him. Her eyes had a steely glint. She definitely wasn't one of the more liberal members.

"You said you can offer some sort of solution to our present situation, Miss Lopez?" said an older man seated in the middle of the table. He looked, and his tone suggested he felt hearing me out was a waste of time. "Let's have it, then."

I was abruptly, sharply aware of the large audience behind us. Finn had told his parents and his sister about the Dulls' magical potential, but I had no idea who else here knew or how the Circle would react to my announcing it.

Well, anyone who hadn't found out already was about to now. If the Circle hadn't wanted them to hear it this way, they should have taken control of the message themselves sooner.

"I do," I said. "It's actually incredibly simple, other than it means you have to admit to the Dull government you've been lying. You need to tell them that you've been covering up the fact that the Dulls have limited magical capacity too. Show them your databases or whatever else you can use to prove it. And then we need to start teaching the regular citizens how to do some basic castings that will help settle down the magic. If we get enough people working on that quickly, we—"

"What's she saying about the Dulls?" a rough voice broke in from behind me. A few confused murmurs rose up in the wake of the question, but not as many as I'd have expected. Finn's family must have started spreading the word among their fellow mages.

A voice I recognized as Finn's sister's spoke up. "The assessments the Confederation has been doing since the early days of the Unveiling actually show that all Dulls have a small amount of magical talent too, just not enough that they'd ever realize it without being guided to it."

"It's not just the Dulls they've been lying to," someone else piped up. "It's most of us too."

"Now, listen," Cunningham said. "If you'd joined the discussion earlier, you'd know we've already been over this." Her gaze pinned me to the spot. "The *last* thing we want to do while the Dull military is rounding us up like criminals is admit that we've been conducting what they'll see as mass fraud for decades. They'll be looking to punish us twice as hard."

I stared right back at her. "Or they'll realize we're all in this together, and they can hash that fraud out with you *after* we stop the magic from either sputtering out or bashing the city to bits, whatever comes first."

"We can't be sure how they'll react," someone farther down the table said. "*You* can't know they won't react with even more hostility."

"I know that telling them will prove I haven't lied to them. That there's no huge conspiracy against them, just one messed-up mage who was angry at just about everyone."

"They might not even believe the Circle at this point," another person in the crowd said. "They could decide it's all more lies."

"We won't know until we try," Finn's father shot back.

"And that could shatter what little peace we're maintaining with them," the man in the middle of the Circle said.

"None of that is going to matter if the magic breaks down much more!" I focused on Leron, thinking of when I'd talked to him in the tea shop, and the moments when he'd seemed to waver. "Is that how you want to be remembered? As the Circle that failed the magic and lost it for *everyone?*"

A hush fell over the room. Leron's eyes twitched. Something like relief came over his face, and he looked down the table at his fellow Circle members.

"We don't have to reveal everything to get to work on this problem with the magic," he said. "We were already going to make a public statement encouraging the use of constructive castings to help restore stability, and we've got plenty of mages here now without much to occupy themselves." The flick of his glance toward the crowd implied some criticism of their extended discussion. "Why don't we have every mage in the college get to work in whatever ways they can?"

The other figures along the table relaxed slightly at that proposal. Cunningham turned to me. "What exact castings do you feel would be most effective?"

I'd been longing for them to ask questions like that for days, but suddenly it felt like too little too late.

"Anything that needs repairs," I said. "In or around the college, as far as people can reach their talents. If anyone needs medical attention, even pain relief from a headache or sealing a scratch. And if we exhaust all of those options, any kind of magic that's creating… I think using castings while making meals, or conjuring temporary bedding for people to sleep on—things like that should help. But at this point, those of us here won't be enough. We have to—"

"We have to see what effect those castings have, and then we can evaluate our next steps," the central Circle member interrupted.

No. The magic around me quavered and pinched at my skin. I'd never felt it so faltering before. I raised my voice. "We don't have time to experiment. We have to do everything we can now, and that includes bringing in *everyone* who can cast."

"How much could the Dulls really do?" someone muttered.

"Why are we even still arguing about this?" another mage said. "Let's get on with those castings. If a couple of you come with me, we can see about fixing the fallen post outside."

The Circle members nodded, looking satisfied. Mages started to cluster and slip out of the room as they murmured about their plans. "Hold on," Finn said.

His father came up to him. "It's a start," he said. "Change doesn't happen all at once. If we don't see a significant improvement by tomorrow, we'll push for more."

He didn't understand—none of them really understood—just how frayed the magic was becoming. The more it'd reached out to me, the more strongly I'd hearkened it. Now I had a connection beyond anyone else's, which only made it harder for them to accept what I was telling them.

"If we wait until tomorrow to even start teaching the Dulls, we'll lose all that time when they could be pitching in," I said.

From Mr. Lockwood's expression, as much as he was willing to support his son, he had trouble imagining the Dulls could summon all that much power either. "I promise you—we'll keep a close eye on this."

I spun toward the Circle, but they were getting up too. "We'll contribute our own skills, of course," Leron said.

I opened my mouth and shut it again at Cunningham's glare. What *was* the point in arguing? I'd lost even the leverage of public pressure. They weren't going to change their minds no matter what I said. They'd found a safe path that let them feel they were stepping up, and that was exactly what they'd wanted.

"What now?" Finn asked, as the rest of the mages left.

I worried at my lower lip with my teeth. "I'm not sure. I need to think. Is there still somewhere around here I could see what's happening on the news? I'd like to know what's going on beyond the college."

"I think the League still has that laptop set up with the feed going." Finn motioned to the hall.

We found the same room where we'd first heard about the mage detainments. Several League members, including Callum, were perched at the desks around the room watching the current reports. A few of them glanced over, and their expressions chilled when they saw Finn.

His mouth tightened. He touched my arm and leaned in. "I'm going to check whether there's anything Luis needs me for. Text me if anything urgent comes up, and I'll be right here."

I guessed the way he'd handled Ary had left some of the League more unsettled than he'd told me. My hackles rose, defensive on his behalf, but he was already ducking out of the room. I sat at one of the desks closest to the computer.

"Possibly of greatest concern to Manhattan residents is the

damage recently done to one of their oldest institutions, the Metropolitan Museum of Art," the reporter was saying. "Recent surges of what appeared to be magic have battered the building, destroying the historic architecture and threatening the collections inside."

The video cut to a shot outside the front of the Met. Two of the stone columns and part of the roof on the righthand side had been bashed in, rubble crumbling across the broad front steps. Cracks spiderwebbed across the face of the building. My heart stuttered. It did look as if the whole place might collapse if the magic struck it again.

"And of course if it topples, the Dulls will put all the blame on us," Callum sneered where he'd come up next to me for a closer look.

I tensed instinctively at having him that close. The last time he'd come anywhere near me had been during the Exam, and he'd been trying to shove me off a tall platform to my death.

"It is partly our fault," I had to point out. "I'm pretty sure some of the Confed authorities have known how destructive castings hurt the magic for a while, but they never spoke up about it or insisted on cutting back."

He glowered at me. "So now you're taking the Dulls' side?"

"I'm on the magic's side. I just don't think it helps anything to be at each other's throats."

"Pacifistic crap."

The words tumbled out before I could catch them. "My approach worked a lot better for me than yours did for you."

I didn't specify *in the Exam* because I couldn't, but Callum's expression twitched with surprise. I could see wheels turning behind his eyes. He touched his Burnout mark. "You're talking about this. You were in there too. Of course. That's how Finn knows you."

"I made Champion," I said, the one detail I was allowed to

talk about. That win hadn't felt like much of a victory when I'd found out what it meant, but right then, it did. I couldn't have been here for the magic if I'd given up.

Callum's gaze slid away from me. In that moment, he looked almost awkward. He couldn't remember what he'd done to me to judge whether I was being fair, but he must have been able to tell that I knew perfectly well how he'd handled himself.

"At least you have a decent reason for acting superior, then," he said after a few seconds, falling back into his sneering tone. "Not like Lockwood, going around as if he's not marked just the same as me, as if he didn't coast along in our classes because the teachers liked his name better than mine."

I'd heard enough from Finn and seen him often enough in the Academy library to know that, whatever Finn's weaknesses had been, he'd never let himself simply *coast*. I doubted Callum would have listened to me about that, though. Instead I said, "The magic doesn't care how much talent anyone has or doesn't have. It wants to resonate with all of us. So I don't see why the level of anyone's ability should matter to *you*."

Callum scowled. "It matters more when a guy says he's all in and then turns on the people he's supposed to be fighting with, just to get a little revenge."

I crossed my arms over my chest. "You know Finn, at least a little. Do you really think he turned Ary in for some kind of personal satisfaction? Can't you *see* how uncomfortable it made him? If it'd been about getting revenge for his granduncle, he'd have gone to the Circle about her right after the attack, not a week later. He let it go until she started acting in ways that would hurt the whole League, not just him. That's the opposite of selfish."

Callum's defiant stance wavered again. He looked away with a swipe at his mouth. "All right. Maybe that's true. It was still kind of sketchy the way he set it all up."

If he wanted to see it that way, fine. I shrugged and turned my attention back to the newscast.

A reporter was interviewing a man who'd worked at the Met for over a decade. "I don't know how anyone can say magic is a positive force when it's ravaging our cultural landmarks," he said tersely. "When are the mages who caused this storm going to be brought to justice?"

An ache closed around my heart. Even though I hadn't liked Callum's tone, he'd been right that plenty of the Dulls would blame us. Would blame the magic. Though I'd also been right in what I'd said to him—the magic, when it was stable and well, only wanted to exist in harmony with all of us.

It still did. It'd thrived with even the minor castings our Dull students had been able to conduct. If the old-magic mages and the new-magic Leaguers, the soldiers rounding us up outside and the Dull government making their proclamations could just *see* how much was possible…

I pushed myself off the chair abruptly and walked out of the room, texting Finn as I went. He met me halfway down the hall. "What's going on?"

I lowered my voice. To see this plan through, we couldn't let anyone who'd oppose us find out until it was too late for them to stop our momentum.

"The Circle won't reach out to teach the Dulls how to cast," I said, "so we will. Every Dull we can reach, every way we can reach them. We can't play it safe anymore."

# CHAPTER TWENTY-ONE

*Finn*

The worst thing about so many of the League members believing I'd betrayed them wasn't the suspicious looks and the wide berth they gave me, or the snarky comments murmured where I could only partly overhear. It was knowing that my misstep with them might make it harder for me to help Rocío now, when she needed me the most.

"We're setting up in room 115," I told Luis in a hushed voice when I'd pulled him aside to tell him about Rocío's plan. There were other League members in the room with us, gathered in a semi-circle while they gulped down the spaghetti dinner someone had prepared for all us refugees, and they shot periodic narrow glances my way. "Any laptops people brought that they're willing to lend to the cause, any people you think would be willing to join in the effort, send them over there."

He nodded. "I think we can manage at least a few of both."

"You can... not mention that I'm involved," I said, embarrassed heat creeping up my neck. "Although it'll probably become obvious before too long."

"There are some people who understand the decision you made about Ary," Luis said. "Or at least who are willing to look past their discomfort to see the bigger picture. We'll do whatever we can. Are you sure the Circle won't shut us down right away like they did with the video, though?"

"Rocío wants to try a more direct approach this time—something they can't shut down. Which means no recordings or 'viral video'—just people willing to trust their friends, give it a chance, and hopefully pass on the word. Once we get the first round of emails out, it'll be mostly up to the people out there to forward the instructions on… but we also want to be able to offer coaching through video chat for anyone who asks."

"That'll be harder to hide."

"Yes." I let out a rough breath. "Once we're really getting started, Rocío or one of her teammates will cast a 'chantment on the doorway to discourage people from checking up on us. The other mages are pretty busy with their current efforts." Which hadn't stopped a different electrical pole from crashing into a storefront on the other side of the college just fifteen minutes ago. "We've got a bunch of her colleagues—other Champions—to help us now. It's mostly a question of how many people we can connect with and bring up to speed as quickly as possible."

Luis gave me a crooked smile. "For every person out there who thinks mages have brought a catastrophe down on their heads, I'd bet there's at least as many who still wish they could discover a talent in themselves. What does your girlfriend think she's going to do with all these people if she can get them casting? Does she figure doing a bunch of small spells all on their own will be enough?"

Rocío had hesitated to get into the next steps of her plan even with me. She might have taken up the mantle of leader in this crusade, but her confidence hadn't totally caught up.

"I think she's waiting to see how far we can get with the first stage before she makes any definite decisions about where we take it from there," I said. "Although if this is enough to calm down the magic all on its own, I doubt any of us will be complaining."

"Too true." He knuckled my arm. "You keep doing what you're doing, and I'll see what resources I can pull together for you. We'll get through this. And when we do, I think we're going to be looking at a very different world—in a way that's better for just about everyone."

I wished I could come by optimism as easily as he seemed to. I wished I could see more for me to do than telling other people how they could contribute. That was the best I could offer right now, though, so I set off for my next destination with my head held high.

The old-magic mages—the only mages in the college who had their full casting abilities, other than the recently arrived special operatives—had spread throughout the building to take up their constructive tasks. I peeked into several rooms before I spotted Margo's ash-brown braid by a window in a second-floor office. She and a few other young mages, friends I remembered seeing around the house before she'd moved out, were whispering in ancient Greek to restore the shattered windshield of a truck parked outside.

I waited until Margo paused to gather herself. She'd always been a strong mage, like every Lockwood I was aware of other than me, but the disruption in the magic was obviously interfering with her ability to cast as much as it had Rocío's. Her face was drawn from the effort, her forehead faintly shiny with sweat. She shook her arms as if releasing tension and noticed me in the doorway.

"Hey," I said. "Can I talk to you about something in private?"

"I'll be back in a bit," she said to her friends, and came over to join me.

There wasn't anywhere all that private in the college at this point. I settled for a windowless corner at the far end of the hall.

"You said before that if there was any way you could help, you wanted me to ask," I started, watching her carefully to judge her reaction. I figured my older sister would come through, but it was hard for me to take anything as certain these days.

What came over her face I could only describe as intense resolve. "What is it?" she asked, brushing a few stray strands of hair behind her ear. "I'm a little worn out from the castings we've been doing, but I've still got a fair bit of energy."

"If we get caught in this operation, the Circle won't be happy. We'll be going against their orders."

She gave a dismissive wave. "They were chosen when no one knew we'd have to deal with anything like this—or knew how they and all the past Circles contributed to this catastrophe. I'm fine with ignoring their authority for the time being."

Relief rushed through me. "All right. We're going to be doing some… work using the college's internet. I'm assuming you did a fair amount of security-related casting in your job. Would you be able to conduct some 'chantments to ensure no one will notice the amount of data we're using, or how?"

She gave me a thumbs-up. "With the current state of the magic, I'll probably need to bolster the castings regularly, but I know a solid technique. I can lay it down right by the tech room where they have everything set up. Do you need that right away?"

"As soon as you can manage it, so we know we don't need to worry."

"I'm on it." She flashed me a smile and set off.

I'd gotten the outcome I'd been hoping for, but that didn't stop an anxious sensation from gnawing at my stomach as I watched her go. I was asking a lot of the people who still trusted me today. If the way I'd handled this situation got Luis, Margo, or anyone else into trouble… then I'd really have let down everyone.

I dragged in a breath against that uncomfortable sensation and headed back to the room where Rocío and her special ops colleagues had been getting organized. I still had one more person to reach out to.

Luis had already come through. When I eased open the door, I found not just Rocío and the dozen or so Champions she'd thought it safe to ask for help, but a handful of League members stationed at the desks as well. The League's leader was just plugging in one of the many new laptops now in the room, using a power bar he'd picked up somewhere or other.

"Turns out there's a whole department for computer-based magic here," he told me with a grin. "They had a stack of computers no one else seemed interested in using… so I figured the Circle wouldn't notice if we helped ourselves."

"I cast an illusion so no one will realize they're gone if they just glanced at the shelves," Prisha announced, looking impressed with herself.

"Perfect." My spirits lifted again as I took in the room and the team we were assembling. It was only early evening—hopefully we could get plenty of eyes on our message before the day was even over. "I need one for just a few minutes. Which should I take?"

"Use mine," Rocío said, getting up. "I'd better make sure the 'chantment on the door is as strong as I can make it." She turned to Luis. "If you send anyone else over to help out, let them know to wait outside rather than trying to come right in. If they get too close to the doorway, they'll feel a very strong urge to be somewhere else. We'll be watching and bring them in."

She sounded nothing but confident now, although I caught the nervous fidget of her fingers before she balled them. Luis tipped his head to her and hurried off again. Rocío positioned herself in front of the door, and I slid into the seat at the desk she'd been using.

She was planning on reaching out to the Dull students she'd already taught herself, but there was one we'd both decided should get the request for help from me. I opened up the video chat app and entered Noemi's number.

My first attempt coincided with a lurch in the magic, and the connection failed before she really had the chance to pick up. The weakening of those energies had one benefit, though. When they quieted back down to recover, my second attempt went through without a hitch.

I'd texted Noemi earlier to expect my call. She picked up with a strained smile already in place, the image distorting for a second before it came into sharper focus. "Hey," she said. "Still camped out at the college?"

"For once, the Circle and the rest of us agree on what's important," I said. "Well, partly, anyway. The other part is what I'm calling about."

"Better you're in there than in one of those detention centers the military is setting up." She shuddered. "What's going on?"

"Well, the Circle still doesn't want to disclose their big secret about all of you, even though getting everyone in the country casting might be what we need to settle down the magic. So we're going behind their backs to get as many so-called Dulls casting as we can."

She perked up. "More lessons? I'm all in for that."

I had to smile at her enthusiasm. "Someone who can actually cast will take you through the strategies we want to focus on a little later. We definitely want you involved on that side too. But we also—we need the people who already know what you're capable of to pass on a message to everyone you can think of who there's even the slightest chance might be open to it. You don't have to say you've already been practicing this stuff if you'd rather not admit to that openly."

The light in Noemi's face dimmed with an anxious flex of her jaw. "What kind of message, exactly?"

"Rocío's written it up," I said. "It's just a quick note explaining that we've discovered that everyone can work with the magic at least a little, and that by working together we can calm the storm. She's including a couple of the basic warm-up exercises so people can try to get in tune with the magic, and then instructions for a mending casting for them to practice if they get the hang of that."

"Okay." Noemi paused. "Before, when we were doing the lessons, you all emphasized how important it was that we *don't* talk to anyone else about this stuff. Is there anything I'd need to be worried about in terms of backlash?"

"The Circle isn't in much of a position to govern anyone outside the college," I said. "And if we can get that message out to people all over the country, even the world… I think they'll be too busy dealing with the fallout to place any sanctions, even if they could."

She still looked uncertain. My hands clenched in my lap. I'd wanted to talk to her because she was my friend, but the last thing I wanted was to use that friendship to strong-arm her.

"I know it's a big ask," I added. "If you don't feel comfortable taking that risk, I won't pressure you. This is an ask, not an order."

Noemi inhaled sharply and shook her head. "No. I've got this. I mean, seriously, you've faced down the Circle and people like them how many times even though you were nervous like hell about how they'd treat you? Any leverage *I* have is with people like me. I can't say I'm truly part of the League and not just some gawker unless I put that to use."

The words hit me like a sucker punch. "I'd never say you're not a real member of the League, Noemi."

She gave me a wry smile. "Of course you wouldn't. That's why we're friends. I'm talking about how I'd see myself. Maybe the thought of helping with something this big makes me a little nervous… but you know what? I've just got to think of it as my chance to be a hero like in all those stories about magic I've read—without needing some grand powers to pull it off. Doing this is a lot more important than making a pencil float."

"I think they're both important," I said stubbornly. "But thank you. I'll email the message to you, and you can pass it on—and encourage others to pass it on too—as soon as you're ready."

"Reporting and ready for duty," Noemi said with a mock salute.

Her image blinked off the screen. I sat back in my chair with the looming sense that I'd set into motion far more than I could ever hope to call back if it all went sour.

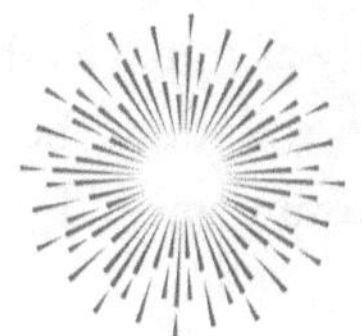

# CHAPTER TWENTY-TWO

*Rocío*

I leaned back in my chair at the polished wooden desk, the waxy smell of the college classroom filling my nose. All around me, voices murmured as my co-conspirators led various Dulls in group video chats through the exercises and castings we'd planned. The buzz of activity in the room made me almost as giddy as what I was seeing on my screen.

Our message—*my* message—had spread much faster than I'd dared to hope. Excited Dulls were passing the information on not just through emails but across social media channels. I'd already been invited to several private groups where hundreds and in one case thousands of members were discussing their progress and encouraging each other in sensing the magic and conducting it.

Some expressed frustration, but plenty were having at least some success. Knowing that took a little edge off my nerves when the magic had one of its sudden spasms.

The efforts of the mages around the college might have had some effect. Now and then the energy in the air felt slightly more settled than before. But I hadn't sensed a big enough shift to believe that a hundred or so mages doing minor castings in a limited area would turn the tide.

I smothered a yawn and checked my schedule. In just a few minutes, I was due to chat with a group of locals Noemi had brought on board. We'd all been offering our lessons pretty much nonstop since last night, grabbing a few hours' sleep when our concentration frayed nearly as much as the magic had.

Sam leaned over in the desk he'd taken next to mine, swiveling his computer toward me. "Take a look at this," he said with a frown.

We'd taken turns checking the local news reports for any of the news *we'd* been making. Unfortunately, the broadcast he'd picked up didn't have anything to do with Dulls using magic. The Bonded Worthy had released a new video.

Sam kept the volume low, but the masked figure's words were subtitled anyway. *The chaos you're seeing only shows how unworthy you are. Soon, you'll have more proof that we are the ones with the real power.*

I shivered. "They can't launch another attack on the same scale as what they did to the Confed building, can they? I wouldn't think, with the magic as worn down as it is, they could pull together a casting that intense."

"I don't know," Sam said. "I've seen how much harder it's gotten even for you. But it'd depend on how many of them were working together and how strong they were to begin with."

Desmond turned where he was sitting in the desk in front of Sam. "No one's caught the insurgents who destroyed the Confed building, have they? We don't know whether they were able to get out of the city or they're still hiding out here."

That thought was even more unnerving. I forced myself to focus on my screen. "We can't do anything about the Bonded Worthy or anyone else until we calm the magic and convince the Confed and the Dull government to sort out their problems. At

least we're making progress on the first part." On the second…
I'd rather not dwell on the soldiers who were now patrolling
outside this building in a sort of blockade, or on whether we'd
managed to gather enough supplies to outlast a siege.

I launched the video chat, several small windows populating
my screen, and let myself get wrapped up in the now incredibly
familiar motions of the initial hearkening exercises. One of the
girls who'd called in was so excited she kept giggling, which was
throwing off her concentration, but I got even her there
eventually.

We'd just started on the practice casting, the same sealing-
paper exercise I'd taken my original class through, when
Desmond sliced his arm through the air.

Every mage in the room understood that warning. Desmond
had been monitoring the hall for any threat of discovery.
Keyboards clattered as we hid our activities. With a hasty
apology, I dismissed the chat and clicked to an innocuous
browser window I'd kept open for this reason. Several of the
mages snapped their laptops shut and lay down on the blankets
spread around the edges of the room as if napping, tucking the
computers under the fabric.

Desmond hadn't been overly cautious, because a second later,
a knock vibrated through the heavy door. Whoever had come
calling had enough magical talent not to be dissuaded by the
'chantment I'd put in place. I couldn't bring too much magic to
bear, or I'd wear myself out completely and risk someone picking
up on the spell and getting suspicious.

Prisha got up to answer the knock, but our visitor didn't wait.
The door swung open, and Ms. Cunningham from the Circle
swept into the room.

Her gaze skimmed over the desks and our apparently sleeping
companions, taking everything in. Her lips pursed. "What have
you all been doing in here?"

"Helping the Dampered and Burnout mages who are farther from the city find places to stay since it's not safe at their homes," Luis said at the other end of the room. That was the official story we'd decided on, although the number of people and computers devoted to that task would still have looked suspicious.

Cunningham's expression stayed impassive. If she didn't trust his explanation, she didn't challenge it. Maybe she had too many other things on her mind.

"Those of us in the Circle are making the rounds, talking to everyone who's taken shelter here," she said. "We've received a new demand—or perhaps I should say 'threat'—from the army." A ragged note crept into her voice. "The president has declared that if we continue to refuse to submit to their assessments, our defiance will be taken as an act of civil war."

Maldita sea. As if we weren't fighting enough battles already.

Prisha made a face. "I suppose it's too much to ask the Dull government to realize their initial demands might have been too extreme and retract them instead."

"No one likes admitting they were wrong," Sam said.

The woman in front of us included.

"Is the president even out of the hospital yet?" Desmond asked.

Cunningham sighed. "He returned to his residence in the White House this morning. I don't believe he's officially fully recovered, but he can still make proclamations."

I resisted the urge to squirm in my seat. "What does that mean for us? We're already under siege. What's going to change if he decides this is war?"

Her mouth tightened even more. "If we don't come to their 'assessment facilities' of our own accord by tomorrow at noon, and the Circle doesn't publicly encourage all other mages to do the same, he's said they'll launch a strike on all of the key

Confederation buildings—this college, the academies, and our primary business facilities."

Luis's eyebrows shot up. "Can they do that? Can't we shield the buildings if we know the attack is coming?"

Cunningham cut a look his way. "A magical shield has limited efficacy against the most powerful military grade weapons even in an ideal situation. Which is far from what we're facing right now given the magic's current… instability. There may be enough of us here to protect ourselves from one missile or bomb, but if they launch several in a row, we won't be able to hold that up. And there aren't enough of us to defend every building they say they'll target."

"We just *saved* the Academy," I couldn't help saying with a pang in my chest. One set of Dulls had failed to burn it down, so now a higher authority was threatening to blow it up. For a second I was flooded with nothing but anger. How *dare* they put us in this position.

"We'd lose an awful lot if this strike happens," Cunningham said.

"If," Sam repeated. "Are you thinking about giving in?"

The idea made me queasy, but then, if the alternative was to be blown up by our own government… I had to admit the Circle wasn't in the easiest position. If they'd told the Dulls the truth before we'd gotten to this point, maybe it would be different, but now the president was already calling us treasonous criminals. Revealing a huge lie didn't seem likely to reverse that opinion.

Cunningham exhaled with a rasp. "We're still deciding our best course of action. That's why we decided to speak with everyone. We want you all to understand the risks and your options." She tipped her head toward the Champions in the room. "Some of you have your full magical ability—and additional training on top of that. If you wanted to help us make a stand here—and if we decide to make one—we'd appreciate your assistance."

*Now*, after everything, the Circle was outright asking our help. I smothered my irritation as well as I could. "What are the other options?"

"If you'd rather present yourselves to the military for assessment or leave and take shelter somewhere that won't be a target, we won't blame you."

How generous of them. My gaze slid to the League members with us. "We can't leave the building without being taken in unless we can teleport far enough to avoid the soldiers," I said. "That'll drain even me—lots of people here can't teleport at all." What would happen to all the Dampered mages and Burnouts under this roof? Were their only options surrender or probable death?

"We do hope that anyone who can help others leave that way will do so." Cunningham gestured toward the hall. "If we feel prepared to take a stand, we'll defend the others as well as we can."

And if they didn't resist, any mage without the talent to teleport out would have no choice at all. They'd be rounded up like my parents, maybe treated even worse because they'd defied the original order. We still hadn't heard of any mages being released from the detainment centers.

Cunningham stepped back toward the door. "In any case, I have more people to apprise of the situation. If you wish to volunteer your talents in one way or another, you know where you can find us."

She slipped out, leaving us in stunned silence.

"Do you think they'd really do it?" Desmond asked, his voice hushed. "Turn a full-scale military attack on their own citizens?"

"I'm not sure they see us as their citizens right now," Sam said grimly. "The Confed has done such a good job maintaining the lines between us and them. The Dull government is afraid of what *we* might decide to do the longer we're stuck in here."

"The more desperate we get," I filled in. "They already assume we're at least partly responsible for the damage the magic is still doing out there."

It *was* desperation clawing up through my chest as I tried to think the problem through. I focused on my breathing to steady myself the way I'd been encouraging my students to practice just minutes ago.

They must be worried after I'd cut off the chat so suddenly. I should shoot them a message letting them know we were okay and offering to finish the lesson.

Or I could send a message to all our students. We had tens of thousands of them now—a whole bunch of those in New York City, since the word had spread from here. It might be too late for the Circle to reconcile with the Dull government by revealing their lies… but we could still prove that the magic belonged to all of us.

A quiver of hope passed through the tangle of nerves inside me. "We have to do it," I said. "The biggest demonstration we can pull together, with all the Dulls who're willing to come. We have to get the word out even farther and prepare them as much as we can, and then tomorrow morning before the deadline, we'll prove to everyone that there's no line between us and them after all."

Prisha was watching me steadily. She hadn't been a part of our earlier lessons or the push against the Academy fire. "Do you think they'll be able to do enough?" she asked.

"With all of us together, I think we have a good chance. And if we don't try, then what?"

Desmond nodded. "It's our *last* chance. If there's a time to pull out all the stops, it's now."

When I glanced at Luis, his expression was set with

determination. Those who'd gone to the blankets sat up, but none of them raised a word of argument.

Sam leaned his elbows onto his desk, his gaze intent on me. "All right, then. What's our next step, Lopez?"

The anxious knots inside me squeezed tighter, but I ignored them. I was in charge of this particular mission, even if I'd resisted taking the lead when we'd started, and I'd better live up to that role. I wasn't doing it alone, not by a long shot.

"We need as many Dulls as possible to get solid on that mending casting," I said. "Focus on that, and give them a heads-up to expect a message tomorrow morning about where to meet. Anyone who can make it to Manhattan before then should come. We'll decide on the exact location then… but I think I have a good idea of where to focus our demonstration."

# CHAPTER TWENTY-THREE

*Finn*

Some sorts of energy, you don't need any magical ability to sense. The whole of the college hummed with tension the morning of the deadline—although I estimated I was twisted in more knots than the whole rest of the building combined.

"I think it'll work," Rocío said, her hand clasped tight around mine. "No one will be able to ignore what we're going to show them."

She made that statement firmly, but her uncertainty showed in the tightness of her mouth. What they showed the rest of the world would greatly depend on how many Dulls actually showed up, and there were no guarantees.

In just a few minutes, she'd be leaving to discover how well her efforts had paid off. The special ops mages who'd go with her had gathered across the classroom from us so she and I could say our good-byes in some privacy.

I offered my best attempt at a smile. "You can't blame me for being nervous. There are a lot of people with guns out there."

"We'll be looking after ourselves. And I don't think the

government is going to want their soldiers to hurt a whole bunch of their own people to get to us, especially when *we're* not hurting anyone."

"We never were," I muttered. We'd already talked this plan through for hours and covered every angle we could think of. If Rocío's demonstration was going to turn this stand-off and perhaps the entire conflict around, she needed to get going well before the missiles started flying in three hours' time.

I gave her hand a little tug, and she stepped into my embrace. It still seemed a wonder that this girl had let herself become—had *wanted* to become—such a huge part of my life. Her hair fell soft against my cheek, and both warmth and strength emanated from her body as I held her. I focused on the moment as intently as I would the most intricate casting I'd ever performed, meaning to memorize every detail so I could always carry it with me, no matter what happened next.

"You're spectacular," I said. "I know I've told you that before, but I figure this is as good a time as any to remind you. I'll do my best to back you up. And I'll be waiting for you after."

"I'll come find you as soon as I can." She eased back just far enough to seek out my lips for a kiss. I touched her cheek as I leaned into it. I needed to memorize this moment too.

Far too soon, she pulled away completely, giving my hand one last squeeze. "To freedom of magic for everyone," she said with a little smile.

I managed to smile back less stiffly than before. "To freedom of magic." One of the ancient lines I'd memorized long ago echoed through my head: perge sequar. *You go ahead; I will follow —in my own way.*

Rocío motioned to Prisha, Sam, Desmond, and the other Champions who'd joined in. They assembled in a line by the outer wall. Prisha gave me a quick nod of reassurance, even though anxiety shone stark in her expression. I waited there, guarding the door, as they closed their eyes and their lips moved in lilting castings.

Rocío vanished first, flickering out of the room like a flame snuffed out. Then the others followed her. They'd picked a sheltered spot to teleport to, beyond the ring of the siege.

Their disappearance was my cue. I checked that the classroom door was securely closed and pulled out my phone.

I didn't have the list of contacts I'd jotted down when I'd tipped off a squad of magic-interested reporters about our protest at the Confed building more than a week ago, but I'd remembered most of the names and had spent some of the past evening looking up their numbers. Now, with polite efficiency, I worked my way through them.

"Hello! I'm calling in a tip about the national emergency. If you head over to the Met, something big will be going on there very soon."

If anyone started asking questions I didn't care to answer, I made a quick excuse and got off the phone. I didn't think they'd skip this opportunity, even in the absence of details. The siege had to have caught the media's attention, and they'd want any scoop they could get.

When I was done, I girded myself and headed upstairs to the room the Circle was still using as a temporary office. The second part of my job was by far the most important, but also the most likely to go horribly wrong.

Voices carried through the door, deep enough in frustrated conversation that they hadn't realized that any muting 'chantment they'd put on the room had disintegrated.

"But the other options—"

"Can you really even call them *options*, Cunningham?"

"Let's be realistic. If we—"

My heart thudded at the base of my throat. The task ahead of me might not only be the most important thing I did today but possibly the most important of my entire life. Not letting myself hesitate, I shoved the door wide and strode in.

The five mages sitting around the table startled. The other two Circle members must have been elsewhere, preparing for the crisis. Well, five was enough for my purposes.

"Mr. Lockwood," Cunningham said, making a sour face. "We don't have time for—"

"You need to listen," I broke in, pleased to hear my voice hold steady despite the jangling of my nerves. "You're going to want to do damage control *right now*. Hundreds of people are assembling down the street by the Met—the soldiers outside won't be able to miss it. They're going to assume it's some kind of retaliatory action unless you tell them the people out there aren't mages and it's nothing to do with the Confederation."

Leron blinked at me. Another man's jaw had gone slack.

"What are you talking about?" one of the women sputtered. "Why is *anyone* assembling there?"

"To make a peaceful demonstration," I said. "But with tensions as high as they are right now, I don't think we can count on the Dull government realizing that soon enough. You wouldn't want them pushing forward the deadline for our surrender—or to launch the attack early without warning— would you? You'd better get on the phone to the highest-level contacts you have immediately."

"How do we even know what you're saying is true?" Cunningham demanded.

I'd been prepared for that question. I motioned toward the door. "You should be able to see some of it for yourself from the windows at the west end of the building. But if you want proof before you act, you'd better go get it fast."

Leron pushed to his feet first. He hurried past me and on down the hall. The other circle members trailed behind him, Cunningham shooting me a glower.

I fell into step at the rear of the procession. Leron knocked on a door at the end of the hall that had been a professor's office and quickly entered. The old magic family bunked down there—a couple and their young daughter—stared at the Circle members who rushed past them to the window.

Leron sucked a breath through his teeth. When he stepped back, I could make out the edge of the crowd forming farther down the street, just where I'd told them it would be. For it to have grown so big already, Rocío must be getting quite a turn out. I had to suppress a grin.

"What's going on?" the man who'd been using the office asked.

"Something we'd better deal with right away," Leron said, and marched out without another word. The other Circle mages hustled after him, and I followed.

"Are you sure they aren't mages?" Cunningham said to me. "Another of your League's ploys?"

"There are mages out there," I said, "but nearly all of that crowd is Dull. Or at least someone labeled as having no magic." *By you*, I didn't need to add.

She cursed under her breath. The second we'd filed back into their room, Leron whipped out a phone.

"General Evans?" he said. "Yes, I'm calling about the assembly you have probably already noticed gathering near the college. You need to understand that they have no affiliation with the Confederation—if you speak with them, you'll find they are all... 'regular' citizens, nonmagical. Yes, of course. No, I don't know what they're doing. We simply noticed and wanted to make sure there weren't any misunderstandings. Yes, I realize that."

He moved into the corner, his voice dropping and becoming more strained at the same time. I watched with my fingers curling into my palms at my sides. The army *had* to believe that the people gathering out there were Dulls. It'd be easy enough for them to check IDs and compare with their databases if they took the time to. They had to believe it so they wouldn't strike out at them… and so they'd recognize the momentousness of the act Rocío was about to lead them into.

Cunningham smacked her hand on the table. "This is ridiculous," she said. "I've had enough of some teenage Burnout trying to push us around, Lockwood or not. Frankly, I've had more than enough of this 'League' interfering with the real mages in this city."

My hackles rose automatically. "The *real* mages?" Even if they weren't a full part of the Confed, Luis and Tamara and all the other Dampered mages still had a connection to the magic. The Burnouts like me used to have it. Maybe sometimes I didn't feel like one myself, but we were all mages

She waved toward the wall. "What's happening out there is all some new scheme by you and the rest of that bunch, isn't it? I'll show you damage control, then. Let's give the soldiers what they've been wanting."

A chill raced down my back as she pushed past me into the hall. "Cunningham!" Leron called after her, just hanging up the phone, but she didn't slow down.

It didn't take long for me to figure out where she was heading. She descended the stairs faster than I'd have expected her stout frame to manage and turned into the hall leading to the college's gym. After their big conference yesterday afternoon, the Circle had directed the Dampered mages and Burnouts to camp out in this space, while assigning the old-magic families to the smaller rooms with more privacy. Rocío had only managed to hang onto her one classroom because there hadn't been enough families here to demand it.

A faintly sweaty smell drifted from inside the gym. We had the changerooms for showers, but a lot of the fugitives hadn't had time to grab a change of clothes. Cunningham strode in and stopped just inside the doorway. I hesitated in the hall, watching her. The rest of the Circle, including the missing two who'd rejoined the group in the midst of the chaos, came to a halt around me.

Cunningham clapped her hands. "All right. Everyone out. You've overstayed your welcome. The Dulls want you, and they can have you."

Heads jerked toward her all across the room. A sputter of swearing and protests rose up in answer. My posture went rigid.

"What are you talking about?" I said. I couldn't call on the magic-bound deal we'd made—they'd only agreed to stop hunting me, Luis, and Tamara, and to talk with us, not to shelter us from threats—but magic wasn't the only force at work here. With a jolt of uncertain inspiration, I pitched my voice loud enough to carry down the hall. "You agreed to help protect these people! How can you turn them over to a government that wants to blow us all up?"

Doors farther down the hall started to open, the mages behind them peeking out. Cunningham spun on me. "These people have already demanded more than they deserved from us."

"Cunningham," Leron protested, "this does seem like a bit much."

She gestured to the gym, lowering her voice. "We couldn't transport them all out of here by magic even if we wanted to. We don't have enough mages strong enough to do that kind of repeated teleporting, especially with the current conditions. If we offer them up to the soldiers outside, maybe they'll back off on the rest of us. And then they won't be hanging around inside these walls making their plans to undermine us."

I raised my voice even more. "So you're planning on sacrificing the people whose magic you've already stolen to save yourselves. Wow. That sounds like some fantastic leadership right there. What exactly have any of us done that was wrong?

Speaking up for ourselves? Pointing out how much your policies are harming people?"

More old-magic mages were coming into the hall to watch the confrontation. I spotted my parents and others I recognized, but I kept all my focus on Cunningham.

I couldn't let her do this. It didn't matter what the League or the Confed authorities thought of my tactics. The old-magic families around me *were* still my people, and I could appeal to them just as I'd used those connections to work around them in the past. Whatever influence I had in the gap where I'd landed between old-magic privilege and Burnout rejection, I had to bring it to bear now.

"You've broken Confederation laws," Cunningham shot back. "You've made a spectacle of our society."

"We have a right to advocate for ourselves," I said. "That's all we've been doing. If we've had to be loud about it, it's because you've tried so hard not to listen. The world is changing, just like it did during the Unveiling. We can't keep going the way we have been. Everyone here knows that."

I flung my hand toward the growing crowd of mages in the hall, and my gaze caught on my sister in their midst. The wry comment she'd made yesterday about the Circle's authority echoed through my head. My stomach flipped over, but before my nerves got the better of me, I hurtled onward.

"If you can't govern us properly through those changes, then I think it's time we elected an entirely new Circle to lead us."

Cunningham's expression tightened into a mask of disgust. "And, what? Do you think *you* should be leading the entire Confederation, Mr. Lockwood?"

I glared back at her. "Of course not. There's hardly a shortage of established mages to choose from, is there? I don't imagine it should be very hard to find ten with a wide range of qualifications who can do a better job than *you* have. Not getting us into a war with the Dull government would be a decent baseline."

Footsteps tapped across the floor. A hand rested on my shoulder as Margo took a spot beside me. "I second Finn's motion," she said, her voice carrying firm and clear. "We survive today however we can, but we decide as a group how we do that, Dampered and Burnouts included. And when we're no longer at war, we elect a new Circle."

"I support that motion," Dad's voice rose up, and then Mom's and then several of their friends. At my other side, a few mages I didn't even know stepped forward and announced their support.

Examiner Khalil—Salma—emerged among them. "I absolutely support that motion," she said, her eyes fierce.

More and more of the mages around me added their voices. The League members in the gym hollered at Cunningham too. "We want a new Circle! And we should have a say in it too."

Mark stood up near the doorway, acknowledging me with a slight tip of his head in a way he hadn't since the truth about Ary had come out. "Maybe the Confed was never the problem," he added to the chorus. "Maybe it was just the ten of *you*."

Cunningham swiveled, her face flushing red, her eyes wild. The other members of the Circle stood silent. Finally, she spun on me with a jab of her finger.

"You—"

"We mages have never been able to fully defend ourselves against the people we've called Dulls because there are so many more of them than there are of us," I said before she could go on. "That's the excuse the Circle has always used to explain why we have to give in to so many things they demand. Well, there are a hell of a lot more of us outside the Circle than in it. And I think you can hear what *we* demand."

More shouts rang out around me. Leron stepped up beside Cunningham. "We tried," he said to her.

"Timothy…"

She didn't seem to know what else to say. Leron turned toward the gym. "We're not forcing anyone to leave who doesn't want to," he said. Then he turned toward the hall. "And the Circle hears you. We govern by the will of the people." He caught the eyes of the other members, and one by one they nodded. "Perhaps it *is* time for a changing of the guard. There have been… a lot of upheavals in the last few weeks."

He hardly sounded happy about it, merely resigned, but I couldn't have expected more than that. My spirits rose with a rush of elation.

Then a massive *boom* echoed through the college, shaking the floor so hard I fell to my knees.

# CHAPTER TWENTY-FOUR

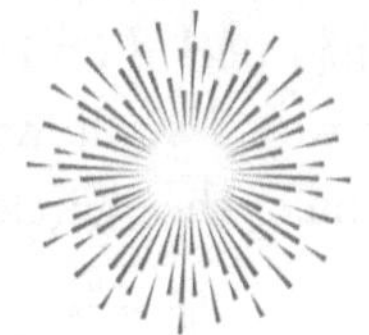

*Rocío*

"Holy crap," Desmond murmured as we took in the mass of people congregating in the street around us. My pulse thumped harder. The magic in the cold air tingled over my skin as if in anticipation, even though it was still tugging at me with erratic twitches here and there. Could it know that what we were going to do here today should be a real start to healing its wounds?

That possibility felt even more definite as I watched the crowd from my position on the Met's front steps. People were gathering all along Fifth Avenue and spilling into the nearby cross-streets—there had to be at least a thousand of them already. They stood firm despite the gust of magical wind still churning around us. More and more joined the group with each passing minute.

Some of the arrivals looked confused, peering around them as if looking for a sign of what was to come, but our more established students like Noemi were moving through the gathering, murmuring instructions and reassurance to anyone who needed it.

"When do we start?" Prisha asked from where she stood farther down our line along the steps. "And can I suggest soon? Because it looks like company is coming."

She nodded toward the street right across from us. Several soldiers who I suspected had peeled off from the siege around the college were heading our way. I swallowed hard. Please, let Finn have managed to convince the Circle to contact the Dull government in time.

The military wasn't the only outside force coming to us. A news van had just parked beside the crowd a couple blocks down Fifth Avenue. A reporter and a cameraman clambered out as a photographer emerged from another car.

"All right," I said to my colleagues. "The people of New York were horrified by the damage done to this institution—let's show them how well magic can rebuild it." I motioned to the chunks of limestone littering the base of the building by the smashed columns and battered roof. "Sam will focus on directing magic to the columns, I'll handle the roof, and Desmond will work on the cracks across the rest of the façade. The rest of you, spread out through the crowd and guide as many people as you can through hearkening the magic and casting it toward us. When you have the chance, use your own castings to help the energy keep flowing. Ready?"

The others nodded and set off. I hopped a couple steps higher so I could easily be seen by the mass of bodies around us. With a brief lyric, I formed a quivering bit of energy into an amplifying cone. I waved to the gathered Dulls, doing my best to ignore the approaching soldiers.

"Hello, everyone, and thank you so much for coming! We're going to do something incredible today. As most of you already know by now, every one of you, no matter what you've been told, has the ability to sense and work with magic at least a little. My colleagues and I will help you do that. The magic has been lashing out, but only because it's hurt and unsettled by the destructive purposes it's been used for. Now we're going to fix the damage done here and calm the magic as well. Who wants to tap into the power inside you?"

Our original Dull students whooped throughout the crowd, and some of the newbies let out a more hesitant cheer. We had to get them started fast before too much doubt set in.

"Follow the instructions you were given, the castings you may have had a chance to practice," I said. "If you haven't managed it yet, that's fine, just give it your best. When you're ready, sing with me and direct any energy you feel toward making this building whole again."

I dragged in a breath and rolled the lyric I'd chosen off my tongue—one that brought me back to the songs my abuela had sung to me when I'd been too little to imagine I'd ever face any challenge like this.

"Dame la mano con un fuerte apretón…"

Dozens and then hundreds of voices rose up along the streets. So many of them blended together that I couldn't have made out any individual one if I'd wanted to. An electric shiver raced through my body. I turned and trained my own attention on the tiny currents of magic flowing toward me, summoning more to join them as they came.

Some of the weak attempts at casting faltered before they had any impact. Some shimmered right into me, rippling through my chest and onto my tongue to join the magic I conducted myself.

Tremors ran through the energy, but the melody of my words cast most of it toward the fallen stone and the collapsed portion of roof. I'd spent most of my time between video chat lessons studying that section of the building from recordings and photographs. Now, bit by bit, the crumbled pieces rose up to be melded back into place.

Magic thrummed all through the air. With one fallen chunk and another, the edge of the roof reformed into its previous shape. Filling in the gap where some had crumbled inside would be harder, but with the lifting of my heart, I didn't doubt that we could manage it.

We were doing it. To fix this damage on my own would have taken hours of concentration. It'd only been a few minutes, and with the hundreds upon hundreds of allies we'd gathered, the historic building was already coming back together.

Gasps and awed laughter reached my ears as the Dulls realized what they were accomplishing too. The wisps of magic they were casting wavered, dropping off here and there as they lost concentration, but new currents rushed in as others made their own attempts.

I was vaguely aware of figures moving along the edge of the crowd—the soldiers, presumably questioning people. We'd prepped our allies for that likelihood too. They'd have their IDs ready if any authority figure wanted to look up their status, and they'd repeat the refrain we'd given them: "I'm not a mage. We can all have magic. And right now we're healing the magic we have."

The soldiers had to believe them. They had to see that all these people couldn't be mages, not when they'd rounded up so many of us already and forced the rest into hiding. And they had to recognize the power the crowd was wielding.

The outer edge of the broken roof was completely rebuilt now. When I stole a glance at the column Sam was working on, it had climbed halfway back to its original height. I just needed to fill in the larger hole across the top—

With a thunderous *boom*, the whole world seemed to shake. I stumbled on the steps and pitched forward, my palms scraping against an edge of stone. The huge limestone façade in front of us split right open, the sections of wall swaying as they started to collapse, and a hot, ashen smell washed over me. Shrieks rose from the crowd.

My lungs constricted so tight I couldn't breathe. It hadn't been a physical blast but a magical one. The energy that had been beginning to soothe around me jerked and flailed with fresh desperation. Smoke billowed up over the gallery, forming the shape of the Bonded Worthy's ghoulish mask.

In the first stunned second, taking that in, my mind latched onto a few fleeting facts: The insurgents hadn't left after all; they'd been waiting for an ideal chance to strike again. They'd picked now—because they'd seen the same news reports and had the same idea to use the Met for a demonstration? Because they'd wanted to thwart our attempt at rebuilding?

It didn't matter. Every part of me simply screamed *No!*

We couldn't let them win. I couldn't let them destroy the moment I'd fought so hard to make happen.

We couldn't let the magic falter any further. It whipped through my hair and smacked at the crowd, but that wobble of frailty was greater and more frightening than ever.

"We can stop this!" I yelled, so loud the words scratched my throat coming up, and pointed to the building as if most of the eyes around me weren't already fixed on it. "We can hold it together. Sing with everything you've got in you and focus on keeping those walls up. We are stronger than the people who want us to fail!"

I inhaled sharply and launched into my lyric, letting my voice peal clear and forceful down the street. Other people were hollering—the soldiers? My colleagues? The Dulls, in fear and confusion? I didn't know, and I couldn't afford to check. Everything came down to this moment, to the seconds slipping by before the building fell apart faster than we could catch it.

The magic skittered away from my intent, but I belted out the words again, winding my melody around the strains of energy, letting my rhythm flow with the erratic cadence that whirled and shuddered against my skin. *I'll work with you, with what you are right now. Just please, please, please, work with me too.*

I hurled all the energy I could gather at the gallery, thrusting out my arms at the same time, as if they could hold up the massive walls. The magic crackled over and through me, and the hairs on the back of my neck rose. The Bonded Worthy hadn't managed to conduct as powerful a strike as they'd inflicted on the Confed building, but the grace that had bought us was nearly spent. The limestone façade shuddered with its slow collapse.

Other voices filtered through the chaos. I thought I made out Sam's and Desmond's on either side of me, Prisha's somewhere deeper in the crowd, familiar in a wrenching sort of way because of our time in the field together. They formed a weird harmony, each with their own melody.

Alongside them, more and more with each passing second, others rang out as well, strained or ragged but belting the lyrics and lines they'd picked to mend the world.

"Sew it all together, and wash it clean…"

"Build it up with silver and gold, silver and gold, silver and gold…"

"I'll heal what I can and take what's left…"

I didn't know half of the songs being sung around me, but all that mattered was that people *were* singing, stirring the magic in whatever minor ways they could. Their voices steadied the energy that flowed through me. As all those tiny pieces merged into one huge force, I propelled the expanding wave of their power toward the building.

I concentrated all my intent on channeling it the same way Finn had acted as a conduit for my cast magic months ago in the Exam. With each word I sang, I aimed the collected energy at the areas that looked weakest, shoring up every piece of the structure I could. Other strands of intent wove around and aligned with mine as my colleagues did the same. A wall of magic, trembling but solid for now, shot up all around the building to hold it in place while we did our work.

That spreading crack—shove the edges of stone back together and bind them. Those splitting supports I could sense all through the expanse of rooms and halls—cool them and push back the heat of the explosion that was warping them. Summon a cold, wet wind to snuff out the flames that had flared up inside. Put that falling statue back into place with a shove.

An ache speared through my skull. Sweat trickled down my back despite the icy bite in the air. I could never have managed a tenth of this much on my own, but the hundreds of people around me, giving their all—they were enough. It didn't matter if they only had a fraction of the ability any official mage did. Even a little magic could tip the balance between victory and ruin.

We couldn't fix the whole structure right now. I didn't kid myself. But I believed with every particle of my being that we could seal it firmly enough that it wouldn't fall, that it wouldn't destroy other buildings or lives in its wake. The terrorists wouldn't get their terror. And then, with the help of experts both magical and Dull, we'd be able to really restore it.

Even the magic felt less terrorized as it hummed through me now. Was it tranquil and joyful, the way I'd hearkened it before my life had become so entangled with violence? No. But we'd caught it before it had broken down completely, stopped the damage it might have caused in its next backlash. It grazed my hair rather than snatching at me now. Its touch against my face caressed more than pinched.

As I sang out my lyric from my hoarsening throat, the energy held *me* like a comforting embrace, not the clinging vise that had demanded so much from me over the last few months.

My headache dug its claws into my forehead and the back of my skull. I lost my rhythm for a second with a hitch of breath at the pain. The rest of my body had gone weirdly numb. I couldn't keep casting much longer.

The people on the streets must have been exhausted too, but so many of them kept singing that they buoyed me along like the swell of an ocean wave. Through the haze of pain, my lips curved into a smile I couldn't have suppressed even if I'd wanted to.

I threw the last of my will into a final effort to stabilize the gallery's outer walls and what I could feel of the inner structure. My voice faltered, and my legs wobbled. I would have fallen down the steps if someone behind me hadn't caught my waist to steady me.

The voices that had risen with mine eased off as mine faded. Despite the throbbing in my head, an unexpected peace settled over me and the crowd, as if we'd all let out one gigantic sigh of relief.

The Met remained, battered and blackened around the edges, but standing. Time had compressed for me while we'd been casting, but obviously a bunch of it had passed, because all kinds of soldiers flanked the crowd now, along with a couple dozen reporters and camera crews. Microphones bobbed, and lenses glinted. Phones flashed where spectators had come and started making their own amateur records of the event.

I had to find a little more strength inside me before I let this moment go. I had to speak to everyone here, to the soldiers and the Dulls and the Bonded Worthy recovering from their own massive casting, to the cameras and all the hundreds of millions of people that footage would reach all around the world. I turned to fully face them, Sam keeping his hand on my side for support.

"Everyone here saw it, didn't they?" I said in my raw voice. "If you're watching this later, you'll see it too. Our enemies tried to attack us, to destroy another part of our city, and that act wounded the magic they want to use as much as we do. The only way to heal it, the only way to make sure all of us—the ones who grew up knowing we were mages and everyone else who was told they weren't—can keep reaching that magic is to direct it toward building and healing like we did just now."

I had to stop and cough before I could go on. "Please. We can't sacrifice the magic to this conflict. We all lose too much that way. Does any one of you want to go without it, knowing you can have that power? I don't want anyone to fight, but if you have to, there are so many other ways. Use them instead. Use magic to protect and to mend, not to destroy."

Someone called out from the crowd of not-really-Dulls in front of me. "What do *we* do now?"

I could have laughed, the answer seemed so easy and so complicated at the same time. I wasn't even sure we'd get there, but while the army hung back simply observing and the cameras filmed on, more than a little hope welled up inside me.

"We teach everyone how to hearken the magic and use it whatever ways they can, however small. And we keep fixing things, keep healing things, until it's as strong as it ever was. There are plenty of broken things in this world that could use attention. And we just proved that if enough of us are trying, we can turn a catastrophe around."

# CHAPTER TWENTY-FIVE

*Finn*

If someone had told me six months ago that soon I'd be standing up before the Circle to advocate for both myself and my most longstanding enemy, I'd have laughed. Here I was, though, about to step into the middle of the ring of broad oak desks in the boardroom serving as the temporary Circle headquarters until the reconstruction of the Confed building was complete.

Several of the League members had come to watch this discussion from the sidelines, as had Rocío. She twined her fingers with mine for one last squeeze of my hand. "They'll listen to you," she said softly, with such utter confidence in my abilities that I'd have kissed her if I weren't worried about professional appearances.

I had better manage to convince the Circle on this matter after how much *she'd* been able to accomplish. Even two weeks after the near destruction of the Met, a pang of gratitude that she was okay, that she was here at all, shot through me every time I looked at her. I tightened my grip in return.

The man serving as moderator for the meetings called out to us. "Ms. Khalil and Mr. Lockwood, you may now have the floor."

I squared my shoulders and stepped forward with the woman I'd first known as Examiner Khalil, who'd offered to take this stand with me. Ten pairs of contemplative eyes fixed on us.

Many of those eyes were familiar, at least. True to their word, the former Circle had stepped back to allow us to choose new representatives—and they'd given all established mages, not just full members of the Confederation, a say. Luis offered me a warm smile and Tamara tipped her head from where they sat next to each other at my right. The Dampered mages and Burnouts had pushed hard for representation within our ranks.

At my left, I had to face the skeptical gazes of Leron and one of the other members of the former Circle, who'd been asked to stay on to help guide the new members. It was hard to mind their presence when next to them sat my sister Margo, her eyebrows arched at a slightly ironic angle.

I knew the prominent Confederation families had asked our father to put his name forward, but Dad had declined, saying he felt he needed to do some work on the ground before he was ready to make decisions for the whole community. The things I'd told him, the problems he'd ignored or failed to notice, obviously weighed heavily on him. Having Margo in the Circle kept the Lockwood tradition alive, and she could provide both a younger perspective and a connection to the people we'd once thought of as Dulls, which was going to be useful throughout our transition.

The other new Circle members were less familiar to me, although I vaguely recognized a couple of them from my parents' socializing. The last few regarded us with sterner expressions. Beside me, Salma stood a bit rigidly, but her dark eyes were set with unwavering determination that bolstered my own.

"I understand the two of you have an appeal to make," Leron said, leaning forward at his desk. I supposed with his established experience, he was still exerting a lot of authority within this room. "Proceed."

"Mr. Lockwood and I came here together because we can speak to two sides of the same issue," Salma said. "I've worked as an examiner and an associate on the Educational Evaluation Committee for three years. You all know now exactly what the Exam involves during the trials and afterward. We submit that the memories of Burnouts should be restored to any who request it. I believe they have the right to know their actions and the tests they had to face. To leave them without that knowledge is simply dodging responsibility for our own actions."

That was my cue. I lifted my chin. "As one of those Burnouts, I second that petition. All of us who entered the Exam took a huge risk with very little disclosure of the dangers. Having a hole in our recollections, forced to merely speculate about what went on and how we failed, only makes recovery more difficult. Anyone who wants them has a right to those memories."

Salma moved around the room to set a small sheaf of papers on each desk. "To support our request, I've brought a collection of reports on the negative effects of memory suppression in relation to trauma."

"We've had some discussions on this subject already," Leron said, which explained why he didn't look surprised by our appeal. He rubbed his mouth. "As I understand it, there are two components to the Exam debriefing process: the memory block on those who were unsuccessful and a silencing 'chantment applied to both Champions and Burnouts. It seems unwise to restore potentially traumatic memories that a person couldn't discuss with anyone else."

I nodded. "We agree and believe removing the silencing 'chantment should be considered as part of the motion."

"We can't remove it completely," said one of the sterner figures at the far end of the ring of desks. "In regard to certain aspects of military strategy and tactics revealed during the Exam, and afterward to our Champions, our accord with the Du—with the common government forbids us from making those public. Without the 'chantment, we'd have no way of ensuring we keep to that agreement."

The "common" government—or people—was our new term for those previously considered magicless. Getting out of the habit of calling them "Dull" was taking some time.

"I believe the silencing 'chantment is reasonably flexible," Salma said. "It could be modified to a narrower range of topics or to prevent only the mention of specifics while allowing room to discuss feelings in the aftermath."

Margo tapped the top of her desk. "We've already agreed that we're abolishing the Exam. We'll need to make an official announcement to the Confederation about why, including acknowledgment of the problems with it. I know we're all nervous about the fallout, but people deserve to know—and if we give former examinees the ability to speak about it without backing up what they'll say, we're just throwing them under the bus all over again."

A murmur of agreement, some enthusiastic and some hesitant, rose up around the room.

"I don't think anything needs to happen *today*," I added. "Most Burnouts have gone years or even decades without those memories. I'm less concerned about it happening immediately than about a guarantee it'll happen within a reasonable timeframe."

"You won't have to make an official announcement about the Exam until close to when the next one is scheduled to start," Salma pointed out. "That gives you several months to decide how to approach the situation—although I'd hope you could manage to agree on an approach sooner than that."

"I think that should be possible," Leron said in a lofty tone.

"Would you please wait in the antechamber—and others not part of the Circle retire to the hall—while we discuss the matter amongst ourselves?"

A security officer ushered Salma and me into the smaller room off to the side. Salma sat on one of the cushioned chairs there. I wandered restlessly around the space for a few minutes before forcing myself to take a seat as well.

"Do you think they'll agree to it?" I asked her.

"If they don't now, we'll gather more evidence to strengthen our arguments, and then go before them again. But I'd expect at least half of the current Circle will be sympathetic. They'll speak up for us and try to convince anyone who has doubts." She paused. "I'm sorry I couldn't manage to let you keep all your memories to begin with."

My throat tightened just a tad at the remark. I'd gotten used to my faded, patchy memories of my five days in the Exam, but fragments drifted into my consciousness at random times that I didn't know what to make of. Sometimes I wondered if getting those scraps was really better than having a blank slate—other than the fact that I wouldn't have remembered Rocío at all without them.

"You did as much as you could," I said. "More than anyone else bothered to attempt—and more than any of the other examinees got. I have no idea where I'd be or what would have happened if I hadn't kept the memories I did."

Salma waved off my gratitude, her mouth slanting downward. "I was part of the system that gave you those horrible memories in the first place. I should have done more sooner. At first I didn't realize the full extent—and then I thought I'd have a better chance if I pushed for change bit by bit instead of arguing against the whole thing—but sometimes you have to make a big statement before anyone will listen."

We'd certainly seen plenty of evidence of that in the past few weeks. My thoughts slipped to the girl who'd stood by me while I waited to make this petition and so many other times before. "The memories aren't all horrible," I said. I never wanted to go through the Exam again, but I couldn't regret going in to begin with, not when it'd opened my eyes in so many ways and brought me to Rocío.

After what felt like hours, the door to the main boardroom opened again. The security officer motioned us in. As I stepped inside, the little smile on Margo's face gave me a boost of hope.

Leron stood up. "The Circle has decided in favor of moving to restore the memories of all burned out mages who have no criminal history, contingent on their request, along with adjusting the silencing 'chantments for both them and our Champions to cover no more than the requirements of our peace accord with the common government—so stated for the record. The proceedings will begin within the next three months, the exact date to be determined after further discussion."

I restrained myself from indulging in a victory fist pump, but I couldn't hold back a grin. "Thank you for hearing us."

A little whoop went up among the spectators who'd been allowed back in at the other end of the room. As we all exited into the hall, my gaze went to the gangly guy with the shock of red hair who'd watched the proceedings in silence. Callum had tormented me more times throughout our shared education than I liked to think about, but I'd made him a promise, and he'd kept up his end of the agreement.

"I'll make sure you're the first one in there," I said to him. "A deal's a deal."

A mix of relief and apprehension crossed his face. The guy had to be worried about what he'd done during that blank in his memory, considering what a jerk he could be even outside of extreme circumstances. That was his burden to deal with, though. I'd done my part, for him and the rest of us.

"Thanks," he said stiffly.

I tipped my head to him before turning away. He and I were never going to be friends, but if the two of us could coexist without outright animosity, there had to be hope for the rest of the world.

Rocío walked out with me, tucking her arm around mine. "That's one relief. I wish I'd been there to see you take on the old Circle and put them in their places."

I chuckled. "You were up to much more important things right then."

"Let's say *different* important things." She beamed at me, and I had to kiss her, just outside the doorway. The brisk but no longer unnaturally wild wind flicked her hair against my cheek before I stepped back.

"I'll see you tonight," I said. "Say hi to Noemi from me." The two of them had combined forces to lead an informal team of emerging mages around the city, making minor repairs to offset the damage the magic had done.

I headed off for a late lunch with Prisha, who met up with me halfway to one of our favorite restaurants. She took one look at my face as she fell into step beside me and nudged me with her elbow. "I take it the meeting went well."

"They're not acting on it right away, bureaucracy being what it is, but they agreed with the motion. It's been written down somewhere. Very official."

"Look at you, Mr. Political Activism."

A faint flush heated my cheeks in the cool winter air, even though her teasing had been gentle. She hadn't been around for most of my participating in the League, so this side of me was new to her. "I'm just trying to contribute where I can. And I had promises to keep."

"I wasn't saying it's a bad thing." She offered me a smile that looked bittersweet. "Just make sure between all your activism-ing and your girlfriend that you still have a little time for your best friend, huh?"

"I'm here, aren't I?" I gave her a playful grimace as we walked into the sweetness and warmth of the café. "How's *your* political activism going? I'm not the only one who's staying busy."

Prisha groaned and dropped into a chair at the nearest table. "So many people with so much magical ambition but so little talent. I guess I should be glad. The worst the squad has had to deal with in the last few days is a guy who managed to conduct enough magic to trigger the coin release on a vending machine. Better that than a whole bunch of new mages who are actually powerful."

In the wake of the near civil war and the revelations that had come with the fallout, many of the Champions, including Prisha and Sam, had accepted recruitment into a growing new field of magical work: policing the former Dulls as they explored their emerging talents. Prisha's squad cooperated with the city's not-terribly-magical police, teaching the officers how to best implement their new skills in the field and dealing with any major magical disturbances—although "major" was clearly relative.

"You could always resign if you don't want to keep doing the job," I reminded her.

"I know. But it's something to do, and it keeps me out of the house. My family has gotten even *weirder* now that they figure they're going to become magical prodigies too." She snapped her menu open. "I have to figure out what I'm going to study at the college when I can properly start next term. After everything we went through in the Exam, I never really knew what I wanted to do with myself after… I just knew I didn't want to lose any of my connection to the magic."

"Is working with the squad giving you ideas?"

"Maybe. I'm starting to think I might actually like teaching.

That's the part I don't mind as much—showing the cops what to do. It's dealing with the idiots who think they can magically get away with crime I could do without."

I cocked my head, contemplating the idea of Prisha as a teacher, and she made a face at me. "I could be good at it."

I raised my hands. "Hey, I didn't say anything! I bet you would. You were always great at helping me practice whatever skills I was trying to develop."

"Indeed I was."

After the waitress had taken our orders, Prisha leaned her elbows onto the table and gave me a sly look. "And how *are* things with the girlfriend?"

My best friend hadn't been all that keen on Rocío at the start, but after their time together in the special ops division, she seemed to have warmed up to her. After all, Rocío had risked her freedom and perhaps even her life going AWOL to try to stop the brutal assault in which many of her colleagues had died, and which had left Prisha with that scar on her jaw. Prisha couldn't talk about her military experiences yet, but every now and then her gaze went distant in a way that wasn't like her former self.

The Champions had all sorts of scars far beyond what the Exam had left on us Burnouts.

I fiddled with my napkin. "The girlfriend is actually, ah, coming over to my house for dinner tonight."

Prisha's eyebrows jumped up. "Her first dinner with the parents? That should be interesting."

"It needed to happen. They really wanted to, I don't know, welcome her sort of into the family. I think they'll be okay."

It was hard to tell. I'd always thought my family was pretty enlightened and that they'd passed those values on to me. That hadn't stopped me from putting my foot in my mouth plenty of times when it came to Rocío's new-magic, working-class background, so I couldn't assume Mom and Dad would handle the conversation perfectly.

They'd just have to learn from their missteps like I had. Rocío was part of my life, and I wanted her to stay part of it for as long as she wanted that too.

* * *

Rocío's eyes widened as she walked into the foyer of my family's home. She shot me a wry smile, and I imagined she was comparing the grand wooden staircase and vaulted ceiling to her family's modest modern apartment. I reached for her hand instinctively.

"It's just— It is what it is," I said.

"You didn't judge my home, so I think I can manage not to judge yours," she said with a wink.

"Rocío!" Genuine pleasure rang through Mom's voice as she came out to greet our guest. "I'm so glad you could join us. Dinner will be ready in just a few minutes. Come right in and make yourself comfortable."

The meal went about as well as I could have hoped, unexpectedly similar to my own first dinner with Rocío's parents a couple of months back. Dad asked her about her plans for the future, Mom inquired after her family, and even though we had a few awkward pauses when one of them seemed to be working out how to avoid *saying* anything awkward, the conversation flowed smoothly enough.

Toward the end of dinner, Dad finally broached the topic of recent events. "I want to tell you that I appreciate the way you stood up to both the Circle and the common government," he said, his voice as solemn as I'd ever heard it. "I have great admiration not just for the magical skill you showed coordinating all those smaller talents, but for your bravery and integrity as well. I hope there haven't been any sanctions behind the scenes?"

Rocío ducked her head at the praise. "Nothing other than a bit of scolding about proper procedures and all that." She caught my eyes, hers shining. "You'd think they'd know by now not to expect me to follow the rules."

I laughed. "If they didn't before, they definitely should now."

Even though the dinner had hardly been fraught, I felt as if I'd been holding my breath for ages by the time we finally retreated to my bedroom.

I sat in my desk chair while Rocío roamed around the space—which, it occurred to me now that I saw her in it, was as large as her apartment's entire open-concept living-dining room. She didn't comment on that, but just browsed my bookshelf and the framed art on the walls.

Her gaze skimmed over my bed, and sudden heat prickled over me. It didn't make sense to get awkward about *that*, considering we'd slept in the same bed more than once in the rooms we'd rented, but the thought of her in relation to my own bed somehow felt more momentous.

I groped for a remark to lighten the mood. "So, you survived parental scrutiny!"

"They weren't that bad," Rocío said. "And it's not like you hadn't already run that gauntlet." She meandered over to me, and I reached to take her hand again.

I traced my thumb over her knuckles, grappling with an emotion that had been growing since the moment she'd told me her big plan.

I'd held myself back before because I hadn't wanted to remind her of how worried I'd been. It shouldn't matter now. She was here. Her gambit had worked. Still, something made the words tumble out.

"I'm so glad you survived everything else. I mean, I should have known you would, but it was hard not to—"

"I know." She leaned over me, touching my shoulder and stealing a kiss from above. I looped my arm around her waist to tug her onto my lap. She nestled her head next to mine. "I was scared about what might happen too," she said. "I'm still scared sometimes. But it's getting less and less."

"Do you think things are going to be okay? That everyone will stick to the agreements they've made?"

"Maybe not forever, but at least for now. It seems like people want peace too much to risk screwing it up. Working on the rebuilding, pitching in with all the volunteers—it feels pretty amazing. The magic isn't completely settled yet, but every day it's calmer. We're really healing it. That's all that matters to me." She shifted back to catch my gaze. "You'll be able to feel it properly soon too. Are you ready?"

A quiver ran through my chest, jittery with anticipation—mostly in a good way. "Of course," I said. "I never wanted to lose the magic in the first place. It's just hard not to wonder it will be after I've gone this long without that connection. Maybe they won't be able to reverse all the effects."

"Hey." Rocío tipped toward me so her nose brushed mine. "From what I've seen, it should work just fine. And if it doesn't, then I'll study until *I'm* a magimedic and figure out how to do it right."

"I'd manage without," I said with a smile. "You really wouldn't have to go to that much trouble."

Her hand rose to my cheek. "Yes, I would," she said quietly, and then we were kissing again, and that was plenty of magic in itself.

When I was holding her in my arms, reveling in the soft heat of her mouth, every anxiety about the future faded away. This was all the sign I needed that we'd be all right—that the world would be all right. The two of us, despite our differences and our initial clashes—one disadvantaged at every turn, one privileged in every way; one of us the most powerful mage of our generation, and the other ending up with no magic at all—had made something stronger together when it would have been so easy to end up on opposite sides of the conflict.

This was the meaning of hope: the affection in this girl's eyes when she looked at me, the tenderness of her touch, and the knowledge that, for all the faith I had in her, she had just as much in me.

Once, what felt like a very long time ago, I'd dreamed of proving my worth and making my mark with magical talent. The truth was that I'd accomplished much more in the five months since I'd lost the magic than the nearly seventeen years I'd had it at my disposal. I'd done something meaningful. I'd made a difference, though not in quite as flashy a fashion as Dad once had.

Now, as I drew Rocío closer, certainty settled over me. I might not ever be a great mage, but I could still do great things, and I'd do them with this girl beside me.

# CHAPTER TWENTY-SIX

*Rocío*

Mom eyed the frost glittering on the living room window and tsked. "January is always the worst. I need a second scarf to go out in that." She tugged her wool hat lower over her ears.

I wrapped my own scarf around my neck, over my down coat. "You don't have to come with me. The presentation is going to be all over the TV."

Dad patted my shoulder. "We're coming, mija. I want to see this with my own eyes, not through a television screen. They owe a lot of us an apology."

My stomach knotted at the thought of the days he and Mom had spent in military custody. No one had hurt them, but no one had done anything to make them comfortable or confirm they weren't some kind of threat to society. What happened today wouldn't make up for everything, but if it turned out as planned, it'd be a big step in the right direction.

We splurged on a taxi to get us into downtown Manhattan with as little time as possible in the crisply frigid air. By the time we reached Times Square, the space was teeming with spectators around the small stage set up on one side. At least all those bodies warmed things up a little.

I wove through the crowd ahead of my parents. Any time people started to look upset about us pushing for a better view, I flashed the pass I'd been given. When we reached the area cordoned off around the stage, Desmond and Leonie were already standing there along with a few older Champions, Desmond with his arm slung around Leonie's waist.

Leonie hadn't come through her last mission overseas unscathed. The bottom of her right coat sleeve hung loose where she'd lost everything beneath the elbow, and from the stiff set of her shoulders, I could tell she was still in at least a little pain. She'd insisted on being part of this presentation all the same, and I'd have fought anyone who tried to take that right from her.

I gave Mom and Dad a quick hug and flashed my pass one last time at the Secret Service guy standing guard by the Champions. He eased open the barrier to let me through.

Desmond grinned as I joined them. "Look at us! From potentially Dampered to standing up with the president in less than six months. They really ought to make a movie about us—with lots more epic magical battles now that we don't actually need to fight them."

"I'd be glad to completely forget the last six months," Leonie muttered, but she tipped her head toward him affectionately.

"Well, maybe they can tell some other stories. You would not believe the stuff I'm digging up in the archives. If it ever stops being top secret, anyway."

"Enjoying the new job?" I asked, and he gave me an enthusiastic thumbs-up. The new Circle had taken on Desmond and another former Champions to sift through all the National Defense archives for anything related to the special ops team. They wanted to build a rock-solid case against magical warfare, should the common government ever think about going back on the word.

"Oh, look, it's the old crew back together again." Prisha came up beside me with a light laugh. She glanced back at the growing crowd. "We're going to have quite the audience, aren't we?"

"Not just them." I nodded to the news vans parked nearby. Some of the reporters were already out commenting on the event and broadcasting it to millions of TV and computer screens.

Sam arrived a few minutes later, as well as several other local Champions. As we welcomed them, the voices in the crowd rose in anticipation. A tall, almost gaunt man with thick gray hair slicked back from his face had climbed onto the stage. He made his way across it, surrounded by Secret Service agents.

I hadn't seen the president in person before. All the planning for this event had come through members of his staff. He didn't look all that intimidating up close. But that was the same guy who'd ordered my parents and so many other mages rounded up and jailed, who'd nearly launched an assault on all the Confed's properties, just a few weeks ago.

He stepped up to the podium, his expression solemn, his deep-set eyes shadowed, and raised his gloved hand for the spectators to quiet down. When the din faded, he leaned toward the microphone.

"Thank you all for coming here today despite the weather. I felt it important to make this statement here, in the heart of New York, because this city has been the hub of magical activity for longer than most of us have known that mages existed. The last time people descended on the city on my orders, it was to constrain those who can use magic. Now, with what we know about our own capability and the good faith the Confederation has shown us, I must formally apologize for the actions taken here and across the country against our fellow citizens."

I caught Mom's eye where my parents were standing near the fence, and she gave me a small smile.

The president went on for a little longer with his apology, and then turned to the subject that was most important to me.

"During these events, one fact has become unavoidably clear. The magic is part of all of our heritage, and the way it's used has terrible effects—on the magic and our world. Never again do we want to see it brought to the violent state it was in after the recent attacks, nor do we want to risk losing this resource completely. As such, I have signed an executive order that the United States military will use no magical assaults during its operations. Magic will only be used to defend ourselves and our allies, to heal the wounded, and to rebuild what is broken."

He held up a paper with an official seal, and the audience let out a cheer. I couldn't hold back a relieved whoop of my own. So many cameras were trained on the stage, recording the president's proclamation. The footage would travel all over the world, just as my demonstration at the Met had.

I doubted those videos and the statements in them would stop all our enemies from diminishing the magic with their own assaults, but they had as much common sense as we did, even if they saw the world very differently. They'd have observed the negative effects on the magic, hearkened its weakening as it lashed out. They wouldn't want to lose it either. And with all of National Defense's energy put toward protection and security, whatever magical attacks we did face would have a much harder time reaching their target.

I had to believe the changes we'd made here would make a difference everywhere. How much of one, we'd have to wait and see.

As the president went on, the Secret Service agents ushered the twenty or so of us Champions onto the stage next to him. My pulse thumped faster at the sight of the vast sea of faces watching us. Our former team stuck together, Sam at my left and Desmond at my right.

I scanned the far edge of the crowd, where Finn had told me the old-magic mages planned to gather, leaving the closest spots to the people who needed this message the most. The glint of his bright hair caught my eye. I sent a smile his way, one he'd know was just for him.

"As we all realize now, every one of us has the potential to work magic, however slight," the president said. "What a wonderful discovery to have come out of so much turmoil. To celebrate that knowledge and to recognize the efforts of the mages who've contributed so much to the well-being of our entire country, I've invited some of those mages to conduct a magical display for you today. Let's work toward a beautiful future together!"

His words were swallowed up by another cheer from the crowd. I raised my voice alongside the other Champions, my choice a simple folk song that flowed right into the thrum of magic around me.

"De colores, de colores."

My voice lifted, and a dragon sparkled into being over the crowd. Not fierce but magnificently gorgeous, its scales glinting blue and purple in the stark winter sunlight, its wings unfurling with a glimmer of orange. It soared up toward the sky, for me, for Javi. For a second, I almost felt my brother beside me.

I was a dragon-tamer, and I was also a dragon, but *I* decided how I used that power.

Other creatures and images floated up around mine: a brilliant soaring Pegasus, a bounding silver kitten, a burst of golden fireworks, the arc of a conjured rainbow. I let my gaze drop from my dragon to the spectators, and my breath caught at the shining wonder on all those faces below. A glow of hope lit up in me, seeing it.

They weren't afraid of our magic or resentful of it. Finally, they could look at the power and recognize the beauty in it—the beauty they'd be able to share in some small part. And I'd helped open their eyes.

As much faith as he'd had in my abilities, I wasn't sure Javi could have believed I would be able to change so many minds. That was okay. I could have enough hope for both of us.

* * *

Finn had tried to keep it cool the whole time we were in the waiting area, but anticipation reverberated off him so loudly I might as well have been hearkening it. His parents had come for the procedure too, but he'd talked to them beforehand about how he wanted it to go. When the magimedic came out to tell him it was his turn, he tugged me onto my feet to go with him. The magimedic gave me a questioning look.

"I'd like to come in too," I said. "To help however I can."

I could tell from her expression that she recognized me. Probably just about everyone in the city—and a whole lot of people elsewhere too—would have after I'd played a starring role in recent newscasts. She glanced from me to Finn and back again.

"It's a very complex process. I don't think there's any part that would be safe for someone without all the training to handle."

My mouth curved into a crooked smile. "Always much easier to cause a wound than to heal it, isn't it? I didn't expect to contribute to the internal aspects. I'd be happy just to channel more magic to you while you're working."

"I'd like Rocío there," Finn put in, his grip on my hand tightening. As eager as he was to hearken the magic again, he'd told me he found the thought of being unconscious with the same magimedics who'd taken the ability away from him unnerving. *When you're knocked out like that, you can't monitor what they're doing—you can't speak up if something happens that you don't agree with.*

I couldn't blame him for wanting someone along who he knew was on his side. And I liked the idea of playing some minor role in the restoration of his connection to the magic after I'd committed to making that happen before I'd even known for sure it was possible.

The magimedic considered. "I suppose that shouldn't interfere with the procedure. If anything, it'll free up more of my concentration. All right. Come along, then, both of you."

The room she led us into looked so much like the one in the Exam building where I'd had the silencing 'chantment placed on me, down to the reclining dentist chair, that I tensed automatically. Finn hesitated for a second before pushing onward and climbing into the seat. His face had turned even paler than usual.

The magimedic sat on a stool near his head. She murmured a few lilting words, and his eyelids dropped down. I took a deep breath, willing myself calm.

No one here was going to hurt him. She was going to give back what'd been stolen from him.

The woman rested her fingertips on the side of Finn's head. She started to croon softly—a verse in what sounded like Latin. I focused on the flow of energy around me and sang out into it, urging it toward her to strengthen her casting as she needed it, keeping my voice quiet and in tempo with hers so the sounds wouldn't clash.

The magic tickled through me with a bubbling of joy. The magimedic sat up straighter as the current I'd directed reached her.

I caught an impression of her own casting, like a weaving together of frayed threads, stretching them out until they connected again, bringing them to life with a spark here and there. She repeated those gestures over and over as I encouraged more magic toward her, until my throat grew hoarse.

Finally, she sat back and swiped at the sweat that gleamed on her forehead. "He needs to rest for as long as the sedative 'chantment lasts," she said. "That will give his nerves more time to heal on their own."

I nodded. "I'll stay with him. I don't mind waiting."

She didn't leave us alone but moved to a desk in the corner of the room, where she started working on a computer. I took the stool she'd vacated and wrapped my fingers around Finn's. Sleep had slackened his face, but I could have sworn I saw happiness in his expression that hadn't been there before.

The magimedic was just getting up from the computer when Finn's eyelids fluttered. It took another few minutes before they opened completely. He gazed vaguely at the ceiling, blinking. Then the most brilliant grin I'd ever seen crossed his face. He touched his temple and looked at me.

"It's back. It's really back."

I had to return his grin. "Of course it is. You never should have lost it."

The magimedic ignored that comment. "During the next few weeks, you may find your connection to the magic is shakier than it was before, Mr. Lockwood. I can assure you that it will smooth out as your brain readjusts to hearkening. If you experience more severe symptoms—headaches, dizziness, vision issues—please contact the center."

"Yes," Finn said, still grinning. "Right."

He hopped down from the chair and met my gaze again. Abruptly, he stepped close and bowed his head toward me. As his forehead grazed mine, he intoned a phrase under his breath that sounded familiar.

A second later, I understood why I'd recognized it. Images and emotions washed over me—Finn's thoughts, Finn's feelings.

He was opening his mind to me the way he had right after the Exam, letting me see everything going on inside him that he didn't know how to put into words.

It was the last casting he'd made before he'd lost the magic, and now the first casting he'd made after recovering it.

Each moment he passed to me brought more of my own emotions into my throat. There was the first time we'd met after I'd been shipped off on special ops duty—his relief at seeing me alive and well, the frustration at not being able to talk about or even remember all the things he wanted to. There was a glimpse of me at the protest at the Confed building, giving him a surge of resolve to challenge the security guard at the door and bring the Circle out.

There we were in one of the hotel rooms we'd stayed in, cuddled together on the bed, cocooned in warmth and contentment despite the enemies closing in around us.

And there I stood on a laptop's screen by the smoking Met building, singing my heart out as hundreds of people we'd believed to be Dull sang with me, holding an entire building together with sheer force of will and magic. So much conviction and admiration pealed through that memory that it squeezed my heart.

An answering conviction rang through me. I grasped both of Finn's hands and leaned in to kiss him as the images faded, not caring about the magimedic nearby or anything else.

It didn't matter what the rest of the world did. It didn't matter who kept their promises or for how long. We'd proven how strong we were together, how much we could accomplish, and if we had to do it all over again, so be it. Neither the beauty in the magic nor the wonder of my bond with the boy in front of me could ever be truly defeated.

# ACKNOWLEDGMENTS

It's been quite a journey wrapping up this series. I'm sorry to part ways with Rocío, Finn, and their friends, but so happy I could give them an ending I think they've earned.

Huge thanks go out to:

Deva Fagan, Amanda Coppedge, and the members of the Toronto Speculative Fiction Writers Group, who helped me find my way from the initial rough drafts to the much stronger book you've just read.

Elsa Viviana Munoz, who offered invaluable feedback on the included Spanish and on Rocío's character throughout the process.

My editors, Rosemary Clement and Alexa B., who whipped my prose into shape and caught the lingering errors.

Jennifer Munswami, whose cover design never fails to catch the eye.

My husband, Chris, who never failed to offer everything from brainstorming help to words of encouragement.

And of course, my readers, who waited so patiently for this final volume in the Conspiracy of Magic series. Thank you for sticking with me and my characters for so long, and I hope this book gave you everything you wished for!

Defy
the
Odds
Defend
Your
Magic

# ABOUT THE AUTHOR

USA Today bestselling author Megan Crewe lives in Toronto, Canada with her husband and son. She's been making up stories about magic and supernatural conspiracies and other what ifs since before she knew how to write words on paper. These days the stories are just a lot longer. Her other YA novels include the paranormal *Give Up the Ghost*, post-apocalyptic the Fallen World series, the sci fi Earth & Sky trilogy, the contemporary fantasy *A Mortal Song*, and the supernatural thriller *Beast*.

Connect with Megan online:
www.megancrewe.com

**Standalone novels**

Give Up the Ghost

A Mortal Song

Beast

**The Earth & Sky Trilogy**

Earth & Sky

The Clouded Sky

A Sky Unbroken

**The Fallen World Series**

The Way We Fall

The Lives We Lost

The Worlds We Make

Those Who Lived